BROKEN LEGACY

WSJ & USA TODAY BESTSELLING AUTHOR

JAYMIN EVE

USA TODAY & INTERNATIONAL BESTSELLING AUTHOR

TATE JAMES

Copyright © Jaymin Eve & Tate James 2019
All rights reserved.
First published in 2019.
Eve, Jaymin | James, Tate

Broken Legacy: Dark Legacy #3

No part of this book may be reproduced, stored in a retrieval system or transmitted in any form or by any means, without the prior permission in writing of the publisher, nor be otherwise circulated in any form of binding or cover other than that in which it is published and without a similar condition, including this condition, being imposed on the subsequent purchaser. All characters in this publication other than those clearly in the public domain are fictitious, and any resemblance to real persons, living or dead, is purely coincidental.

Cover design by Tamara Kokic
Book design by Inkstain Design Studio
Content editing by Heather Long
Line editing by Bookends Editing

BROKEN LEGACY

For those that race through life like Riley.

Never ease up on the gas until you cross the line first.

Or die trying.

Chapter 1

Shock held me immobile for many long moments. I'd just seen Catherine Deboise—my birth mother—kissing her brother. Graeme Huntley. And not a kiss-on-the-cheek-happy-to-see-family sort of kiss. Nope. This was some *Game of Thrones*, incest as fuck, brother and sister making out.

My stomach lurched, and I swallowed hard to stop the bile from rising any farther.

A million questions ran through my head, and the general theme was making my stomach churn even harder.

Was I the product of an incestuous relationship?

Was Oscar?

Did Richard know about the relationship?

Was Catherine the spy?

She had to be the spy.

She was kissing the man who ran the company trying to destroy Delta. What the fuck else could that mean?

After Graeme left in a rush of expensive sports car, I remained where I was, pressed into the grass of the Deboise estate, hidden behind some well-trimmed hedges. Thankfully, Catherine didn't linger on her doorstep, returning inside before his car had even cleared the gate. Somehow, she hadn't figured out that I was out here—for once, the laziness of the guards was working in my favor.

Or maybe Richard told them not to announce me. Who knew what that crazy bastard was up to?

A slight scuff of dirt behind me alerted me to the new presence, and I managed not to scream as I swung my head toward the noise, already reaching for the gun tucked into the front pocket of my hoodie.

Their faces were creased in hard, angry lines.

"Riley," Beck murmured, his gaze running across me like he was assessing for injuries. "What the fuck are you doing here?"

Dylan was right beside him, both of them in a similar position to me, pressed close to the ground.

"I came to see Catherine," I started breathlessly. "I was going to confront her about Dante. Get the truth out of that slimy bitch."

I sounded shocked, my voice vapid.

Beck immediately noticed. "What happened?" he demanded, somehow managing to keep his voice low despite his obvious pissed-off-ness.

"Catherine and Graeme," I whispered, the images of them kissing strong in my mind. "Catherine and fucking Graeme Huntley," I finished louder.

Both guys turned to look toward the impressive mansion, their eyes tracking in that hunter survivalist way they had.

"I thought that was his car," Beck muttered, "when we were jumping the fence."

I nodded like a bobble-head toy. "Yep, he just left."

"She's in shock," Dylan said softly. "We need to get her out of here. Give her a chance to calm down."

Beck found his feet and lifted me with ease, cradling me against his chest.

"What about Catherine?" I gasped, because we were not hiding at all.

Beck made a disparaging sound. "Fuck Catherine. She doesn't scare us. We were in stealth mode until we knew you were okay, but now..."

Fair enough.

He followed Dylan; they moved fast and soundlessly, able to step in just the right way as to not create any sort of disturbance. I did not have this skill. Which was the only reason I didn't ask him to put me down. Right now my body felt like jelly, and I'd probably trip and break another limb if I was left to my own devices.

I gave Dylan the front gate code, and he entered it so we could leave. Beck's Bugatti was parked right beside the butterfly, and he dropped me into the passenger seat before holding out a hand for my keys. He wanted Dylan to drive my car.

I started to shake my head—I was the one who drove the butterfly. She'd only just been returned to me after being totaled, and I was feeling a little possessive, but as my head spun, I realized that I wasn't really in the best position to be focusing on things like traffic and pedestrians. Plus, I wanted to be close to Beck. I needed the comfort.

When I surrendered the keys, Dylan shot me one last worried look before he turned and hopped in the butterfly.

"Talk to me, baby," Beck said as he started up his Bugatti. "Tell me what you saw."

The burn of acid assaulted my throat again, my stomach contents wanting to expel from my body. I'd never quite realized how weak my stomach was until I entered this world. I'd probably thrown up more in the last few months than I had in the ten years before that. All of this insane shit was really taking a toll on me.

Beck had his unfathomable expression focused on me still, and I tried to organize my scattered thoughts. "When I got there, Catherine was standing on the front porch with a man. I knew immediately it wasn't Richard, and I figured she was having an affair. You know, rich wife cliché that she is."

Beck nodded, slowing down as we exited the main gates of the Delta compound.

"Then he turned around and … it was Graeme," I whispered.

Beck's expression twisted slightly into confusion, and not because I said Graeme, he'd already known he was there, but because of the *way* I said it.

I turned in my chair and met his gaze full on. "She kissed him, Sebastian. Kissed him passionately… like a lover."

I waited for him to flinch, or call me crazy, or act disgusted.

But he did none of those things.

Either his mind hadn't immediately gone to me being a possible incest baby, or he was much better than me at hiding his emotions, because right now, his expression was unreadable.

I jumped when he reached out and captured my hand. "We will get to the bottom of this, Butterfly," he told me, his voice as serious as I'd ever heard it. "And I promise you, Catherine Deboise is going to fucking pay for what she's done to you. To all of us."

I squeezed my eyes shut tightly, trying my best to get those images out of my head. "She's literally the most fucked up human I've ever met. And considering the world I've been in lately..."

That was really saying something.

Actually, Graeme Huntley was about the same, so there were two fucked up Huntleys wandering around. Fucked up Huntleys that might be my pare—

I gagged again, and knowing I couldn't live like this any longer, I reached into the center of the car and grabbed for Beck's phone. He didn't question me or try and take the phone back; he just let me scroll through until I found the number I needed.

The phone rang three times before a deep, familiar voice answered.

"Beck!" Richard Deboise said quickly. "Is everything okay with Riley?"

Hearing his voice had my stomach churning once more, not just because the last time I'd seen him he'd tried to drug me, but because he might not be my father, and if he wasn't, that meant…

"I need you to tell me the truth," I said without preamble. "For once in my life, I need the honest truth. You fucking owe me after our last meeting."

That got Beck's attention—I could practically feel his steely gaze slamming into the side of my head, but I ignored him, waiting for Richard's answer.

There was a beat of silence and then: "Okay."

"Did you know about Catherine and Graeme Huntley?"

The silence was longer this time. Much longer.

"Yes. I have known since before we were married."

The phone was on speaker, and Beck's angry sound reached Richard.

"Who is with you, Riley?" he asked, more bite in his tone.

"Just Sebastian," I replied.

"It's not safe to talk on the phone," Richard continued then. "Meet me at the red-zone Delta house. Beck knows what I'm talking about."

The line went dead, and with trembling hands, I dropped it back where it usually sat. "He knew about it." My voice rasped. "He knew she was fucking her brother, and he still married her."

Everything about this day was blowing my mind, but there was one positive in Richard already knowing—hopefully he would have some answers to the many questions spinning around my head.

Beck was the one to reach for the phone this time. "Can you send Dylan a text? I'm not going in there without backup. Not when your safety is in question."

With a nod, I took the device and opened his messages. "I need you to use these words only, okay?" Beck said before he rattled off a bunch of shit that made no sense to me.

"Are you sure?" I said, almost smiling at the gibberish in the text.

Beck managed to curl one corner of his perfect lips. "Yeah, we have our own way of communicating, Butterfly. Unless you're a codebreaker, you won't figure it out."

I chuckled this time. "How did you know? Codebreaker is my middle name."

Yeah, right? This life of crime was definitely new to me, and I doubted I'd ever catch up to my guys—the experts.

"What did you mean about Richard owing you?" Beck said, diverting our conversation. I managed not to groan, because I'd been hoping he wouldn't really catch onto that … or at least not push me about it.

I should have known better.

"The truth, Riley," he added when I didn't answer straight away.

I could tell by his tone that he was not going to let me get away with any half, bullshit type answers.

Deep breath. "Turns out Richard is as much of a psycho as the rest of you all," I said quickly. When Beck's eyes darkened, I continued in a rush, "He didn't hurt me, just scared the fuck out of me. And he threatened you, Beck, so I think it's best if I don't tell you all the details."

I waited for him to explode, and there was definitely a tense moment of silence, but Beck surprised me when his grip on the wheel loosened and he let out an amused, derisive laugh.

"You are going to have to have more faith in me, Butterfly. Richard thinks he has it over me and the guys, but he doesn't have a fucking clue what we're capable of. He's never bothered to pay attention." I got his full attention then, and I was slightly afraid for anyone on the road, because Beck was not watching it at all. "Don't ever keep anything like this from me again."

I returned his glare with one of my own.

"You keep shit from me all the time in the pretense of 'protecting me.' I was just doing the same fucking thing."

Beck's lips twitched, and he nodded. "Touché, baby."

I thought that was the end of it, but I should have known better. "You're not to be alone with Richard again."

Arrogant fuck.

I hadn't even told Beck what happened, not specifics, but somehow, he still knew that it was something fucked up and weird. Enough to make his demand. I didn't bother to answer, because today, I couldn't make that promise.

With a shake of his head, he let it go, and silence fell between us as we crossed through the main town of Jefferson. We left suburbia for a less urban area—long fields of green and crops that appeared to be in the early stages of sprouting, spring only just making an appearance.

"What does the red-zone mean?" I asked Beck, needing to break the silence.

He stared ahead, relaxed as we sped along. "We have multiple safe houses, drop off zones, and delivery routes mapped around Jefferson. Red-zone is for private use only. Delta meetings mainly. It's regularly searched for wiretaps, bugs, and unauthorized surveillance equipment. It's probably the closest thing we have to a safe place to talk."

Good. That meant Richard had something important to say. Or he was luring us out here to try and kill us. I wouldn't put it past him, but at least we were prepared now for his underhandedness. Neither of us trusted Richard and that gave us an edge.

Beck turned off the main road, entering a small cleared area surrounded by trees. Unless you were looking for it, you'd never have seen it there. We followed this path through the trees for a long time, and as I sat higher in my seat to look around, I was relieved to see Dylan behind us, the butterfly gleaming in the early morning sunlight that filtered through the dense vegetation.

Seeing him reminded me of something. "How did you know to follow me to Catherine's?" I asked as a building appeared in the distance. I'd been so sure Beck was sound asleep when I'd left this morning.

His expression darkened—I'd just reminded him that I'd snuck out into danger. "It was a combination of things. You asking about your gun was the first tip off, and then when we were kissing, there was something *off* in your expression. Like you thought it was the last time we'd ever touch. My mistake was in expecting you'd get some sleep before you snuck out—that's why I was a few minutes late catching up to you. And Dylan heard your car and was down in the parking lot at almost the same time as me."

Fuck. I was never going to be able to hide anything from them.

"I'm sorry I took off," I told him, recognizing that it had been pretty stupid. "I just figured that Catherine would never talk to me truthfully with you guys there. Like everyone else, she would be scared that you'd kick her ass or something."

Beck's chest rumbled, and it almost looked like he was counting to ten in his head to try and calm down. "Don't do that again, Riley. Catherine is dangerous. Everyone in our world is, and you shouldn't trust any of them except us. The four of us will always have your back."

After everything that had happened in the last few months, those words had my body warm and glowing. Somehow these rich, arrogant fuckers had buried themselves deep in my heart.

Beck pulled to a stop in front of the safe house. "We're in this shit together," he said as he turned the engine off. "I would have gone with you. Any of us would have."

"I thought you'd stop me," I admitted. "You can be pretty bossy when it comes to safety."

Beck shifted around so he was facing me fully, his beautiful eyes awash in gray storm clouds. They got like that when he was pissed or upset. Right now I was pretty sure he was both.

"I'm bossy because I fucking love you, Butterfly. I'm not letting anyone take you away from me. But … if it was important to you, I wouldn't have stood in your way. I would have just made sure that we were prepared for anything. I would have had backup." He reached out and cupped my face, his hand rough and soft at the same time. "I won't stand in your way, baby, but I will stand at your side, where I belong."

Well, fuck. What did someone say to that?

"I love you, Sebastian."

The words slipped out. I hadn't said it back to him earlier, even though I'd felt it, but now there was no way to keep it inside.

He stilled, the storminess of his eyes fading to something almost silvery. That was how they looked when he was happy. Content.

He reached up, his other hand cupping my face, too, and in true Beck style, he slammed our mouths together. The kiss was hard and punishing at first before it gentled to loving touches of lips and tongue and hands.

A firm knock on the window beside my head was the only thing that pulled us apart, because we were not stopping on our own. Dylan stood there with an exasperated look on his face, and he jerked his head toward the door of the safe house, indicating that Richard was already there waiting for us.

Reluctantly, I pulled away from Beck, and climbed out of the car. The safe house was small, looking a lot like an old brown barn that had been sitting out here in the elements for decades. It was run down on the outside, but something told me that was part of its "blend in and not get found" camouflage.

"Stay close, Riles," Dylan said when Beck crossed behind the car to join us.

"And don't forget to use your gun if you need to protect yourself," Beck murmured, his eyes hard as his gaze landed on my father.

Richard looked like shit, eyes bloodshot, wrinkled suit on. His gaze found mine, and for a moment, I struggled to breathe.

What truth was I about to find out? And would I be able to handle it?

Chapter 2

"**H**urry inside," Richard said, and it astonished me again how chameleon like he was. One minute kind and caring, the next psycho and scary, and right now he almost seemed frail and afraid. Maybe he had multiple personalities.

Beck and Dylan fell in on either side of me. "Stay together," Beck said under his breath.

Dylan nodded, the perfect lines of his face hardening, making him look older than his twenty years. I always felt safe when I was with these two. And especially when I was with all four of the heirs, but I was also determined to feel safe just with myself. Which meant I had to stay in control of this situation.

I had my gun. Maybe I'd use it.

Stepping through the front door, I let out a low gasp. Okay, I might have expected that the outside was a "front" hiding the true inside, but I had not expected this.

Inside was a fortress. The walls lined with what looked like steel: silver, shiny and thick. There were no windows, and it appeared that the front door we'd just used was the only way to get in and out.

"It's virtually bomb and earthquake proof," Richard said, smiling at my undoubtedly shocked expression. "Nothing can get in once it's locked down. We've used it a few times over the years."

The front door was closed by Beck, and then we followed Richard through the entrance and into a steel-lined living area I'd caught glimpses of. There were multiple couches, a thick cream rug, and three shelves teaming with books.

Richard sat in a high backed leather armchair, and the three of us ended up in a tan leather couch across from him. "Now we can talk, Riley," Richard said.

Okay then. "Are you my father?"

First thing was first. Dylan shot me a side-eye, and I remembered that he didn't know of Catherine and Graeme yet, but he'd catch up quickly, because I would definitely be asking more about them.

"Yes," Richard said without preamble. "I've had DNA tests done and our match was conclusive. I'm your father."

A relieved gust of air left me. That's how fucked up my world was—I was relieved that the psycho drug-his-own-daughter was my father.

"Was Oscar your son?"

Richard's face fell. "In every way except blood."

I wasn't exactly shocked, but somehow I still was…

"He's not a Deboise?" Beck asked, shrewdly watching Richard, assessing each and every answer.

Richard shook his head. "No, he's a Huntley. Catherine was already pregnant when she came to me and begged for help. Her life was in danger. Her son's life was in danger. We'd always gotten along well, she was attractive, and this alliance suited me. I wasn't sure I could have children after an accident when I was younger, and this way I was assured an heir to carry on the Deboise name."

Dylan sat straighter now. "I never knew of the accident."

Richard laughed. "Yes, well, one doesn't exactly advertise that he might not be able to have an heir. Tends to bring out the vultures. You three are the only ones who know. Oh, and a doctor who stitched me up."

"You did have a kid though, so that's a moot point, right?" I pushed, needing more evidence that I wasn't a Huntley. Richard hadn't exactly proven himself to be trustworthy and right now I only had his word about this "DNA test."

Richard reached around to the small side table I hadn't noticed and lifted some papers. "Figured you'd want proof," he said.

He handed them to me, and Beck and Dylan moved in closer so the three of us could read through the papers.

I noted the official seal first, and more official numbers and such that indicated this was a legit test. I then focused on the results ... and it was exactly as he said. My DNA proved Richard was my biological father, beyond doubt.

"So, Oscar was Graeme Huntley's child?" Beck said, while I continued to stare down, my knuckles white where I held the edges of the paper.

Dylan startled next to me, but that was the full extent of his shock. I doubted that anyone else would have even noticed.

Richard's expression shuttered. "No. Oscar was not Graeme's. He was

Reginald Huntley's child."

Beck and Dylan were so still, and the energy that was coming from both of them was dark. Really dark.

"I don't understand," I said, finally meeting my father's eyes. "Who is Reginald Huntley?"

There was another player in this game I didn't know about? Was she fucking another one of her brothers? Or … a cousin, maybe?

"Catherine's father," Beck snarled. "An evil old fuck that thankfully died a few years ago."

Catherine's father…

Somehow I wasn't sick. Somehow.

"Catherine was sleeping with her father and her brother?" I asked, swallowing hard to stop the bile. What the fuck was happening here? Had I stumbled into some sort of dark romance story where crazy shit kept happening, even when it made no sense?

Richard shook his head, eyes sad. "No, she didn't sleep with her father … he raped her. For years. She was the victim of his assault night after night from when she was about ten. When she got pregnant, she found the strength to escape him. She went for the only people powerful enough to take on Huntley."

"Delta," I breathed.

Oh my fucking god. That was absolutely horrific, and for a split-second, I felt sympathy for Catherine. It actually explained a lot about the fucked up person she was, why she acted so horrible. But … at the end of the day, I couldn't forgive her for what she did. Especially with whatever was going on with her and Dante.

That was a question to deal with after this one.

"That's why you've always been so sure about her loyalty to Delta," I said, focusing on getting whatever information I could. "Her hatred toward her father."

Richard nodded. "Hate and fear. She would never go back near them."

But… "She was kissing her brother." I shook my head. "And she definitely didn't kiss him like he was someone that assaulted her. Or like she was afraid of him. She kissed him like he was the one person in this world she loved."

At this, Richard looked upset, maybe for the first time since I'd walked in here. "I knew that her brother received abuse from the father as well, in a different way to Catherine, but it drew them very close together. She told me that he'd saved her, and that they briefly had a sexual relationship, but that it was all done. She was done with Huntley."

"It's not done," I assured him. "Catherine has to be your spy."

Richard looked like he wanted to protest, but he didn't, sinking into his chair. "I will look into it. From now on, you need to be extra careful around Catherine," he said weakly. "She brought you back here for a reason, Riley. If it's to ensure that we can vote in this upcoming meeting, then that means she is going to vote Huntley into Delta."

"Remove her as your proxy," Dylan demanded. "Do it immediately, otherwise you cannot guarantee the safety of the vote."

Richard shook his head. "If I do that, and Catherine is our mole, then we will all be in danger. She knows too much. She has power now she didn't before. It's better if we draw her out, and then when we have the evidence, we'll go to the board and have her taken down."

Something told me that whatever Catherine did to make Richard take her in to his life, to protect her, was still there for him. Maybe he loved her fucked up ass. Or maybe he liked the drama. Either way, he wasn't ready to just throw her under the bus yet.

Richard glanced at his watch and stood rather gracefully. "I have a meeting to get to. Seems I need to become more involved in the company again, at least in small increments, until we figure out what to do about Catherine."

We all stood as well. Richard gave us a nod before bestowing a sad smile on me. "You probably don't believe this, Riley, but I'm not your enemy. I don't always make the right decisions, but I do always have the well-being of my family and company at heart."

With that, he turned and left, and I just shook my head, as information overloaded my brain. Dylan asked Beck a few questions about the Catherine and Graeme thing, mainly what I'd seen. I just tried to work out my next move.

"We need to talk to Dante," I said when they'd finished their rushed discussion. "He knows something. Maybe it will help us get to the bottom of whatever fucked up shit Catherine and Graeme are up to."

Right now my best friend—or ex best friend depending on what secrets he was keeping—was sitting in Jefferson lockup as a murder suspect.

"Yep. Good idea," Dylan said.

I had a dark thought. "Do you think Graeme knows about Katelyn yet? I mean, he didn't look upset or anything, but surely he'd care that his daughter died."

"His phone was off," Beck said. "One of the officers told me that as they led Dante away. So I doubt he knew."

Clearly turned off so they could have their clandestine affair or whatever.

I almost wished I could see Graeme's reaction when he found out, because I was starting to suspect that no one in this world had normal emotions. Or normal relationships with their children. What was to say that Katelyn was even biologically his. Was there anything we could believe about the relationships we'd learned of so far?

We left the same way we'd entered, and this time Beck pushed the Bugatti harder and faster, especially once we were back on the main road. Both of us needed the speed. A moment where we could forget the mess of the world we were firmly stuck in.

Forget Delta, just for five fucking minutes.

Chapter 3

A different person was on the front desk at the police station this time. A man who didn't look much older than us, with dark skin and pretty blue eyes. It was a nice contrast, and I wondered if he'd be easier to deal with than the last gatekeeper.

"Beck," he said, nodding respectfully when we stopped across from him.

"Johnson, didn't know you'd started work here," Beck said, sounding like he didn't hate this guy. Which was a very good start. "Heard you transferred out of state for a few years. Good to see you back."

Johnson nodded, looking relaxed and happy. "Yeah, I started at another station on beat duty before finally working my way up the ranks and ending up back here."

His eyes brushed briefly over me, but didn't linger, and I didn't bother to engage in any sort of conversation. A need to talk to Dante was starting to eat away at my insides. Like, I could not wait one more second to get the truth from him. Even with all of the truths I'd gotten tonight, this one was probably going to be one of the biggest. One of the most important. Life changing.

"You were always interested in law enforcement," Beck said, not sounding surprised. They shot the shit for a few more minutes before Beck got to business. "We had a friend brought in earlier on some bullshit charges. Do you think you could get us in to see him? Dante, the gangbanger."

I arched a brow at Beck while Johnson tapped at his computer for a moment then let out a low whistle. "Arrested on charges of aggravated assault, rape, and murder in the first degree. Uh, those are hardly bullshit charges, Beck." He gave us a pained look. "You sure don't want to make my first few weeks on the job easy, huh?"

Beck gave him a charming smile. "Just a misunderstanding," Beck replied. "We just need ten minutes with him. My girlfriend has a couple of things to ask him."

Johnson's blue eyes flicked to me again, and this time there was something in that gaze. Curiosity no doubt about the chick who finally got the "girlfriend" label from Beck. Just when it started to get uncomfortable, he sighed and checked his watch.

"Five minutes," he said in a no-nonsense tone. "That's the best I can do. If Saunders comes back from his lunch break early, he'll kick you out. So get your answers quick."

Johnson buzzed someone on the intercom and a few moments later a bored looking middle-aged woman in uniform escorted us through the station to a vacant interview room.

"Just wait here," she told us. "Your friend will be brought in shortly."

She left us, shutting the heavy metal door behind her with a heavy sound.

"Sit down, Butterfly," Beck urged, guiding me toward the uncomfortable looking chair on one side of the table. I shook my head and started pacing. There was no way I could sit still, not at a time like this. My head was so full of secrets and revelations it felt like I might explode if I didn't keep moving.

Dante working for Catherine.

Katelyn's murder.

Catherine and *her brother*.

Catherine and her father.

Richard's confession about Oscar.

It was all so freaking much. Just when I got past the fact that Delta—and my *friends*—had coerced me into murdering a man. Just when we worked through all that betrayal and broken trust ... this happened.

My mind was officially blown.

The door clicking open jolted me from my thoughts, and I gasped as Dante was brought into the room. My hand flew to my mouth in horror as the uniformed police officer escorted my oldest friend to the table and handcuffed him to the bar running down the middle of it.

"Mr. Beckett." The officer nodded to Beck and offered me a polite smile. "You have five minutes, please knock on the door if you want to leave prior to that. Otherwise, I'll be back shortly."

"Thank you," Beck responded, leaning his back on the mirrored glass and folding his arms over his chest.

The officer left, and I flew across the small space to hug Dante.

For a moment, he froze. Then his uncuffed hand came up and patted my back as I sobbed into the side of his neck.

"Hey, Riles," he whispered, "it's okay. I didn't do anything that they're saying. This will all get sorted out, don't worry."

Hearing his voice helped me pull my shit together a bit, and I released him. Only to crack my open palm across his face in a violent bitch slap. As much as I hated to give that bitch credit for anything, Catherine had helped me improve my slapping form.

"You fucking lied to me, Dante," I accused him in a harsh whisper. "My whole damn life. It was all a lie. How could you do this?"

"Riles—" He tried to grab my hand, and I snatched it out of his grip as I backed away.

"No," I snapped. "Don't fucking 'Riles' me. You're a fake! How long, Dante? How long have you been working for that bitch?"

I was mad as hell now, my fists clenched at my sides as I glared down at him. We'd been friends for a very long time—almost ten years. One day he just showed up and we'd been inseparable since. Now every memory of our life together was under scrutiny.

Dante dropped his head to his hands, the metal cuffs jangling against the bar as he rubbed his hand over his shaved head.

"The whole time," he finally said, his voice thick with ... I didn't know. Regret? Surely not. Otherwise he would have *said something sooner!*

"The whole time," I repeated in a horrified whisper. I'd had my suspicions but to have him confirm it. "The *whole* time. You've been spying on me for Catherine the entire time we've known each other?"

He nodded, his eyes full of pain.

"No." I shook my head, denying the truth of his words. "No, that's not possible. You were just a kid when we met. You were only—"

"Nine," he finished for me. "Yeah, I know. In case you haven't noticed, Catherine Deboise doesn't exactly have many moral boundaries. Blackmailing a nine-year-old is hardly the worst of her sins, don't you think?"

My brows shot up, and I grabbed that glimmer of hope with both hands. "Blackmail?"

Dante nodded. "Will you sit down and let me explain it? I swear I won't hold anything back, I'll tell you everything."

I wavered a moment, wanting to tell him to go to hell. But this was why I'd come to the police station, wasn't it? To get these answers?

Swallowing past the hurt and anger, I bit down on the inside of my cheek and slowly sat my ass down in the chair opposite Dante. Beck remained where he was. Silent and stoic. That was all I needed from him, too. He was there, he was supporting me, but he wasn't fighting my fights for me.

"Thank you," Dante whispered as I clasped my hands in front of me on the table. "Riles, I need you to know ... I didn't kill Katelyn. That whole thing is a fucking set up. You know I wouldn't do that. Right, Riles?" His eyes implored me to believe him, but my trust had taken one too many beatings for one lifetime.

"Why don't you start at the beginning?" I suggested, my voice a husky whisper as I dodged his eye contact and looked to my hands. "How did this shit with Catherine start?"

"Selene." He uttered his sister's name with such choked up pain that I instantly regretted judging so harshly. He was nine years old when Catherine got to him for fuck's sake.

I sucked in a deep breath and nodded. "You said Catherine blackmailed you. What did that have to do with Selene?"

Dante shot a quick look at Beck, then at the door. "I don't imagine we have a huge amount of time, so I'll give you the quick version and beg you to go and speak with Selene after this. I gave her some documents in case of an emergency." He grimaced and looked down at his handcuffed wrist. "I'd call this an emergency."

"No shit," I agreed. "So...?"

Dante scrubbed his free hand over his head again. "You remember how my old man was in the Grims before me, right? That's how I ended up involved?" I nodded. "Right, well when Selene and I were kids, we were out playing in the yard, just messing around on our bikes, and someone with a grudge against my dad decided to drive by and start shooting. Just... opened fire with an AK-47. I don't think they were even really aiming for anyone or anything, but they hit Selene."

I sucked in a breath, pressing my fingers to my lips to keep from screaming or crying or something. What the fuck was *wrong* with this world? The only thing that kept me calm was knowing that she had survived.

"She got taken to the hospital, but..." He trailed off, his head bowed as he picked at his fingernails, clearly remembering the day. "There were complications. She needed more surgeries and rehab. It was all so expensive, and my parents had no insurance, no way to pay. The best the hospital was offering was palliative care. Selene was dying, and they wouldn't do anything to save her unless we could pay."

"And that's where Catherine stepped in?" I breathed out, partly horrified and partly grateful. Catherine's obsession with control had saved my friend's life.

Dante nodded. "She wanted someone to keep an eye on you, make progress reports, shit like that. It seemed like such an easy gig, you know? Make friends with some kid and check in with this rich bitch every now and then. In return, she'd see that Selene got all the care she needed to make a full recovery."

I licked my lips, stunned. "Why you?"

Dante shrugged. "Gang connections. My dad had been doing dirty work for Delta for years, and we were so close in age..." He sighed. "I guess it wasn't hard for her to assume that the son of a gang leader might value money higher than morals."

"Stop it," I scolded. "You didn't value money over morals. You valued your sister's life. I can't..." I broke off, my voice cracking. "I can't blame you for that."

My best friend's gaze shot up to my face, his eyes full of hope and desperation, and I clenched my fists tight to steel my resolve. "But that was almost ten years ago, Dante. Ten *years*. Did my friendship mean so little to you that you kept this secret all that time? That you *kept reporting on me?* Do you have any idea how violated that makes me feel? How used, and how downright *stupid?*"

His face had fallen with every word, and my heart cracked further. "I know, and I can't even begin to apologize to you, Riles. By the time I stopped seeing you as a job and started seeing you as..." He paused, flicking a lightning fast glance at Beck. "As a friend, it was too late. Anything I said would have ruined what we had, and I wasn't willing to risk that."

I gaped at him. "So you're saying if I hadn't found out, you never would have told me?"

"Never." His jaw was set, and I couldn't totally wrap my head around what I was hearing. "Catherine made my dad sign a contract. If I told you everything, or refused to keep working for her, then my family would need to pay back the cost of Selene's health care. Millions of dollars. But if it was just money, I probably could have handled it."

I let out a heavy sigh, feeling my shoulders sag even more than they already had. "She threatened someone you love. I'm starting to understand the way Delta works, now. When money isn't enough of an incentive, threaten to kill people." As I said those words, another horrible, bone-chilling thought popped into my head. I was almost too scared to ask, not wanting to hear the answer... but all the same, I needed it.

"Dante," I croaked, licking my lips again. "Did you ... did Catherine kill my parents?"

The pained look on his face said it all, and I dropped my face into my hands with a shuddering sob. Almost instantly, a warm body wrapped me in a tight hug, and I knew it was Beck. His smell was so familiar now, it might as well be my personal fragrance, not to mention that instant feeling of calm and safety that his touch brought to me.

"I'm so sorry, Riles," Dante whispered, and I cried harder. "I didn't know for sure. I swear, if I'd known for sure I would never have let you go out that day. I would never, ever intentionally let her harm you."

I pushed back from Beck, wiping my eyes with the heel of my hand and glaring at Dante. "But you knew something was up. You tried to stop us that day, I remember. You came over and asked my dad if he could help you fix your heating. You *knew* and you still didn't say anything!" Tears were pouring freely from my eyes, so much that my vision was blurring and my nose was all blocked up.

Some girls could cry and still look pretty. I wasn't one of those girls.

"Riles, I swear I didn't know for sure. And your father seemed determined to ignore me," Dante insisted. But it was too late; my rage monster was in full beast mode.

I detached Beck's arms from me and stood, my chair scraping across the floor with a harsh sound. Just as I was about to really blow my fuse, the door opened and that same uniformed officer sauntered back in.

"Everything okay here?" he asked, eyeing my aggressive posture and Dante's tear-streaked face. "I gave you extra time, but Saunders is on his way back and he won't be happy to find anyone questioning his suspect."

I stared down at Dante a moment longer, dimly noticing the scratches on his forearms. "We're done," I snapped, storming from the room and not totally sure whether I meant that we were done talking or done with our friendship. Or both.

Beck paused me with a hand on my arm as I made to leave the station, and I frowned at him in confusion.

"I just need a word with someone," he told me with a quick smile. "Will you wait in the car? It'll only take two seconds." He held out the keys to the Bugatti, and as much as I didn't want to be alone, I also didn't want to stay in the police station a second longer.

I grabbed the keys from his fingers. "Sure."

But if he thought I'd be waiting patiently in the passenger seat, he was sorely mistaken.

Chapter 4

When Beck joined me a few minutes later, my hands were caressing the Italian leather steering wheel. My feet sat lightly over the pedals, and I was listening to the sexy, low rumble of the engine idling.

"Baby, were you thinking about taking off without me?" Beck teased, sliding into my usual seat and closing the door. "I wasn't that long."

I flashed him a quick, humorless smile. "No, but I *am* going to drive us home."

My shoulders were tight, and I was ready to put up a fight. After everything I'd been through, I deserved a quick drive in Beck's gorgeous car.

"Okay," he replied, shocking the shit out of me. "Take the long route. I want you to savor this." His grin turned wolfish. "Because it's the only time I'm ever letting you drive this car."

I snorted a laugh as I threw the gear shift into reverse and hooked out of the parking lot we were in. "We'll see about that, Sebastian. After all, I am your *girlfriend*."

Yeah, I'd been in a state of shocked numbness earlier, but I'd still picked up on Beck calling me his girlfriend to that cop. It was a bit dumb, given everything else going on, but hearing that title made me go all tingly.

Beck didn't reply to my teasing, just waited until I'd gotten us out on the freeway and at breakneck speed, then reached over and wove our fingers together.

I glanced down, startled, and couldn't help noticing a smear of blood on his first and second knuckles and the swollen redness around them all.

"Quick chat, huh?" I muttered, shooting him an accusing look before returning my eyes to the road. He'd punched someone, and I'd bet my car that when I next saw Dante he'd have a black eye.

If I saw him again.

I wasn't sure I could ever look at him and not see my parents' faces now. Their death was preventable. A part of me had always known that there was something off about the accident, but I'd been too afraid to look closely at it, because how did I live with that knowledge?

Suddenly I was sobbing. Huge, gulping, heart-wrenching sobs that actually hurt my chest they were rattling it so hard. Somehow Beck took control of the car, easing us to the side of the road as I lifted my foot from the accelerator.

"Catherine killed them," I choked out. "The only fucking people in this world who ever loved me. She just wiped them out like they were nothing more than an animal in the middle of the road, stopping her from where she was going."

Beck wrapped his arms around me, pulling me from my seat and into his lap. His heat and energy surrounded me, and I cried against his chest for so long, that by the time I lifted my head, I was exhausted and his shirt was soaked.

When my eyes met his, I was not surprised to see brimming fury there. His hands slid up and cupped my swollen, tear-stained face, and he brushed away the trickling moisture with his thumbs. "There are two things I need you to remember, Butterfly," he said softly. "One: Catherine is going to pay for what she has done. In every way possible, she will regret the day she hurt you."

For some fucked up reason that actually made me feel better. I knew all the stories about revenge not soothing the soul, but for now, it gave me a fucking focus, and I was all onboard for Beck's plan.

"And two?"

His grip tightened slightly, and he pulled me closer, our lips touching, his tongue darting out to slide across some of the tears that had caught on the corner of my mouth. "Two: your parents loved you very much. I didn't even have to meet them to know this, because you are so fucking lovable. But, and I don't say this to take away from them .... you have so much love and family in your world still. I fucking love you. An unconditional sort of love. It doesn't matter how you fuck up, Riles, you'll always have me. I'm your family."

His gaze never left mine, and I could not have looked away for anything in the world. My heart was hurting and expanding and shaking, all at the same time. Beck was unraveling me at the very seams of my being, but he didn't let me fall apart. Somehow, he was putting me back together. Better.

"Dylan, Jasper, Evan, and even Eddy," he continued, in that same soft, sexy rumble he did so well. "They're your family. You will never be alone again."

Well, fuck.

I chuckled through fresh tears—pretty amazing I had any moisture left in my body to cry at this point, but apparently there was some. "You're quite the poet when you're not punching people or shooting someone in the head."

Beck shrugged. "What can I say ... I'm a man of many talents."

That was very true. Very, very true.

"I love you too, Sebastian Roman Beckett," I said, sliding my hands up into his thick dark hair. "Thank you for being my family. For having my back." I kissed him gently before pressing my lips a little harder to his. Some of the sadness in my soul eased again, and I started to breathe more freely. I'd never forget my parents, the pain would not go anywhere, but I wasn't alone dealing with it. And that meant a lot.

Clambering back into the driver's seat, I took a few deep breaths, swiped at my face, and then shifted her back into gear. "I need to talk to Selene," I said softly, pulling onto the road.

Beck nodded. "That's our next stop, but you need to sleep first."

I shook my head roughly. "No! No time for sleep. I need all the information so I can decide how to proceed from here. Taking down Catherine is going to take a serious sort of plan. I already have a few ideas, but I need to speak with some people. There's no time to screw around."

Beck's chest rumbled as he shook his head. "Baby, come on. You can't do this on no sleep. A few more hours is not going to change anything. Take care of yourself first, or you'll be in no position to take anyone down."

I wanted to growl back at him, but unfortunately that wasn't something I'd mastered. Instead I sighed, because... he was right. Bastard. Spinning the Bugatti around, I put her on the road back to our apartment.

"Can you send someone to watch over Selene?" I asked as we neared town. "Somehow Catherine is going to find out we talked to Dante. She's a slimy bitch who always has her finger on the pulse. If we're not going there right away, someone should watch over her. Maybe even warn her."

And I didn't trust the phone.

Beck didn't look worried. "I sent the guys there the moment we walked out of the police station. Selene might have vital information. She's to be protected until we figure out what to do next."

I nodded, relieved that he was taking this seriously. In my chest I felt a new urgency. We'd just entered the final phase of whatever bullshit Catherine had been planning for twenty years. This was her long game, and I was going to do my best to ensure it never came to fruition.

Debitch was going down.

Chapter 5

BECK

Controlling my temper was something I'd been working on most of my life. I was born to violent and volatile parents. It was my mother's milk, my nutrition, my lifeforce for so many years that it was second nature for me to hurt first and ask questions later.

My father had taught me to hide my violence, because the CEO of the top Fortune 500 company could not lose his shit and start throwing chairs across the boardroom. It was also *frowned upon* to shoot assholes in the head. I'd learned that my temper would stop other companies doing business with us and that would hurt our bottom line.

Everything in Delta's best interests, of course.

It took a long time, but eventually, I got very good at hiding the darkness in my soul. The predator inside. But, in this moment, as I stared down at

Riley's face, still stained with the tears she'd cried on me, a black wave of fury settled into my soul. The sort of fury that had me wanting to start a goddamn war for her, to wipe out any fucker who'd ever dared hurt her.

Dante was lucky that all I'd done was rough him up a little. I could have killed him. I thought about it, and it was only that I'd be leaving Riley out here unprotected with whatever bullshit was going on that stayed my hand. Even Delta's power would take some time to clean up murder at a police station.

"You better pray that we win against Catherine," I'd murmured to Dante just before I left the room. "Because if Riley is hurt again, I'm coming after you."

Just before I had stepped out the door, Dante called out my name. I could barely stand to look at his fucking face for another second, but I turned. "Catherine needs the vote to go her way," he said. "Check your board members. She thinks she has the votes to get Huntley in, and if that happens, they're going to kill you all."

I didn't acknowledge his words, just shook my head and left the room, my hands itching to go back and hit him again. The weak fucker hadn't even tried to defend himself. He'd screwed up, and he knew it. I would not pave his way back to Riley either. If she forgave him, I would let him live, but I'd never trust him around her again.

Now, as I sat beside her, watching Riley sleep, all I had were the dark emotions churning in my soul. An anger that would not abate.

My phone buzzed in my hand, and seeing the familiar name pop up, I got to my feet and stepped out of the bedroom. "You get there?" I asked Jasper.

"Yep. We just got to her house. She's home, and so is her cop husband. Everything is quiet, so Evan and I will just keep an eye out until you get here. Dylan is waiting to drive with you both tomorrow."

"Right," I agreed. "Laying low is a good plan. It'll go smoother if Riley breaks it to her. We don't want her to run without giving us the information we need."

Jasper made a sound of agreement. "Let us know when you guys leave," he said and hung up.

I was about to slide my phone back in my pocket when it rang again. *Beckett Snr* flashed on the screen, and I stared at it for a long moment before ignoring the call. I didn't have time for his bullshit today, and if anything was designed to snap the sliver of control I'd gotten back over my emotions, it was talking to my father.

My mother was the same. Popping prescription pills like they were the air she needed to breathe, thinking no one knew she was shacked up with her masseuse. Riley had said that Catherine was a rich woman cliché. Well so was Magdalena Beckett.

She sure as fuck was never a mother.

"Beck," Riley called out, and the urgency in her voice had me moving my ass to get back into the room. I burst through the door, gun in hand, eyes taking in the scene in one quick sweep.

I'd learned to catalog a scene in five seconds.

But there was no one in the room other than Riley, and she wasn't even awake.

Her arms and legs thrashed about on the bed, and she was crying in her sleep again. Placing my gun on the side table, I climbed in with her and wrapped my body around hers. Holding us both the fuck together.

"It's okay, baby," I soothed softly. Riley always joked that she couldn't sleep without me. That I kept her nightmares at bay. What she didn't realize, though, was that she did that for me as well. That and so much more. I'd barely slept more than a few hours a night before I'd met Riley, my brain and body constantly on alert.

Pretty standard when you were on edge waiting for your sociopath of a father to drag you out of bed and beat the fuck out of you. Dylan and I had that in common. Evan's father was more about psychological abuse. Jasper's was neither; he just ignored his son.

In our world, that was a blessing.

But when I was with Riley, my body was content.

Whatever the fuck was between us, that shit was soul deep. Riley was in my blood, and I wasn't sure I could live without her.

She'd stopped thrashing about now, content in my arms, her smaller body wrapped around mine as I held her close. My chest ached in the way that only she brought about. Like her tiny hand was around my heart, gripping the fuck out of it.

I had one thought: we had to take these motherfuckers down before my girl got hurt.

If it meant I had to single handedly kill them all one by one, then I would do that for her, consequences be damned.

I'd leave that as plan B though, because I was hoping that there was a way this could all work out and I wouldn't end up spending the rest of my life in jail. That there was a path that ensured I got to keep Riley, and that we'd have a fucking chance at a normal future. Riley said she had a plan. We'd try it her way first, and maybe, just maybe, there would be some sort of future left for us all when the dust settled.

Chapter 6

"Get in here," Selene ordered, grabbing me by the arm and yanking me through her front door. "Not you, tough guy." She blocked Beck's entry with her body, placing her hands on her hips and glaring.

Beck opened his mouth—undoubtedly to argue—but I gave him a stern headshake. I'd already warned him that Selene would likely want to talk with me alone.

"I'm fine, Beck. Just wait with Dylan." I indicated to our friend's car parked inconspicuously in a driveway across the street. Or as inconspicuous as a half million dollar car really could be in a middle-income neighborhood. He'd driven us, seeing as both Beck and I only had two-seater cars and it was way too much of a battle to argue he stay behind. Jasper and Evan had already been here keeping watch, and they'd taken off now to get some sleep. I was fucking lucky to have these guys in my world.

"Butterfly..." he growled, giving me a *look*.

"I'm fine," I repeated. "Go."

He looked like he was going to argue the subject, but Selene didn't give him a chance. Planting her palm in the middle of his chest, she shoved him out of the doorway then slammed the door in his face.

For good measure, she flipped the locks before she turned to face me.

"Start talking, Riley. Why the fuck is my brother in jail under suspicion of murder right now?" Her fists were planted on her hips and her scowl fierce, like I was to blame for all the bad shit in Dante's life.

Maybe I was.

"Babe, don't interrogate her in the hallway," Selene's husband yelled from the living room, then appeared a moment later, looking rough. "Hey Riley, come in."

He indicated for me to head through to the sitting room and I did so. The shit I needed to ask them—or to tell them—it wasn't standing conversation.

"Sorry about Selly," Rob apologized with a pained smile when I sat down. "It's been a long night. For all of us, I'm sure."

The way he phrased it sounded like he understood what a spectacularly crappy night it'd been for me, but Selene just snorted and glared at me. She'd sat down but her arms were folded tightly over her bathrobe. Her hair was a mess and plaid, flannel pajama pants showed between her robe and her slippers, but I'd hazard a guess that she hadn't slept all night.

Neither had her husband if the bags under his eyes were any indication.

"Can I get you some coffee, Riley?" Rob offered. "I suspect this chat needs the caffeine boost."

I gave him a nod and a tight smile. "That'd be great, thanks Rob."

He left us to make the coffee, giving Selene a kiss on the forehead as he passed, but she just glared harder.

"So, you had goons watching my house all night," she stated. "I take it that means Dante's arrest was something to do with your new life?"

Her aggression was starting to piss me off. After all, she'd known about all of this a hell of a lot longer than I had.

"You tell me, Selene. I'm not the one on Catherine's payroll." I snapped the words at her, and she visibly paled. Her frown slipped and her eyes widened with... fear?

"Neither am I," she spluttered, her cheeks blooming with warmth and her gaze ducking away from me.

"No, but Dante was," I whispered, feeling sick just saying it out loud. "Did you know?" My voice cracked but I powered through. "Did you know that Catherine killed my parents?"

Selene's gaze shot back to me in horror, and she pressed a hand to her lips. "Oh my god, Riles," she breathed. "I'm so sorry. No, God no. I had no idea..."

Tears were rolling down my face again, and I swiped at them with the back of my hand. The relief that she hadn't known was almost staggering. "That's not why I came here. Dante said he gave you some evidence? I need to see it."

She shook her head in confusion. "Wait, what about Dante? All Rob could find out is that he got arrested at some rich kid house party where a girl was raped and stabbed to death. Riley, you *know* he didn't do that. He wouldn't."

I hesitated a moment before I replied. "Yesterday I would have agreed with you. Now I don't know what he's capable of."

Selene gasped, and Rob paused halfway back into the room with a tray of mugs.

"You don't honestly think he's guilty, do you?" Rob's smile turned into a scowl. "I know he's not exactly on the right side of the law in everything he does, but you and I both know Dante has a good heart. He just had a shitty upbringing and a crappy role-model."

Rob plonked the tray down on the table, sloshing coffee out of the mugs before taking a seat himself.

"I don't know what to think anymore," I admitted, looking down at my hands as I picked my midnight purple nail polish. "I just need whatever evidence he left with you, Selene. This shit... it's bigger than just a murder charge."

"What could possibly be bigger than my little brother getting framed for murder?" Selene demanded, her hands shaking as she clutched at her robe. "He's in this mess because of me! None of this would have happened, he wouldn't have ever got mixed up with you, if it wasn't for me." Her voice was shrill and pained, and I could see tears welling up in her bloodshot eyes.

Rob must have seen she was about to lose it, and he wrapped her in a side hug from where he sat, smoothing her hair with his hand and shushing as she sobbed into his shirt.

"It's not your fault," I whispered, anxiety twisting my stomach in knots. "It's Catherine's fault. It's all Catherine's fault, and we're going to make sure she doesn't get away with it."

Selene was still crying, but she nodded and mumbled something about getting the documents before shuffling out of the room in her slippers.

"How do you plan to do that?" Rob challenged me when Selene was gone.

"Catherine sits on the board for one of the world's most powerful companies. There isn't a single industry, legal or not, that Delta doesn't have its fingers in. Do you have any idea how many agents from every area of law enforcement have tried and failed to take Delta down? The whole world knows they're dirty, but they practically own the world, so they keep getting away with it." He paused, his lips tight in anger and his nostrils flared. "Framing Dante for murder is just a game to people like Catherine Deboise."

I nodded. I understood what he was saying but...

"That's all true, but have any of those agents had insiders? Me, Beck, the guys... we have access that law enforcement doesn't have. What if we had the evidence which would put Catherine and the other board members in jail?" I was grasping, hoping that something in Dante's documents would help. But even if it didn't, I'd keep trying.

Catherine was going to pay for what she'd done to my parents, one way or another. Even if I had to kill her myself.

Rob seemed to be thinking about what I'd just said as he sipped his drink, staring down at the floral sofa cover. "You'll need someone in law enforcement that you can trust," he finally said, and hope flared inside me.

"I trust you," I said, nervously tapping my fingernail on the side of my own mug.

Rob shook his head. "No, I'm just a beat cop. I mean, someone with the power to make something happen *if* you get any usable evidence."

Selene came back into the room then, clutching a thick brown envelope to her chest. "I've never opened this," she said softly. "He made me promise. He said that I was only to give it to you in the case of his death, because he couldn't protect you any longer..."

My heart was hurting so badly, my chest ached like I'd been punched right in it. "He lied to me for years. *Years!* I don't know how to move past this."

Selene looked like she wanted to argue with me again, that fierce look in her eyes as she opened her mouth, but then she just shook her head. "Sometimes people fuck up, Riles. But he did it for the right reasons, I promise you. Deep down, his intentions toward you have always been pure. He loves you."

I didn't reply because I really couldn't talk about it any longer. Turning to Rob, I changed the subject. "Talk to me about finding someone in law enforcement."

His expression was calculating, and it was obvious why he'd been such a tough beat cop for years. "It doesn't have to be in law enforcement. Just find someone with a working knowledge of the justice system, even better if it's a judge or lawyer, to help you build the case. But keep in mind, no one will take you on unless you have irrefutable evidence of their corruption."

That didn't surprise me at all. And since we had one shot at taking them down before they buried me, I would not screw it up. *Lawyer or judge…*

A memory hit me. A memory I hadn't wanted to dwell on because it required me to think about the day I almost got raped, but that girl in my class … she'd said her father was a high-powered lawyer in New York City. Maybe she was my answer, but how could I tell if he could be trusted?

"Is there an easy way to see if someone is on the payroll of Delta?" I asked Rob, not expecting he would have the answer.

He shrugged. "They'll have files on everyone they do business with. Your boys should be able to get access to that."

Especially Beck. Or maybe Richard would allow me access as well. We had to do it without arousing suspicion though, because as I'd thought before, the moment the board got wind of us trying to take them down…

It wouldn't be pretty.

I stood suddenly. "I've got to go," I said before I finally met Selene's red-eyed gaze. "I'm sorry this is all happening, girl, and I might be angry with Dante, but I won't leave him there to rot. I'm going to figure out how to fix both of these things, and ensure Catherine can never touch us again."

She nodded, her arms wrapped tightly around herself. For the first time she looked her age, sorrow weighing her down.

"If you need our help, just ask," Rob said, standing with me. "You're not alone."

A tear tracked down Selene's cheek. "We're family," she whispered.

I smiled best I could before I turned to leave, brown envelope clutched in my hands.

As I expected, Beck was right outside the door, his expression dark and scary. "Let's go," I said softly, and his cheek twitched as he fought to get himself under control.

"I don't handle it well when you're out of my sight, Butterfly," he said with a soft menace. "Not with everything that's happening."

I patted his shoulder. "I know, babe, but it's going to be okay. I needed to talk to them alone." He fell in beside me as we walked from their apartment. It wasn't until we were in the car with Dylan that I spoke again.

"Rob said we need someone in either law enforcement, a judge or a lawyer to try and take Delta down, and we need irrefutable evidence of their corruption or wrong doings. He said so many people have tried to prove this before and all have failed."

Beck and Dylan snorted. "It's almost a running joke on the board now about how they're untouchable," Dylan said.

I nodded. "Yep, but they've never had people on the inside go up against them. We're in the perfect position to take the bastards down, we just need to find the right person to help us."

Beck eyed me closely. "You have someone in mind?"

"Remember that girl, Sami, from class. She said her father was a high-powered lawyer in the city. Maybe we should look into them … you know, see if they've done any business with Delta before."

Beck nodded. "That'll be easy to check into. I have access to all of the servers as Beckett proxy."

"We could also look into some of the officials who tried to take Delta down recently," Dylan suggested. "See if any name stands out."

I nodded, and Dylan started the car so we could get out of this area. "What's in the envelope, Riles?" Beck asked, his eyes falling to the brown package I still had clutched to my chest.

I swallowed hard. "Whatever Dante left for me. He asked his sister only to give it to me when he was dead, but apparently in jail for murder is close enough."

Neither of them pushed me to open it, even though I could see the curiosity in their eyes. "Should we wait to be back with Evan and Jasper? I asked. "Do they even know everything that's going on?"

"They know," Beck said shortly. "I filled them in while you were asleep. Right now they're running interference with the board, making sure they don't look too closely at us."

"They'll meet us back at the apartment," Dylan said softly, typing into his phone. "We should wait for them."

I settled back, relieved that I had a few more hours before I had to face whatever was in this envelope. Something told me, it would be devastating.

Chapter 7

"Riles, you don't look so good," Jasper said, and I hated how uncharacteristically serious he was right then. Not even a sliver of humor danced in his eyes. No teasing. No sexual innuendos. Nothing.

"I'm nervous about what might be inside," I admitted. "Like, I already know Dante betrayed me. I know that he was working for Catherine. But part of me is still making excuses, and maybe those excuses are right—he was forced, he was a child, he didn't want to betray me, he still fought to protect me as much as he could. Or… maybe all of that is bullshit and he's just a lying bastard. Either way, the answers are inside."

Jasper wrapped an arm around me, and I sank against him. "We've got you," he murmured. "Whatever is inside, we'll face it together, because that's the only fucking thing that has kept us all alive over the years."

Evan snorted, his expression dark. "Yeah, except for Oscar."

Oscar! Fuck. I'd forgotten that he was another piece of our puzzle to investigate. "Guys! We forgot to follow up on his missing body." Seriously, how the fuck did we forget that?

"We need to figure out what happened to him."

They nodded. "We're still looking into it," Jasper said. Maybe I was the only one who forgot. "But there's not a lot to work with right now. When we get past this Delta situation, we can focus on the Oscar thing."

Yeah, I supposed that was fair. Oscar was dead and nothing would bring him back. But the rest of us … we hadn't kicked the bucket yet, and to ensure we stayed topside, we had to take Delta down.

Beck walked out of the kitchen, handing me my cup, filled with beautiful, perfect, lifesaving coffee. "Figured you could use that," he said, sitting beside me so I was sandwiched between him and Jasper. Evan and Dylan were on the couch across from us.

All of us stared at the envelope on the glass-topped coffee table.

No one pushed me to open it, which was so unlike their normally impatient selves, and it made me put on my big girl panties and reach out to grab it. I ripped the top off the seal before I could think twice about it.

Upending the contents onto the table, I found a cell phone: small, black, and totally beat up. One of those cheap burner types you'd get from Walmart. Thankfully, it powered up immediately when I pressed the button. There were also assorted pieces of paper; some that I could see looked like records of bank transfers.

Dylan immediately flicked through the paperwork, while I opened the messages on the phone. There was only one contact that messaged or called this phone, and it was not Catherine's number. Or at least not the number I had for her. I scrolled back to the very earliest message, noting the year on the timestamp was 2009.

Unknown: You have your first assignment: befriend the girl. Remember. You fail, and your family will suffer. Your sister will suffer. This is a job, and I expect you to do it right.

This was it, the moment that Catherine blackmailed someone into keeping tabs on me. Someone who would become my best friend and one of the only people I'd ever trust.

Beck and Jasper leaned over to read with me as I scrolled through the messages. Most of them were standard stuff, but there were a few which turned my stomach.

Collect blood samples. Collect urine samples. Collect DNA.

"Dante refused to do some of them," Jasper pointed out. "Like the DNA one."

That was true, I could see the return messages where he'd argued with her. Catherine had allowed him some leeway in what he did, and I could see that some of the answers he gave her were modified. Some even false.

"He lied to her a lot," I said, "about me. I can kind of see where he was trying to help me."

I kept scrolling, my heart pounding harder because we were coming up to the dates close to my parents' deaths.

Unknown: Weekly schedule of the parents. Condition of their car. I need both immediately.

Dante: Why?

Unknown: It's not your job to question me. Just know that circumstances

47

have changed, and I have need of this information.

Dante: *Are you going to hurt them? Or Riley?*

Unknown: *Falling in love with your job is a bad idea, gangbanger. Remember that everything you have in this life, is because of me, and I can take it all away. How's your niece?*

"She doesn't even try to be subtle," I choked out before scrolling farther down. Dante had listed my parents' work hours, my after-school activities, and our weekly dinners out.

I paused at a text to a different number. The first number that wasn't Catherine. A number I knew very well. *Dante: Riley is in danger. Stay put for more instructions. This is a life and death situation. Trust me.*

My breathing came in and out in gasps.

"What is it?" Beck asked sharply.

"That's my dad's number," I whispered. "He texted that to my dad on the day we crashed."

My head felt light and airy, like my brain had disconnected from my body. "That's why my father made us go out. He insisted on it despite the crappy conditions. Dante had tried to warn him, but instead he'd scared him."

"Weren't you going for dinner or something?" Evan asked, his eyes locked on me.

"Yes," I started before more of the memories from that night came back to me. I'd deliberately not thought about it, which was stupid considering I was a key witness to what had happened, but who wanted to relive the worst day of their life? "We were going in the wrong direction. I didn't really question it at the time, but … we were kind of heading out of town."

My dad had seemed somewhat agitated.

I almost dropped the phone in my haste to get to the next text.

Dante: How could you? How could you kill her parents? They were all she had in this world. You've destroyed her. You've destroyed your daughter.

I could feel his anger and anguish in that message, and all of a sudden I couldn't breathe; my chest tight, I attempted to suck air into my lungs. This was my irrefutable proof that it had been Catherine.

"Breathe, baby," Beck said in his soothing voice. "In and out, count in your head, one, two, three, four, five. You're having a panic attack, and you need to ground yourself."

At first, I could barely hear him, but after some time, his words penetrated, and I started to count in my head, forcing the air in and out, forcing my body to stay alive because I needed it to finish this. To stop Catherine. Destroy her.

"My mom was alive when we crashed," I said softly when I was able to breathe easily again. The memories were hitting me now, hard and fast. Flashes of that night. That chill in the air. The screech of our tires. My fear as we tumbled down the embankment.

"When our car stopped in the embankment, she was alive." I was almost positive.

"You said her neck was broken on impact," Dylan reminded me gently.

I shook my head. "That's what they told me, but I was there. I might have blocked out what happened at first, but … I remember now. I heard her voice and her gasp. Someone got to her just after we crashed. Probably my dad too. They were murdered."

And those fucking seatbelts. Definitely the work of Debitch.

Pain twisted inside me, and a small sob escaped my lips before I clapped a hand over them. Now wasn't the time for weakness. There was a long, weighted silence while the guys clearly scrambled for the right thing to say. But there was no "right thing" in this situation. Catherine had orchestrated the murder of my parents—my *real* parents—and this was proof.

"I'm going to make that bitch pay," I whispered into the conversation void. "She's not getting away with this. Not this time. She's pushed her luck too fucking far."

Beck made a small sound, smoothing his hand down my spine. "Don't plan anything rash, Butterfly. We're in this together, remember? We'll take her down *together*."

No doubt he was thinking about how I'd run off in the middle of the night with no plans past possibly putting a bullet in my bio-mom's skull. Put like that, I guess he had a point.

Leveling a hard stare at Beck, I took a deep breath, considering our newfound *togetherness*.

"Promise me," I ordered him. "Promise me we'll make her pay for this, Sebastian."

His huge palm cupped my cheek, his steady, unguarded gray eyes meeting mine for long enough that I couldn't doubt his sincerity. "I swear to you, Butterfly," he vowed, "Catherine's going down."

I'D THOUGHT IT WOULD BE such a simple thing. We were all in agreement that Catherine—and the rest of the Delta council—had abused their power for way too long. They all needed to answer for their various crimes, and the successors would be the ones to see justice done.

But apparently, it wasn't as easy as just marching up to a judge and presenting our evidence. For one thing, we still didn't know who was on Delta's payroll, and for another, how would we prove the legitimacy of our evidence?

"I knew this was too good to be true," I groaned, tossing the stack of papers back on the coffee table some hours later. I collapsed back into the couch and scrubbed at my sleep deprived face with both hands. We needed ... more coffee. Yes, maybe more coffee would make more brain power.

"Hey, Jasper?" I called out, knowing he was rustling around in the kitchen a few moments ago. Hopefully he was still there and could sort out the caffeine situation. "Can you—"

"No!" he shouted back, then appeared in front of me with a slick smile and a handful of sandwich. "You're cut off from the coffee pot, hot stuff. Orders of the big man himself."

I shifted in my seat to glare at Beck who was engrossed in some financial document that had been in Dante's folder of dirt. He didn't even look up from his page, but I saw his lips twitch with a smile. "You're exhausted, Butterfly. You need to sleep." He looked up then, casting his tired eyes around the room. "We all do."

Feeling stubborn, mostly at being told what to do, I shook my head. "No way. We have a board of megalomaniac assholes to take down and a murder charge to overthrow. Do you really think Dante is getting much sleep while being held for rape and murder?"

Beck arched a brow at me in challenge. "He betrayed you. Lied to you for your entire fake friendship. Why do you care if he goes to jail for killing Katelyn?" He paused, narrowing his eyes. "What makes you so sure he didn't do it?"

I glowered back at him, my anger simmering beneath the surface. "He didn't do it," I snapped. "The betraying me was because of Catherine. Not a life he chose. Besides, I know him. It wasn't all an act."

Please don't let it have all been an act.

Beck stared back at me for a long time then gave a cavalier shrug. "If you say so, sweetheart."

The tone of his voice raised my hackles, and I pushed to my feet. My hands were propped on my hips and I glared down at Beck. Fucking Beck. "What the fuck does *that* mean?" I demanded.

His flat look only served to enrage me further.

"Nothing at all," he replied with a sharp edge of sarcasm. "Only that you clearly know him so well. If you say he wouldn't assault, rape and murder a girl, then clearly you know better than us."

I didn't know what the fuck had gotten into Beck, but I was too fucking tired—physically and emotionally—to put up with his drama. The heavy sarcasm said pretty clearly he thought Dante *was* guilty, so what the hell had given him that impression?

It didn't matter. He was probably just letting his dick do all the talking and seeing how jealous he'd been of my friendship with Dante since day freaking one…

But it was a fake friendship. Wasn't it? So maybe he had a point.

"Fuck you," I snarled.

"Okay," Jasper interrupted, physically stepping between me and Beck and breaking the death glare staredown we were engaging in. "That's enough of that. Weren't you two all loved up and confessing undying vengeance on our parents a few hours ago? What the hell happened while I was making a sandwich?" His accusing glare shot between Beck and me, but it was Evan—who'd been standing behind Beck's chair—who replied.

"I'm guessing it has something to do with Dante's assault conviction from three years ago," he announced, reading from the paper still clutched in Beck's hands. I guess he must have moved on from the finance docs. "Aggravated sexual assault against a Miss Hailey Tabot, age fifteen. Looks like the charges were dropped after a healthy donation into the Tabot family trust account. Courtesy of Catherine, I'd guess." Evan flicked his gaze up to me, but I couldn't speak past the huge lump in my throat.

Holy shit.

Aggravated sexual assault? No way. This had to be one of Catherine's set ups.

Still, a little voice in the back of my head whispered poison, reminding me of a night three years ago...

"What date?" I croaked out, scarcely capable of words. "What date was the report?"

"December twenty-fourth," Beck answered my desperate question, his jaw set in anger. "He attacked that girl on Christmas Eve."

It was like my strings had just been cut, and I dropped back into my seat when my legs gave way. Fucking Hailey Tabot. Dante's only serious girlfriend and my arch-nemesis. We'd all been at a party on December twenty-fourth, three years ago. Dante had given me my butterfly a few months back, and I was taking *every* opportunity to race her ... to Hailey's disgust.

Some shit about how he clearly loved me more than her, and how everyone could see it. Total bullshit. Dante freaking *loved* Hailey... it's what made me so fucking sure that assault was another Catherine stunt. Except, on *that* night I'd had a huge fight with Hailey. She'd been caught tampering with my car before an impromptu race, and when I'd confronted her, shit had turned nasty. Like bitch fight level nasty.

Dante had pulled her off me and driven her home. I hadn't given it another thought ... not really. Not when Dante showed up at my place the next morning with scratches on his face, or even when Hailey and her parents suddenly moved to live with her grandma in Florida.

Had I just been a stupid trusting dickhead?

I mean, I had missed the whole "paid to keep tabs on you" thing.

Fuck. How dumb had I been all these years?

Chapter 8

Beck and I didn't talk for the rest of the night. Eventually I ended up in bed, and I had no idea when he joined me, but he was gone by the time I woke the next morning. The only evidence he was there at all was the fact I'd had no nightmares, that comforting "Beck scent" still surrounded me, and his side was warm—I'd only just missed him.

With a groan, I pulled myself up. It sucked that we were mad at each other right now, especially when we were in the midst of trying to take down Delta, but despite all the evidence presented to me about Dante and his possibly evil side, I couldn't bring myself to write him off completely. Not yet. He deserved a chance to explain himself, especially about Hailey. She was a bitch of the worst kind, and that in no way meant she deserved to be sexually assaulted, but it did mean that I wasn't going to just blindly trust the allegations against Dante. Hailey had lied to me so many times that I wasn't sure she could actually tell the truth.

Entering the bathroom, my sleep-addled brain finally registered the fact that the shower was running. Through the top of the glass, I could see his broad, muscular shoulders. Hands against the glass, his head was resting forward as the water beat down on him, and before I could stop myself, I was padding quietly toward the glass door.

When I stopped on the other side, Beck's head lifted slowly, and he turned to face me fully. It was like he knew I was there, even though I hadn't made a single sound approaching him. As our eyes locked, my body tightened, the tiny panties I'd worn to bed already damp. Beck fucked me with one look. The rest was a pure bonus, because there was no one in the world that could do to me what he could.

His face was expressionless, but his eyes were blazing, storm clouds building there as the gray darkened. I wanted to step inside, but I couldn't fucking move. He slowly pushed the glass open, skimming past my body, and in a split second, I was jerked into his hard, wet body.

"Fuck," I groaned, arching into him. Jesus fucking Christ. I needed him. Right now. We could be mad at each other later.

"You belong to me," Beck said softly, that expression never wavering from me. "Dante might have some of your past but that's all it fucking is. The. Past."

I probably should have been arguing with this possessive Neanderthal, but I was beyond the wording and the sentences and the arguments. There was still some fire in me though, as I lunged forward, slamming him into the tiles, and taking him completely by surprise. I practically climbed him to get to his face, and then we were kissing, hard, punishing kisses. Sometimes kissing Beck was like waging war, each of us trying to come out on top. War with a hell of a lot more pleasure involved.

Beck's hands wrapped around my thighs as he yanked me up into his body. I tried to wrap my legs around him, but the wall got in the way, so Beck move forward slightly. I arched again and again, rubbing myself up and down his naked body. It was slippery from the water, and I needed to get my clothes off right now.

I needed more.

"Fuck..." I was all but begging him.

Fuck me, Beck.

My underwear and top disappeared in a heartbeat, Beck managing to both tear and drag them off me in the same instance, then he kept me elevated with one hand, while his other slipped up my thigh and grazed across my pussy.

"Butterfly," Beck said, and I somehow managed to pry an eye open and try to focus on words.

"What— Fuck!" I cried out as his fingers slid inside of me, first one and then another, The thumb on his other hand, the one holding me, shifted so it was pressing against my ass, circling in teasing strokes.

"You belong to me, Riley Jameson. Say the fucking words."

I shook my head, and his thumb pressed harder, and I was about to fucking combust at the feeling of his fingers stroking me.

"You're not going to win, Sebastian," I said, unsuccessfully keeping the moan from my words. "I will submit to no man."

He stopped moving his hands and slowly dragged them away from my aching center, and I tried really hard not to punch him.

My head shot up so I could meet his eyes. "Don't use my body against me," I said, huffing every word out in forced anger. He watched me for many long moments, still holding me like I weighed nothing, hot water beating down on us as we waged this dominance war between us.

I caved a little. "Please, Beck."

His jaw twitched and he didn't look happy. "Don't call me Beck."

It was the very thing I used to distance myself from the over-fucking-whelming emotions he created in me. And he knew it.

"I love you, Sebastian Roman Beckett," I said softly, "but that's not going to be enough for you to control me. If that's the sort of chick you want, you're with the wrong fucking person."

I wiggled down, and for a beat, as his hands tightened on my thighs, I didn't think he'd let me go. But then he did.

Stepping out of the shower, I was wet—really fucking wet—and pissed off, but I knew I'd done the right thing. Beck was strong, a leader … someone used to getting his own way no matter what, and I couldn't let him take whatever sliver of independence I had left. If he knew—truly knew—how much he affected me, then it would all be over for me.

"Just remember, Butterfly," Beck said to my retreating back, his words soft but there was no mistaking the darkness underlying them. "Dante is the one who has lied to you for half your life. Consider this when you take his side."

I wanted to scream and yell and cry and punch walls—I was starting to act like Beck in that sense. Maybe it was because I partly knew he was right, but I also was loyal to the fucking bone. I would not give up on my best friend. Not yet. And Beck was going to have to learn to live with that or … I wouldn't even consider the *or* in this situation because I was pretty sure, despite all of my strong independent stance, I couldn't live without Beck.

I took a few minutes to get dressed, then made my way out into my kitchen. I could not function today without coffee. Hopefully, we hadn't used it all last night because it was the only way I was waking up even though it was— Holy shit, 12:30 p.m.

We'd wasted another day and that was not okay with me.

My movements grew faster as I started to get all of the coffee goodness together, pausing at the doorbell.

That's odd.

None of the guys would ring the doorbell, and since we'd taken over the entire building, there shouldn't have been anyone in here. Deliveries even went downstairs.

I was just about at the door when Beck appeared like the silent ninja he was, stepping between me and the door, knocking back my hand that had been reaching out to open it.

"You didn't even check the peephole," he muttered, his jaw clenched. "You're going to be the death of me, Butterfly."

Even pissed at each other, he still cared. Fucker.

Beck lowered his head and peered out for a second before he pulled back, an odd expression on his face. I noticed the gun in his hand, and when he gestured for me to get behind him, I didn't argue. Something was bothering him, and that meant whoever was out there was not a friend.

He opened the door slowly, his eyes assessing every inch like there was a bomb or tripwire that would blow us up if he opened it too quickly. I tried my best to peek around him, but he was too fucking huge, his broad shoulders mostly blocking the opening.

When the door was finally open, he didn't say a word, and I wondered if he was doing a silent stare off with the person. Then he stepped aside.

Nobody?

Just a vase of flowers sitting innocently in the middle of my mat.

"What the…" I trailed off.

Surely Beck didn't have enough time to order me flowers, and it was totally not his style anyway. Not to mention he was currently stalking along the hall, knocking on the doors of our friends, and checking in the stairwell and cleaning closets.

Leaving him to … whatever that was, I turned my attention to the flowers. Four blood red roses, two pure white ones, and a black rose dead center. A splash of red lower down caught my eyes, and as I leaned closer to peer through the glass vase, a gasp left my lips. The roses were covered in thorns, and each of the thorns was dripping red.

It spilled into the water, one droplet at a time, before sinking to the bottom, which I only just noticed was completely red. What the actual fuck? Was that blood? Or maybe paint?

Please let it be paint.

"Don't touch them," Dylan said as he rushed along the hall, wearing nothing but a pair of soft sleep pants. His body was ripped as fuck, just like Beck's, and I felt marginally safer knowing these badasses were here to protect me from whatever fuckhead decided to leave me morbid roses.

It was probably Catherine, trying to freak me the fuck out.

And if that was the case, it was working.

Chapter 9

By the time the guys returned, I'd managed to brew an entire pot of coffee, drink that pot, and then get a second one on for all of them.

I was a jittery, hyped-up mess.

"Did you find anything?" I said, jerking to my feet when they all filed in. Dylan held the flowers in his hands. Evan had been waiting outside the door while they searched, and I smiled gratefully at him, because he'd been the only reassurance I had that Dylan, Beck, and Jasper weren't being murdered in the street.

"Nothing," Dylan growled, his eyes locked on the roses. "Whoever left these knew what they were doing. Front security didn't see a thing."

"Is it blood?" I had to ask, even though I wasn't sure I wanted the answer.

Dylan gave a single nod. *Holy fucking shit.*

Jasper whipped out his phone then hit two numbers and then a second later: "We need to add some security to our building." There was a short pause. "Only those vetted through the network." The other person must have said something, and Jasper's face darkened. "Yes. That's what I fucking said. I want it done today."

He hung up the phone then, and I shook my head at their demanding nature. Beck's gaze was on me, like he knew exactly what I was thinking. Especially how it related to this morning in the shower—the control he sought. But I was determined not to give any of them an inch. I couldn't.

"Coffee is over there," I said, waving to where I had all their cups lined up. I'd already added sugar to those that took it and milk to Evan's—he was the only one who didn't drink it black.

Dylan dropped the flowers on my coffee table, kissed my cheek as he passed, and the rest followed suit to get their morning shot of energy.

"Can we assume these flowers are some sort of scare tactic from either Catherine or Graeme?" I asked, following them into my small kitchen. "And can we also assume the blood is from an animal or something?" *Please.* I wasn't sure if animal or people blood was worse, actually. I liked most animals, humans on the other hand…

I hovered just outside, because the kitchen wasn't really big enough for the four of them to fit comfortably, but they made it work, moving around each other with the ease of people who had spent a lot of time together.

"We can assume nothing," Dylan said, taking a long sip of his coffee. "We have multiple enemies, and with the vote drawing closer, a lot of those assholes will crawl out of their gutters to try and take us down."

"But what is the point?" I asked. "I mean, the flowers aren't taking anyone down, right?"

All of our eyes shot to the vase on the table.

"Maybe we should leave them outside," Evan suggested, and I wondered if they were also imagining some sort of toxic gas secretly emitting from them.

"I'll call the captain and get him to test them to see if there is anything to worry about," Dylan said, moving to make the call.

It wasn't like them to involve the police, but in this situation, we could let someone else do the grunt work.

Once the flowers were outside for the police to collect, we finished our coffee and had some toast and cereal to keep us going, and then we got back to the research. Two hours passed in silence, and I tried my best to focus on the spreadsheets and not Beck, because I was really hating this tension between us.

"I don't know if we have enough here," Jasper said, stretching his back. "There's a lot of circumstantial stuff. Lots of incriminating numbers, but nothing to specifically tie Delta or Huntley to any of it. Dante could testify, but it's going to be his word against Catherine's unless we can make some of this evidence link them as well."

I hadn't forgotten what Rob said: we needed our smoking gun. Irrefutable evidence.

"How would Dante even have this information if he wasn't somehow part of it all?" I asked, dropping a folder back on the table. "Maybe that's evidence in itself and will give his word some more credibility."

Beck placed both hands on his knees and leaned forward in his chair. "This could have all just been doctored or typed up by anyone. We have no original documents. Nothing that their computer techs could search. The phone is a burner, and can't be connected to anyone. This is all just circumstantial stuff and will end up being a known gang member's word against Catherine Deboise, of Delta corporation."

Evan rubbed a hand over his face before ruffling up his hair in a tired manner. "We need help. We're in over our fucking heads with this law shit. We've always fought with our hands, this is something different. We need to find an expert."

I waited to see if anyone would speak first, and when they didn't, I decided to remind them. "What about Sami from school? Her father is supposedly a big shot lawyer in New York, remember? Can we check and see if he's on the Delta payroll? And if he isn't, maybe he will help us. Or at least point us in the right direction."

The guys exchanged a look, but no one argued. "If he's based in New York, there's a high possibility that he's on the Delta payroll," Beck warned me. "But it's still worth checking out."

"One issue though," Dylan said, standing in one smooth movement. "The true client files are only on internal servers. We're going to have to get into Delta offices and go from there."

The others stood as well, and I followed suit. "I'll get the car," Jasper said.

Beck nodded. "Are we going to sneak in or make this an official visit?" he asked us, leaving the choice in our hands. "I have access to the files, all of them, but it is going to leave a trace that I was there."

I raised my hand and then felt like a fucking idiot when they all smirked at me. "Maybe Richard will help. I don't have to tell him what I want his login for, but he owes me. Or more importantly he owes us all for bringing Debitch into our lives. Maybe it would be safer to use his login."

Beck's attention was fully on me then and heat flared through my stomach, wrapping around my arms and legs, holding me immobile. Fucker always knew what he was doing.

"You might be placing your father in danger," he said softly.

I shrugged. "Honestly, I'd prefer he was versus any of you. And I'm really not that worried—Richard is a secret psychopath like the rest of them. Nothing will take him down easily."

Beck nodded then, and I ducked off to grab my phone and make a call. Five minutes later I was back, code written in a small notepad and nerves fluttering in my stomach.

"He didn't even question me," I told them, lowering my voice. "And he said he'd keep the board busy for the next day or two in the safe houses, going over their game plan for the vote."

No one looked hugely reassured by this, which didn't surprise me—Richard wasn't exactly trustworthy, but I hadn't told him our plan, so there was a minimal risk to asking for his help.

Beck extended his hand to take the notebook from me, and without really thinking, I moved it out of his reach and pressed it to my chest. The motion made us both pause, and Beck arched a brow at me in askance.

"Butterfly?" he prompted. "I need the code if I'm going to search the database."

I frowned, mostly at myself, and glanced down at the notebook pressed into my shirt. "Yeah, I know. But you don't need it until we're *at* Delta HQ, right?"

At this, Beck's other brow shot up to join the first, and he looked legitimately startled. "So you're going to keep it secret until we get there?"

I nodded, not totally sure what I was doing.

Beck's gaze darkened. "Don't you trust me, Butterfly?"

My mouth opened, but no sound came out. His glare held me frozen to the spot like I'd been doused in liquid nitrogen, and I flailed for the right answer. Obviously, yes, I did trust him. Sort of. With some things ... like my heart, I guessed. But did I trust him to take Richard's login code for Delta and not use it past this one task?

"Well, that's a question asking for trouble," Dylan muttered, saving me from an actual response as he physically stepped between us and wrinkled his nose at me. "You have every reason not to fully trust *any* of us, Riles. Beck shouldn't be pressuring you when he's the one at fault." This was delivered with a sharp glare in his friend's direction, to which Beck just grunted and sank back into his seat.

"It's not that," I tried to salvage the situation before it got out of hand. "I'm not holding old grudges, it's..." I trailed off with a helpless shrug. I didn't really know *what* my issue was. Maybe I was just being a bitch to punish him for leaving me high and dry in the shower?

Dylan shook his head and smoothed his palms over my shoulders, rubbing my upper arms in a comforting, friendly way. "You don't owe us explanations. If you don't want to hand over that code, we won't make you. When we get to Delta you can input it yourself then tear up the paper, okay?"

I nodded, not wanting to dig myself any deeper into the hole I'd created. Already, I could feel Beck's angry glare and see the worried frowns on Evan and Jasper's faces. When I glanced over at them, though, they were quick to fade into easy, reassuring smiles.

"Okay," I agreed, giving Dylan a grateful smile. He'd diffused what was potentially heading for a nasty fight with Beck, and all of our energy was better spent elsewhere. "So when do we leave?"

Dylan deferred to Evan for that question, who checked his heavy Tag watch. "Like, two hours? The police haven't grabbed the flowers yet, and I'm sure they want to ask a few questions."

While they were distracted, I ripped the page with Richard's code out of the notebook and tucked the paper into my front pocket. Beck watched me do it, though, so I made a mental note to just memorize the damn thing.

"We also need to document these flowers in our database," Evan added.

This clicked something in my brain. "You have a database of creepy gifts and threats? Does that apply for all of you or just me?"

Evan looked startled at my question, and I figured he didn't know Beck had told me about the other threats left at the Deboise manor after I moved out.

"All of us," Jasper answered with a lazy grin. "Some of us have thicker files than others though." He winked, like it was some kind of competition to have the most death threats. Crazy fucks.

"That's nuts," I muttered. "But if you guys have this many threats, wouldn't Katelyn? She was a Huntley heir, after all. Shouldn't she have had just as many crazy fucks leaving gifts on her doorstep?"

The guys considered this, and Evan nodded. "Yeah, I wouldn't be surprised to find they do. Most people with considerable wealth, influence, power, or status get death threats; it's just part of the gig. Anyone would have to be dumb as fuck not to keep a record of them though. You never know when a harmless stalker will escalate." He must have just seen where I was going on this line of thought, and he gave me a long look. "You think Katelyn could have been killed by a normal crazy?"

Heat bloomed in my cheeks, and I folded my arms over my chest. "I just know it wasn't Dante. So shouldn't we see if anyone has checked her 'database' for any threats of stabbing?" I had air quoted the word "database" then immediately felt like a child, so I tucked my hands back under my armpits.

"Someone at Huntley probably already checked it," Dylan offered, but the frown on his face said he was thinking about it.

I snorted a sound of contempt. "I bet they haven't. Everyone is so fucking sure Dante killed her, why would they bother looking for another suspect?"

"She's got a good point," Evan backed me up. "Not saying the killer *had* sent Katelyn a threat, but if there is enough reasonable doubt, then they surely can't convict Dante."

"Unless he really is guilty," Beck snapped, standing up from his chair and stalking closer to me. "After all, he has a history of violence against women."

Anger burned through me, and I snarled at him. "He didn't kill that bitch, and you know it. I don't know what the fuck he did to get your panties in a wad since he's been in *jail*, but you need to get over it." I poked him in the chest, refusing to be physically intimidated by him.

Beck just glared. Typical.

My phone buzzed then, and I realized it was Eddy.

Eddy: Get me out of here, girl! I can't do the family thing any longer.

Eddy had been with her grandparents in Texas since the Dante thing, and even though she complained, I secretly thought she was happy to get away from all the Dante drama.

Another buzz. *Eddy: Grandpa just challenged me to chess. Fucking chess!*

I laughed. "Good news?" Beck said, arching an eyebrow at me.

"Just Eddy," I said, shooting back a quick text before pocketing my phone. "She's dying at the ranch."

Jasper snorted. "Glad they stopped inviting me there. Only so many times I can see our grandfather bang the maid and grandma take sixteen different pills with breakfast before it starts to get old."

I rolled my eyes at him. "Dramatic much. At least Eddy has been safe with your fucked up family. Away from Jefferson."

Jasper nodded. "There is that. But she'll be back soon, and then we'll have to make sure this doesn't touch her."

Keeping my friends safe was the top of my list, and I truly believed the only way to do that was to ensure that all of Delta's board was gone.

Permanently.

Chapter 10

Rolling up to the Delta office some hours later I felt like I was playing a role. I wasn't Riley Jameson, chick racer and poor orphan. I was Riley Deboise, heir to the Deboise family fortune and future leader of Militant Delta Finances. This time I'd dressed the part. Power suit, black and white, with my favorite heels.

I looked rich and successful, my long dark hair slicked back in a high ponytail, the ends dead straight from my flatiron. Still, when my heels clicked across the marble foyer as I followed Beck with Dylan beside me, I couldn't help feeling like the worst kind of imposter.

Three months ago I'd been a teenager living in a low-income area. Now I was an heir to a fucking billion dollar company full of sociopaths.

Weird.

The doors to the elevator slid open soundlessly and the three of us stepped into the mirrored box and remained silent while the doors closed again behind us.

"Something on your mind, Sebastian?" I whispered, getting sick of the cryptic looks he'd been shooting my way when he thought I wasn't looking. In a fully mirrored elevator, though, there was no hiding the direction of his gaze.

Beck's jaw clenched, but he said nothing in reply. Dylan's soft snicker sent my suspicious look his way, and he just gave me an unapologetic lopsided grin. "Beck's just pissed off that I was already tagging along and he can't do all the dirty, depraved things he wants to do to you in that outfit." Dylan smirked in the direction of his friend, who glared death back at him but didn't deny the truth of it. "Beck's not good at dealing with the fact that he's stuck with that hard on until we get the info we came for and get home."

My brows shot up and my gaze went straight to Beck's crotch. Well, I mean, that was like waving a red flag at a bull, wasn't it? He made a frustrated sound in his throat and angled his body away while he rearranged his pants to—I assume—hide the boner in question. What kind of addicted bitch did it make me that I wanted him to just whip it out and let me deal with it right then and there? Dylan could watch for all I cared. Hell, that could be kinda—

"Butterfly," Beck snapped, a throaty growl underscoring my name. "If you don't stop looking at me like that, your dress isn't making it out of this elevator in one piece."

My cheeks flamed, and I very deliberately dragged my gaze away from Beck and peered at the carpet. Damn that was nice carpet.

Seconds later, the doors slid open on the top floor, and Dylan snickered a laugh. "Shit, I was really hoping you'd push that a bit further, Riles."

The startled look I gave him as I stepped out into the corridor was nothing on the warning glare Beck shot his friend. None of us had forgotten that kiss at the gala it seemed.

"Come on," Beck growled. "We need to get this done before any of the board catch wind that we're here."

He led the way down the hall, and into an office the size of a studio apartment with floor to ceiling windows offering breathtaking views over the city. It was way excessive for one person's office.

"This is your dad's office?" I wrinkled my nose at Beck as he powered up the integrated computer at the massive desk. "Kinda compensating for something, huh?"

Beck flashed me a quick smile. "Actually this is Richard's office. Soon to be yours."

"Oh." I looked around again. "Well, it's, uh, lovely."

Beck shook his head with a grin, and Dylan covered a laugh with a cough. Asshole.

"Here." Beck indicated for me to sit in Richard's desk chair. "Put the access code in, and then I'll find the files."

I did as he asked, sitting down then very deliberately withdrawing the slip of note paper from my white lace bra. It was just visible over the top of my dress shirt.

"What?" I asked, acting innocent when Beck let out a frustrated groan and Dylan scrubbed a hand over his face. "This outfit doesn't come with pockets, okay?"

Funnily enough, it actually did have pockets in the jacket. But I was enjoying the sexual power play even before seeing how Beck would react to my clothing choices.

Peeking at the note, I quickly typed the code into the computer then watched with satisfaction as the screen changed to display a desktop with just a few icons on it. It took me another moment to recognize the image Richard had used as wallpaper, but when I did, my heartbeat stuttered.

"Oscar," I whispered, staring at the image of my half-brother. I'd seen a handful of photos of him around the Deboise manor, but this one was totally different. He was relaxed, his arm thrown around Richard's neck as he laughed toward the camera. Richard in the photo had his face turned away from the photographer, looking down at his son with total love in his face. "Richard really loved him, huh?"

I glanced up at Beck and Dylan who'd come around the desk to see what I was looking at, and they both seemed grim. Sad, even.

"We used to joke that Oscar won the lottery with Richard." Dylan's voice was quiet and nostalgic. "All the bullshit we went through growing up, all the training, the punishments, the mental torture... Oscar never suffered as bad as the rest of us. Richard shielded him as much as he could." His words cracked with emotion as he remembered my deceased brother. "His death broke Richard. So much more than he's showing."

An uneasy feeling twisted in my gut at his words, and I fought the urge to bite my lip. I wore bright red lipstick and the last thing I wanted was to pop out of Delta with smeared makeup.

"Do your thing," I said to the guys, rising from the chair and leaving them to find the files we needed. Computers were far from my forte, and the uncomfortable feeling under my skin was making me jumpy.

I hated that I was questioning my friends, but Dylan's comment sparked a question. If Oscar was spared the awful upbringing that the other heirs were subjected to ... did any of them hold a grudge? Would they have had motive to hurt him?

Horrified at my own train of thought, I shook my head to clear it. That was just crazy; I'd seen their emotions at the cemetery. Surely none of them were that good at acting. All the murder and intrigue of late was making me more paranoid than I really cared to admit. How the guys all managed to hold their sanity after spending their entire lives in this world ... it blew my mind.

"All done," Beck said softly, brushing a hand over my lower back as I startled.

"That was quick," I observed, "did you get it?"

Dylan flashed me a little USB stick in his palm before pocketing it and a chill ran down my spine, which I quickly ignored. Stupid Richard and his suspicions now had me seeing monsters in every shadow. Just because Dylan had the flash drive didn't mean he was doing anything bad with it. Same as the one from the gala.

"You okay?" Dylan asked, giving me a quizzical frown.

I shook off Richard's doubts about Dylan's loyalty and gave him a tight smile. "Of course. Just thought it would have taken longer."

"No hacking necessary when we have a top-level clearance access code, Butterfly," Beck explained, opening the door and holding it for me.

"Besides," Dylan added as he followed me out of Richard's office, "we figured it was better to just copy the files and look through them later. Would hate to get caught by security and need to pretend we're in the middle of a threesome or something." He shot me a sly wink then headed back down the corridor toward the elevators.

"He's joking," I murmured to Beck when he glared after his best friend.

Beck's attention shifted to me. "That's the problem. He's not joking at all."

He slung his arm over my shoulders, pulling me in close to his body as we slowly followed Dylan. "Maybe my little chat with him didn't sink in as well as it should have."

I whacked his stomach with the back of my hand and tried to ignore all those rock hard abs. "Stop it," I snapped. "He's just messing with you, and I don't blame him. You seem to be turning into more of a possessive asshole with every day that passes."

I'd meant it as an off-hand commentary about Beck's extreme jealousy issues—and I thought *I* needed therapy—but apparently he took me more seriously than that. In the blink of an eye, Beck had me pinned to the wall beside a gold framed oil painting with his body pressed to mine.

"I'm a possessive asshole?" he growled, crushing his hips to mine and dropping his lips to the curve of my neck. My breath caught in my throat, and I swallowed a lusty whimper before replying. "Yes, Sebastian. You are."

His teeth scraped over my skin like a threat, or a promise, and my pussy clenched with need. "You're damn right I am, Butterfly. You *belong* to me, and the sooner Dylan and the whole fucking world learns that, the better." He was using my body against me again, but that was a two-way street. The hard length of his cock trapped between us was clear testimony to that fact.

His lips worked up the side of my neck until he reached my earlobe, which he grabbed with his teeth.

Oh fucking hell.

"That's where you're wrong," I informed him in a breathy, sex-drenched voice. My hand trailed down his muscled side and slipped between us to grab a firm handful of his crown jewels. "*You* belong to *me*, Sebastian Roman Beckett." He groaned but didn't move away. "Even when you are acting like a fucking Neanderthal. Now, go tell Dylan to catch an Uber home because I want you to fuck me at least twice before we start looking over those stolen documents. Got it?" I gave his junk another squeeze to reinforce my position of power, but judging by the ragged breath Beck sucked in, it was only turning him on harder.

When he shifted away from me, a dazed sort of smile danced across his lips. "Yes, ma'am," he murmured, then dragged his tongue over his lower lip *slowly*. Before I could pounce and climb his body like a spider monkey, he swaggered off to deliver my orders to Dylan.

Chapter 11

"All right," the silver haired, sharp suited man across the desk said with a heavy sigh as he tossed down the papers he'd been looking at. "Do you want the good news or the bad news?"

My stomach sank. I knew it wouldn't be so easy to nail Catherine to a wall and watch her squirm. "Whatever," I replied with a wave of my hand. "It's all the same."

I sunk back in my seat, feeling thoroughly dejected and not at all surprised at what he said next.

"This isn't enough." He tapped Dante's files in front of him. "Not even close to enough. For one thing, there are no clear ties to Catherine Deboise or really *any* of the Delta board members. For another, the origins of this information is circumstantial at best. You got it from a known gang member, with a criminal record, who is currently being charged with murder?" He grimaced and shook his head. "I'm sorry, this 'evidence' isn't worth the paper it's printed on."

I sighed heavily to myself and looked out the window of the high-rise office building. I needed a hot second to pull my shit together before I did something embarrassing ... like cry. When Sami's father had checked out in the Delta records, I'd arranged the meeting. A meeting I'd come to alone, utilizing the time that the guys had been summoned for a dinner party. As far as Richard and Catherine were concerned, I was holed up in bed with a nasty cold.

"So what's the good news?" I asked, turning my attention back to Jarred Wells, of Wells, Banksy and Thomas. The Delta files had showed him—and his partners—to be one of the very, *very* few top tier legal firms in New York to not be accepting payments from Delta in some way, shape, or form. So I'd had Sami set the meeting up. Of course, she thought I was pressing charges against my would-be rapists, not spearheading the internal takedown of the largest criminal organization in North America. Semantics really.

Jarred Wells gave me a shark-like grin. "The good news is that if knocking Militant Delta off their pedestal is your goal, you came to the right man."

I arched a brow at him, curious at the bloodthirsty tone he used. "I sense a history."

"Most certainly," he replied, but didn't elaborate further. "This evidence isn't enough, but you're in a much better position to get what *is* enough. You said you had access to the secured files in their head office?"

I shook my head. "I did, briefly, but Richard would have changed his code since then. We may be blood-related, but we are far from family."

Jarred nodded, like he'd expected this answer. "I can understand that.

Well, I have no doubt you can find something they're hiding. Criminals or not, they're all still businessmen. And woman, if you count Catherine as anything more than a perpetual nuisance."

My jaw clenched hard. "She killed my parents. That's considerably more than a nuisance in my eyes, Mr. Wells."

His expression softened for a moment. "Of course, I'm sorry. I simply meant in the sense that businessmen typically keep records of *everything*. It sounds stupid, given all the illegal activity Militant Delta is involved with, but the more powerful a person is the more indestructible they see themselves. Their arrogance alone would see that they've kept records on every dirty little secret they have. If you can find that..." He shrugged, and I didn't need him to say the rest.

If you can find that... you can see the entire board behind bars.

I knew what he was saying. The guys had already demonstrated a thousand times over how many fucking records were stored on various servers, but I knew of one place that held the absolute motherload of dirty secrets.

The vault.

"You've thought of something," Jarred commented, watching me with sharp, intelligent eyes. A slow smile crossed his lips, and he nodded. "Good. I look forward to our next meeting, Miss Deboise." He stood up with me and offered his hand to shake.

"It's Jameson," I corrected him, but he shook his head.

"No, dear. It's Deboise. Whether you like it or not, if you topple a king or queen their subjects still require leadership. When you achieve your goals, the weight of cleaning up Militant Delta will fall to you and the other successors. Make sure you're ready for that." His handshake was firm. Professional.

"Good luck, and don't get killed. I've waited a damn long time to see those bastards receive their karma, and I have a good feeling that you're the one who can make it happen."

I cleared my throat nervously. "No pressure, though."

Jarred Wells barked a laugh as he walked with me to the elevators. The whole office floor was empty, silent except for his assistant who had earbuds in, listening to music while she worked way past close of business. "No pressure." Jarred laughed, indicating for me to step into the elevator then giving me a warm smile as the doors slid closed.

Alone for a few moments, I released a huge breath and scrubbed my hands over my face. He hadn't said anything I hadn't expected. Dante's file *wasn't* enough to lock Catherine up and throw away the key, but just in case, I'd had to try. And this was also a test. If Delta came after me now, I'd know that Wells was on the take, secretly.

And if they didn't, we had an ally. Someone who was willing to help, and hadn't been corrupted by greed and power.

The foyer of the tower Mr. Wells had his firm located in was just as quiet as the office upstairs. To be expected, I guessed, at almost nine at night. Good thing I had moved out of the Deboise manor already, so no one would see me sneaking home in the early hours of the morning by the time my car got back to Jefferson.

Beck and I had a rip-roaring fight about me going alone, because he was an untrusting bastard, but in the end, he'd had no choice. He had to be at the Delta party as the Beckett proxy, and I wasn't willing to wait any longer. But I'd conceded on allowing his driver to take me in a town car—which had been waiting outside for me for at least the last half hour.

"Have a good evening, miss," the security guard called out as I walked across the marble foyer and past his desk.

I flashed him a quick smile then stepped out onto the street. My car—a dark silver Rolls Royce Phantom—waited exactly where he'd dropped me off, and I clicked open the back door and hopped in without waiting for the driver to open the door. It always made me uncomfortable when they did that, like I wasn't capable of doing it myself?

"Sorry, that took longer than I thought," I apologized to my driver, Carl. "I hope you didn't get grief from anyone for waiting here?"

No response came. Not even a nod of acknowledgement, nor did he start the engine.

"Carl?" I prompted, peering at the back of his head. He hadn't even looked back to greet me when I got in, which was odd. It'd been a long drive down to the city, and I'd gotten a pretty clear sense of what a good guy Carl was.

A chill ran through me, and I sat forward in my seat.

Carl's head was lolling to the side, and at first, I thought he was asleep. I wouldn't have blamed him; it had been over an hour since I went into my meeting. But then I saw the smudge on his collar. It was just a shadow in the dark street, but when I lifted my phone and shone the light on it, red blazed at me.

I choked back a cry, slamming into my seat, my heart racing and limbs shaking.

Dead.

Sorrow for the man I'd only had a short time to get to know rose up in me. Carl had been a nice guy, older, with a couple of grandchildren. Some asshole had ripped him out of their world without a second thought, and it was my fault.

Flashbacks of my parents' crash hit me, and a keening cry rose up in my chest. I tried to stop it from emerging, but I was fighting a losing battle. Delta had brought darkness into my world, a darkness that was threatening to consume everything and everyone.

What if I lost Beck and the guys? Eddy? I wouldn't survive it.

My door wrenched open, and I screamed until the familiar dark lines of Beck's face flashed in the limited light.

"Butterfly," he bit out, his eyes running over me.

"You—" I coughed. "You followed me?"

He shook his head like I was a fucking idiot. "Of course I did. You demanded your independence, and while I accepted it, there was still no way in hell I was going to leave you to travel into the city without one of us."

"Carl's dead," I said softly, my voice husky with tears. "Someone got to him while I was in my meeting."

Beck's eyes briefly flicked toward the driver, but then they were back locked on me. "I missed it because I was keeping an eye on you. We need to get out of here, Butterfly, and we need Carl and the car moved to another location. If this law firm is actually going to assist in taking Delta down, then there can be no ties to us found close by."

I grabbed his arm, some of the clawing pain and panic in my chest easing at the warmth of his body. "We should go inside and ask Wells for help," I said softly. "He'll know … legally, the best way to deal with this. You know, before we all get charged with murder."

Beck laughed darkly. "Being charged with murder is the least of our worries if Delta finds out we're trying to take them down."

His eyes rose to the impressive building I'd just left. Somehow, there was no one on the street still, but it was New York, and even though this law firm was down a side street, someone was still going to come by soon. We needed to get out of the car.

I pushed against Beck. "Come on, let's get inside."

He didn't look happy, and that particular flat, furious look was one of his scariest. "What makes you think we can trust this lawyer?" he said softly, stepping back and drawing me with him. "He might be the one who killed Carl. He might have orchestrated all of this to leave you alone and defenseless."

I nodded. "Already thought of that, oh suspicious one, but ... my gut is telling me that we can trust Wells. Fate landed him in my lap. We shouldn't go against fate."

Beck shook his head, but he didn't argue any further. When we were standing on the street, cool wind whipping across us, sending my coat billowing out, he drew my gaze away from the body visible through the front windscreen.

"Wait here for a second," Beck said. "I'm going to wipe our prints from the car."

Of course. Why didn't I think of that? I mean, unlike Beck I didn't end up in life or death situations on the regular, but I was a huge aficionado of CSI.

Beck pulled a white cloth and small spray bottle from his pocket ... why the fuck was he carrying around a cloth and spray for removing fingerprints? I probably didn't want the answer to that.

For the first time he shot me a slow smile. "I had a feeling."

When Beck was just about done wiping the car down, I wandered a little closer to the sidewalk. The few street lights above us were out, which was in a way ominous. Had Beck done that? Or the killer?

And was the killer around here somewhere still.

My eyes darted about, trying to take it all in, but it was so fucking dark that visibility was almost nil...

Wait.

A shadow across the front windshield caught my eye, and I stumbled closer, careful not to fall down the gutter. It took my eyes a few minutes to adjust, and when they did, I somehow managed not to scream, pressing a hand tightly over my mouth.

Black rose.

A single black rose was tucked into the wipers. I fumbled with my phone again, raising it so there was a very low light across the car. My hands trembled at the red running in lines down from the thorns. *Carl's blood.* I knew it was Carl's blood, just like I knew the killer was leaving me a message.

You're next.

Chapter 12

Sometime later, could have been minutes ... or hours, Beck appeared at my side.

"Butterfly?" he said, barely a whisper of my name.

"Windshield," I choked out.

He turned away from me, and I could have sworn that the heat he always threw off rose a few more degrees.

He wrapped an arm around me and practically lifted me from the sidewalk, taking us out of the cool wind and into the Wells building. The security guard rushed over to offer assistance, but Beck waved him off, leading me to the elevators and putting his phone to his ear. He was right beside me, but an incessant ringing in my head was making it hard to focus on what he was saying.

I heard the words *rose* and *blood*, probably because those two words were already running around my head, filling me with fear and anger.

If Catherine was doing this, I was going to fucking kill her. Jail was too good for her, she needed to die. More voices were talking around me, and it wasn't until Beck sat and pulled me into his lap that I snapped out of whatever shock had taken hold of me. He had his arms wrapped around me, and I pressed my face into his wool coat.

"The guys are on their way," Beck said softly, and I lifted my head to meet his eyes. Needing the reassurance I often found in his gaze. Of course, the storminess of them should have scared me, but I was way past that with Beck. I was safe with him.

"Ms. Deboise," Jarred Wells said, drawing my attention to him. "Tell me exactly what happened."

Steeling myself, I nodded, trying to get my head on straight again. Thankfully the disorienting shock in my body started to fade as the adrenaline died down. "I went out to the car and my driver was dead," I started before quickly filling him in on everything else that happened.

"Delta can't know we're here," was Beck's only contribution to the conversation, his body tense under mine, that heat still pouring off him.

He was pissed. Mega pissed. I couldn't really blame him either. I'd stood my ground and demanded independence, coming into the city on my own, and my fucking driver had been killed. I was sure Beck was thinking how easily it could have been me. Alone, defenseless in New York city, with a killer clearly after me.

We were one step from him telling me "I told you fucking so," and he would have had every right.

The fine skin around Jarred Wells eyes tightened, the only sign he was at all concerned. "We must work quickly so that Delta doesn't find out. I have a friend on the police force, a rather high up detective, who hates your company as much as I do. He can help us out in this situation."

His eyes met mine directly and he paused for a moment. "This situation and the other one we discussed Ms. Deboise."

I nodded.

It was nice that he was still treating me as his main point of contact on that situation; usually Beck would have just taken over. But for once, he didn't flex his alphahole personality, allowing me to remain in control.

His gaze never left Jarred, though, watching as he called his detective friend, waiting for the car and the body to be removed, and all the while, Beck continued to observe everything in his quiet, deadly way.

Then we waited until he got the text. "The guys are here," he said shortly, standing and lifting me with him before I was dropped gently to my feet. It was *very* late now but Jarred had not made one move to get us to leave. Instead, he'd stayed silently waiting with us.

"I'll be in touch soon," I said softly, and he just nodded.

"Take the back stairwell. Even if my friend can smooth over any witnesses, we don't want word to get back to Delta…"

We really fucking didn't want that to happen.

Beck and I left via the back stairwell, and as we descended, I realized something. "How did you get here? You clearly don't have a car nearby if we had to wait for the guys."

"Friend gave me a lift from the dinner."

"What friend?" I pushed.

Beck shook his head. "No one you know. Let's just call it someone who owed me a favor and knows it's worth more than his life to talk about anything to do with Delta."

I was really too tired and freaked out to question him further. Loving and trusting someone didn't mean you had no secrets, it meant that you trusted them to ensure their secrets never came back to hurt you. Beck and I might have finally been at that point.

Or maybe I was just beyond giving a fuck. There was only so much one person could worry about, and I had reached my limit.

A familiar dark SUV was waiting in the shadows outside the stairwell. Beck had somehow found the time to let them know where to pick us up.

"Riles," Dylan said as I climbed in the back. "Are you okay?"

His concern was obvious, and I felt marginally better just being back with them all. "Yeah, not really."

Beck pushed in on the other side of me, and I was between him and Evan. Jasper was driving with Dylan in shotgun.

"Tell us everything that happened," Evan said the moment we pulled away. "Beck only gave us the highlights."

Probably worried about the phones being tapped, even though they apparently had "untappable" phones. Untrusting bastards were starting to make sense. I could finally see just how fucking scary this situation was.

I told them quickly about my meeting with Wells. "He said the evidence from Dante is not enough. He's apparently been looking for a way to take Delta down for years, and he won't go after them with anything that circumstantial. We have one shot at this, and he won't waste it."

Which had been what Rob said also.

"This Wells kind of seems too good to be true," Jasper said dryly.

No one disagreed. "I got the vibe that he had some sort of beef with Delta in the past. Maybe we should check him out?" I suggested.

Beck shook his head. "We'll know soon enough if he's playing us. Delta will come at us with all of their power."

"So we just wait and see," Evan said, sounding relaxed enough.

"Wells is right," Dylan said darkly, and I wondered why he wasn't looking back at me. Usually he faced me directly when he spoke. Lots of eye contact. That was Dylan's thing. But now he was staring out the window. "We all have one shot, and if we fail, they will bury us. Heirs or not."

It was a heavy feeling, the pressure grinding us down. But I was not giving up.

"I have a plan regarding that," I said in a quiet voice. "But before I go into that, we should discuss this fucking rose killer asshole."

Evan snorted. "Rose Killer. Sounds like a pussy-ass bitch with a name like that."

"Have you guys gotten anything back on the other flowers?" I asked, ignoring Evan.

"No." Dylan said shortly, and I could tell I wasn't the only one noticing his weird attitude.

"What about information on gifts Katelyn received?" I pressed.

"Graeme is blocking all access to his family and the police files," Jasper answered this time, and the stark contrast between him and Dylan made the tension skyrocket. "But we're working on sneaking in through … let's just call it a side access."

Which was probably a good idea since we now knew this "rose killer" was an actual killer.

"Poor Carl," I said softly, my chest aching again. "He has kids and grandkids. I mean had. He had…" I broke off.

"For what it's worth," Beck said gently, "his family will be compensated."

It wasn't nearly enough, but it was something at least. I had no idea how Beck was going to manage that without tipping Delta off to our involvement, but he'd figure out a way.

The bright lights of the city hit me as we finally left the back streets where the Wells building was. Despite the fact it was the middle of the night, there were people everywhere, and I blinked at the sudden noise and activity. I'd been sitting in a dark murder bubble for too long, and I almost couldn't correlate the two worlds.

"What's your plan?" Beck broke the silence, and I jerked in my seat.

"Shit, you scared me," I said, pressing my hand to my chest. "Sorry, I must have been in my own world."

His thumb brushed across my cheek. "You're in shock still. Give yourself a break."

I nodded, my head bouncing up and down even though I wasn't sure what the fuck I was feeling. "So the plan."

I took a deep breath, wondering if they would think I was a fucking idiot or not.

"I think we should vote Huntley into Delta."

I let that sink in for a moment, wondering what their initial reaction would be.

"Are you out of your fucking mind?" Jasper asked, sounding almost amused by my crazy suggestion. "Beck, you need to get your woman checked. She's fucking crazy."

I held a hand up, even though Jasper was watching the road and couldn't even see me. "Hear me out before you dismiss my brilliance." My attempt at a joke fell very flat. "There's more to it than just voting them in and hoping that the board goes to war and kills each other."

Evan snorted, shaking his head. "That actually might not be a bad idea. Wars within Delta would weaken them a lot."

"That's not enough for me," I said, letting some of the dark anger that had been simmering inside since I was first brought into this world spill out. "I want them to suffer. I want them alive, stripped of their money and power, at the mercy of the criminals in whatever horrible jail we arrange for them to be at."

They had destroyed so many lives. It was time to pay.

"And how do you propose letting Huntley win the final seat will ensure that?" Beck asked, sounding like he was taking me seriously.

I cleared my throat. "We need access to the vault. That's where all the evidence is. Decades of fucking evidence."

My body was tense as I waited again. "No one knows where the vault is," Dylan said, pensive and still doing the weird stare out the window thing. "No one. It's the highest guarded secret Delta has."

"Someone has to know," I told him just as thoughtfully. "Someone deposits the evidence in there."

Beck's hand gripped mine, his thumb brushing over my skin. "One of the elders is the secret keeper. There is always only one and no torture would make him give up the location—upon his death, there's a fucking ceremony and everything where they use his thumb to open up a safe that gives direction to the next secret keeper."

Jasper snorted. "That old fuck wouldn't break. He's not human. But I suppose we could knock him off and remove the thumb."

I shook my head. "No, we aren't there yet. Plus, I'm guessing he's pretty heavily guarded."

The grim silence told me that I'd hit the nail on the head there.

"Okay, so he's the only one that knows. Is he unguarded when he puts the video in the vault though? Like … when he put mine in there?" I was trying to piece it all together.

Beck shook his head. "Nah, he hires a runner who he kills after the fact. Promises someone money, and then when they do their task, he gets rid of them."

Disgusting. The Delta board needed to go down.

"Why doesn't he just do it himself? Would be easier."

Dylan finally turned around, and I flinched at how hard and dark his face was. "When have you ever seen Delta get their own hands dirty? The elder will want no tie to the vault, no matter what, and he's ensuring that by using his disposable lackies."

Fuck. "Even more reason to use my plan. If we can't torture the information out of the old fuck, we need to ensure that there's a new recruit who requires an initiation video. There are no more heirs, so the only option is Huntley on the final seat. Then we follow the lackey, somehow, and find the location and requirement for entry into the vault. It's our only shot. The vault is the one place that will have what we need. Evidence that cannot be disputed."

I crossed my fingers on the hand Beck didn't hold, praying that this plan might be viable. Because I needed something. And I needed it soon. Even if the five of us eventually took over our roles as heirs, with our parents and the elders still there calling the shots, threatening our loved ones, we'd never be free. The danger would never wane. We had to end this shit once and for all.

"It might work," Jasper said softly, able to turn a little now that we were almost out of the city. "There's a chance at least."

"If it doesn't work," Dylan warned, "We've added a very dangerous person to our board, and we will lose some control."

Beck was silent, all of us waiting for his opinion. He was the unspoken leader of this merry band of assholes, and his opinion held a lot of weight. "I think we should give it a shot," he finally said, and I let out a relieved breath. "Huntley won't add much more danger to our position—Delta board and our parents have always been the true threats. It's worth it to see if we can take them down."

"This will be interesting," Dylan murmured so quietly I think I was the only one who heard him. For whatever reason, it sent a shiver of apprehension through me.

Chapter 13

I clenched my jaw and tried to drag myself out of the foul mood I'd woken up in, but it was no use. I sighed heavily and slammed my locker door shut, just barely missing Eddy's fingertips—she had only just gotten back from her week at her grandparents, and was as annoyed as me to be at school.

"Sorry," I muttered to her when she yelped and glared at me.

"No drama," she replied with a cautious side eye. "Someone have a rough night?"

I heaved another sigh and tossed my hair back over my shoulder. As if the weekend hadn't been bad enough—what with Carl being murdered and the ominous rose left for me—my hair-tie had snapped on the way to school and I didn't have a backup. "Yeah, you could say that," I agreed. Without even meaning to, I searched the halls for Beck.

When the guys had told me the plan for this week, I'd pitched a shit fit that had ended up with Beck sleeping on the couch and me staring at the ceiling all damn night.

"Do nothing." That was what the plan had boiled down to.

"Hey, why don't we cut out and go get real coffee?" Eddy suggested, linking her arm through mine. "You look like you could do with a break... from everything, and I missed you while I was gone."

I almost waved her off, but the odd note to her voice had me looking closer at her. "I'm fine," I assured her with a small frown. "Just not sleeping well since... you know."

Her lips pursed, and she nodded. "Since your best friend and my casual lover got accused of murdering one of our classmates? Yeah, that's sort of what I meant."

She paused, spotting the guys coming toward us down the hall. "Have they...?" she broke off, biting her lip as she kept her eyes on the four kings of Ducis Academy. "Are they being assholes about it? I know they're the ones who beat Dante up back when you took that week off school."

Startled, I stopped walking, spinning her to face me. Something else was pushing this doubt from her, something more serious than she was letting on. "They're totally fine," I replied, "they're helping to come up with a plan for getting Dante released, seeing as we all know he didn't do it." I peered at her closer. "Is everything okay with you? Was it okay at your family's? Your parents haven't been causing drama have they?"

Eddy shook her head and gave me a tight smile. "Nah, all good. Grandmother was same old—busybody bitch. But it was a nice escape. Parents are MIA as usual." She eyed the guys one last time. "Anyway, I better get to history." She hurried back down the hallway right before the guys reached me, and I frowned after her, confused as fuck.

"What's her deal?" Evan asked, wrinkling his nose as Eddy disappeared into the swarm of uniformed students.

"I have no idea," I murmured in response. I didn't bother telling them she'd just said she needed to get to class when it was the beginning of the lunch break. She was avoiding the guys for some reason ... I made a mental note to corner her later and find out why.

Beck slung his arm around my shoulders, tugging me in close and nailing me with a seriously intense kiss. Startled, I let out a squeak and pushed him back. Eventually. It wasn't like I didn't want him kissing me, I was just confused as to why PDA was suddenly a thing for us.

"Uh, hi?" I squinted up at him, even as he tucked me into his side while we headed for the cafeteria.

"Hey," he replied with a cocky smirk.

Shithead. He knew exactly what I was asking.

Jasper snorted a laugh as he held the lunchroom door open for us, and I speared him with my suspicious glare.

"Start talking," I demanded, knowing he was the easiest target.

Jasper gave me a wide, smug grin. "Beck overheard one of the guys in social studies talking about your tits. Looks like he decided to stake claim."

I spluttered a shocked noise and poked Beck in the side. "Is that true? Did you just publicly piss on me because some guy complimented my rack?"

He gave no response, but when we reached our usual table, he sat and hauled me into his lap and proceeded to make sure the entire fucking academy knew we were together. His grip on my ass only let up when I was groaning softly into his mouth and fighting the urge to grind all over his hard cock.

"You're damn right, I did," he told me in a voice drenched in sex and need. "Now no one can pretend they don't know."

I arched a brow. "Know what?"

Beck's gaze was blazing hot, setting my whole body on fire. "That you're *mine*."

I bit my lip to hold back the elated smile that wanted to burst free.

"Now, Sebastian," I scolded teasingly. "We've been over this. But I guess we can settle on mutual ownership ... until I can get you alone for a power struggle later." I suggested the last in a breathy, lust filled whisper, and Beck's hips jerked slightly.

"Guys. Point made." Jasper threw a balled up napkin at Beck's head in a playful gesture, but when we turned to look, his eyes held a little more seriousness.

Clearing my throat in embarrassment—suddenly remembering that the entire freaking academy was watching me dry fuck my boyfriend—I made to get off Beck's lap. He grabbed me around the waist before I could make it far, spinning me around to face the table but keeping me on his lap.

"Just for a couple of minutes," he growled softly in my ear. "Give me a moment to think about really unsexy things so I don't sit here with my boner on display for the whole school."

I snickered a laugh, grabbing a fry from the tray of food Dylan had just delivered in front of me. "Case in point of who owns who," I whispered back to Beck with an evil smirk.

"Guys, serious chat time," Evan said, drawing my attention away from Beck's erection pressed against my ass. "Beck staking a public claim sort of drops Riley in the cross-hairs for Delta, doesn't it?" He shot a glance at Dylan as he said this, and I was curious to hear the answer.

We *had* been keeping our shit low key so that Delta wouldn't try to use our feelings for each other against us. Me being the weak link in the group and all, it was not a good idea for them to know that I was a weakness for any of the guys. So what changed?

"Doesn't matter," Dylan muttered, sounding just a little bit sour. "Everyone with eyes can tell they're fucking, even if they're not making out in public."

"True shit," Jasper laughed. "The sexual tension is electric." He poked me in the arm and made a zapping sound, which made me grin like some kind of loved up fool.

Damn it. Beck was totally ruining my chill.

"Besides," Beck added, reaching around me to snag some fries for himself. "My dad already has us figured out. Not much point in hiding it when the biggest wolf of all has our scent."

"Makes sense, I guess," I commented. The tension seemed to have faded from Beck, but I gave him a quick glance to check he was cool with me getting off his lap. At his small nod, I slid over into my own seat.

Don't get me wrong, I loved sitting in my boyfriend's lap as much as the next girl, but given all the heavy shit going on in our little crew, I preferred to feel like an equal player, not a cheerleader.

"So, did we make any progress on accessing Huntley's files?" I posed the question to Jasper, and by "we" I really meant him. I'd found out over the weekend that the back door they planned to use to access the files was actually some genius hacker chick that Jasper had hooked up with a while back. The holdup wasn't in gaining access to the server, it was in Jasper convincing this chick to actually help in the first place.

"Uh, yeah, it's getting there." His cheeks flushed pink, and he suddenly became very interested in his lunch for some reason.

Evan covered a grin with his burger, and I narrowed my eyes at him. "Spill it."

"Jasper tried his usual routine on her this morning in economics, and she slapped him." Evan was practically gleeful with the information, and Jasper's face darkened further.

"Wow," I said, a bit shocked. "Is that a first for you, Jas? Your face says this is maybe a first, which kinda surprises me."

Jasper looked genuinely offended at that. "What the hell does that mean?"

I shrugged. "Just that I figured you'd been slapped plenty of times. You're kind of a man-whore."

At this, even Dylan and Beck laughed. Or ... as much of a laugh as either of them were capable of in public, which was more of a smile than anything. Still. Enough to have Jasper outraged.

"Harsh, babe," he commented, defensive. "This *is* the first time I've been slapped. Supposedly after I hooked up with Layla last year, I stood her up on a date and then she found me in bed with her roommate."

I spluttered a laugh. "I'm not even surprised. You deserved that slap, so good for her."

Jasper scowled. "I don't even remember doing it. There was a rough patch with some shit at home... I was drinking a lot, among other things."

"Well..." I wrinkled my nose and tried not to laugh at his sulking face. "You better get down on your knees and grovel. If this chick can hack a system that none of you three James Bond wannabes can hack ... then we need her. Fast. Dante's hearing is set for this Friday." It actually should have happened already, but Beck was using his influence to push it off as long as possible. Yesterday—which was what sparked our argument—that influence had run out.

"I know, I know," Jasper moped. "I'm mostly pissed at myself for doing that in the first place. When she stopped flirting with me, stopped going out of her way to run into me in the halls, I figured she was just one of *those*, you know?" As he said this, he gave a subtle head jerk toward the gaggle of girls whose skirts were always too short, their shirts too tight, and their eyes permanently lingering too long on my guys. I hadn't really interacted enough with other students in Ducis Academy to know them by name—except for Brittley, of course—but I got his point. He thought this Layla was just a social climber who wanted to tick off "fucking a Delta heir" on her list.

"It never occurred to you that you'd fucked up?" I pressed then regretted it when Jasper grimaced. Maybe he actually liked this girl more than the rest? Either way, he needed to start making amends.

Wiping all traces of teasing from my face, I reached across the table to take his hand in mine. "How can I help you, Jas? I could be a pretty great wingwoman."

"It's fine." He sighed and gave me a grateful smile. "I'll sort it out. Don't worry, all we need is enough reasonable doubt that they drop the charges. I'm sure a whole death threats file will do that."

My stomach twisted with worry. "I hope so."

Under the table, Beck reached over and took my hand in his, threading our fingers together. It was a small thing, but it reminded me that we were in this together.

Chapter 14

The afternoon passed quickly, and as I was exiting my last class, I spotted the bathroom and nodded my head. "Be right back," I said to Dylan.

He just grunted, and I paused. "Dude, I'm going to need you to stop fucking grunting at me and start using your words. Clearly something is going on with you, and I'm here if you need to talk about it."

Dylan just shook his head. "Not ready to talk about it, Riles. But I will try my best to limit the grunting."

I sighed. "Cool with me." Even though it really wasn't. On instinct I leaned forward and wrapped my arms around him. Hugging him tight. I loved Dylan like a brother, he was a solid friend and a loyal person, but whatever was up with him bothered me. He'd been acting weird for days. Instinct told me that I needed to get to the bottom of it before it escalated any further.

Dylan's arms tightened around me, lifting my feet off the ground.

"Whore," someone coughed as they passed us, but I didn't give a fuck. They could think I was fucking all four guys as much as they wanted. Even if I was, that didn't make me a whore—I loved the Delta heirs, every single one of their spoiled, entitled, dangerously scary asses, so it would never just be about sex.

Unfortunately, I didn't love the other three like I loved Beck.

He was it for me; I was a fucking goner.

Dylan held on longer than I expected, and I didn't try and break his hold. He needed this hug a whole lot, and I was here for him. When he finally let me go, I headed into the bathroom, desperate to pee. When I was done, I washed my hands and straightened up my mess of hair. It was everywhere—probably had been since Beck mauled me at lunchtime. No one was in the bathroom with me, courtesy of Dylan no doubt, and I was actually expecting it to be him when the door opened and a figure stepped inside.

It wasn't.

It was Sami.

She met my gaze in the mirror before quickly checking every stall, and then she pulled out some sort of small devices that she ran around the room. I stood there wide-eyed, wondering what the fuck was going on, when she stopped at my side.

"Sorry for all the cloak and dagger bullshit," she said quickly. "My father is paranoid at the best of times. And when it comes to Delta, he's paranoid on steroids."

I nodded quickly, because that sort of paranoia might just keep us all alive.

"You have some information for me?"

She nodded. "Yes. The body was taken care of and has been linked to another crime. The NYC police department already have it filed away and nothing should come back to you."

I swallowed, thinking of poor Carl.

She pulled some files out of her satchel and handed them over. "He also found some stuff that he thinks might help with Dante and also with whoever killed your driver."

I glanced at the plain yellow folder with not a single identifying mark on it. "Is this Delta stuff?" I asked.

She shrugged. "I'm just the messenger. But I got the feeling that maybe your driver had nothing to do with your company at all. Dad seemed to indicate that it might be something related to you."

The folder seemed to burn hot under my hand.

"He wants another meeting soon with your progress," she said. "I'll let you know."

I nodded, and then she spun and disappeared. My hands trembled as I stared at the folder again. I wanted to rip it open and see what he'd sent me, but I also knew the boys would be pissed if I looked without them.

Case in point when Dylan stuck his head inside the door.

"Everything okay in here, Riles?"

Taking a deep breath, I slipped the folder into my own bag and nodded. "Yep, all good. Just some girl talk."

I winked, but no doubt he could see the serious expression hidden behind my pretend.

"That's good," he said with his own fake grin. "There's a bit of a lineup out here though. You ready to go?"

I snorted at the fact that he kept everyone out so I had privacy. And safety, no doubt.

"Yep, let's do it."

I received multiple glares when I emerged, but all of them managed to keep their mouths shut. Dylan's scary scowl probably had something to do with that. But I like to think it was me.

"Thinks she's the fucking queen," some bitch muttered near the end of the line. "Nothing but a used up whore."

She glared at me from under her platinum blonde hair and thick black eyebrows, and maybe it was the fact we were dealing with so much shit and these cunts would just not stop with the fucking name calling, but I'd had enough.

Spinning away from Dylan, I advanced on her. My expression must have clued her in on how angry I was … that they'd pushed and pushed and now I was about to show them what happened when Riley went over the edge.

"What the fuck did you just say?" I bit out when I was a few feet from her.

She opened and closed her mouth before turning to her friend. Clearly hoping for some support, but the friend was already backing away.

My hand snapped out and grabbed her chin, holding her tight as I forced her to look at me. "You shouldn't call other women whores," I said softly. "We should be sticking together in this fucked up world, not dividing amongst ourselves through petty jealousy. My shine doesn't dim yours, love."

Some fire came back into her face as she struggled to free her chin from my grip.

"I call it like I see it," she snarled. "You're fucking four guys. You had a fucking group of guys at school get a shot with you. You. Are. A. Whore."

A rumble from behind told me that Dylan had had enough of this bitch.

He wasn't the only one. I released her, and just as the guys had taught me, I swung my body forward and slammed my fist into her face, knocking her back and to the ground. She started screaming and crying, pressing her hand to her cheek as she scrambled away.

I followed, not giving her an inch. "Anything else to say?" I asked. "I mean, any chick that talks about gang rape as having a 'shot' at me, doesn't really deserve to speak, so I can break your jaw. If you'd like some help staying quiet."

She shook her head frantically, eyes still filled with angry tears. Now though, there was a healthy dose of fear in there as well.

In fact, as I turned around, none of the chicks in the hall looked directly at me. Like they were afraid to catch my eye. That made me grin because apparently the psycho gene was in all Delta heirs.

Linking my arm through Dylan's, we strolled out of the school to find Beck, Jasper and Evan waiting for us by their cars. All of them had their phones out, and I wondered what the fuck they were watching, until we got close and I heard my voice.

I jerked my head to Dylan. "You filmed me? Asshole."

He shook his head. "Riles, it was hot as fuck. The guys needed to see you in action."

I shrugged, not really caring. When I looked again, Beck's eyes were on mine, and his eyes were blazing hot. He dragged his gaze across my face and down my body, and I actually shivered. My knees felt a little weak, and Dylan was half carrying my weight by the time we got there.

"Butterfly…" Beck drawled.

Jesus. Just … I really needed a come to Jesus talk because I was basically fucking Beck in the parking lot. With my eyes. But if we didn't get out of here soon, the "whore" slurs would be coming a lot more frequently.

Beck reached out and lifted me clean off the ground before he deposited me in the passenger seat of the Bugatti. His fingers brushed across my nipples as he clicked the belt in, and I groaned, this low breathy, needy sound.

We'd been fighting a lot lately, but in no way at all had that diminished our attraction. If anything, it was heightening it—we were just that fucked up. Beck slid into the car, and the throaty engine roared to life. I moaned again because I wasn't sure I'd been this turned on for a while, and this car … it was basically my aphrodisiac.

"Hold on, Butterfly," Beck said, shooting me his perfect smile.

"Bastard!" I bit out, clenching my thighs. "You started this at lunch time."

He chuckled, and I moaned again as he spun out of the parking lot, slamming his foot down as soon as we straightened. I had to close my eyes and think unsexy thoughts, or I was literally going to climb onto Beck's lap and fuck him in a speeding car. Both of us would probably die, but it'd be worth it.

The only thing that wouldn't be okay was if we killed an innocent bystander, so I'd have to keep it in my pants until we got home. Beck's hand slid across my thigh, and I thanked whatever gods there were that I hadn't worn tights today. His fingers caressed the bare skin, sliding up to brush across my aching center. Stroking my clit through the silky fabric.

I arched my back, letting my legs fall open as much as I could. "Beck, please." I was all but begging as he teased and played with my body like it was one of his guitars. An expert at using his fingers to create art, magic, beauty.

His finger slid in under the side of my panties, and I was so wet that his fingers glided across my body like we'd used lube. He circled my clit once, and then again, and I cried out. He increased the movement until I was a writhing, sobbing mess.

"Come for me, baby," he whispered in a low husky voice, and I shattered, riding his hand the best I could, all the while craving more. It wasn't enough. I needed Beck inside of me. I wanted him to fuck me over and over until I forgot our mess of a world, and all I could think about was the way he destroyed my body.

And my soul.

He worked me until I was basically dead, my body falling limply in the seat. "You're really good at that," I whimpered.

Beck lifted his finger and licked across it, eyes hooded. He dropped that gaze to mine, and I shivered at the heat there. "Next time it's my mouth," he promised, and my pussy basically jumped to attention, ready for everything he was offering.

His gaze went back to the road, and mine went directly to the very obvious erection straining against his pants. Shit. That was not going to waste. Just as I reached out to wrap my hand around him, Beck cursed, his face hard as he stared out to the left. I turned in that direction too, frowning at the sight of the police cars lined up in front of our building.

This can't be good.

Somehow, I managed to push my sexual urges aside, straightening myself so that I didn't stumble out of the car, vagina flapping in the wind. Beck had on his "Delta face," and since I still hadn't perfected one, I worked to just appear normal and unfazed.

We parked in our normal spot in the secure garage. Dylan entered a minute later with everyone else, including Eddy, who was back living with us. I loved having my best friend close, but knowing we were putting her in danger tainted it slightly. When she'd been in Texas, she had been out of the line of fire.

"What's with the PoPo?" Eddy asked, dragging herself out of the car, her school bag coming with her. "There were police and detective cars out there."

Dylan lifted a hand, his phone pressed to his ear as he listened intently, and nodded a few times. We waited, and when he finally hung up, he turned grim faced. "That was the Delta board. The flowers we sent in triggered something in the police database and they're here now to question us. We're not supposed to say a word until our lawyers arrive, but I figure it's safe to suss out what they know."

The other guys nodded, none of them at all concerned about being questioned by police. They were the fucking experts at lies and deceit, so this was an average day at the office for them. "You should get out of here, Edith," Jasper said, turning to his sister. "This isn't about you."

She crossed her arms. "The fuck it isn't. Anything to do with you five is about me. You might consider me an outsider because I'm not a magical fucking heir, but I am your family. All of your family. I won't be left out any longer." She jabbed a finger in my direction. "Like what you did to Dante and Riley. I should have known about that!"

The anger I'd seen earlier in her face returned, and it all made sense now. "You found out. How?"

She snorted, arms once again bound tightly over her chest. "Fuck yes I did. Our cousin told me that the four heirs had fucked over the fifth heir to get her to join their group of fucking assholes. Hurt her friend. The whole family was impressed with how brutal you all are. Shares are going to skyrocket on Delta apparently." She looked disgusted. "It all makes sense now. Dante's injuries. The way Riley hated you all. Her anger."

She snarled at them. "How could you do that to her? How? I encouraged her to go back to you guys when I should have been encouraging her to stab you all in the chest."

Stepping forward, I wrapped my arms around my best friend. "I love you, and I appreciate your anger on my behalf, but we've moved past it. Just trust me when I say that the guys are as much victims of Delta as I am. We're working toward ensuring this shit never happens again."

Her face remained furious as she stared at me, trying to discern if I was lying to her. Finally, some of the anger died away. "They're still assholes," she finally said.

I nodded. "They absolutely are. The biggest assholes. But they're our family and we need to accept that while they may act like dicks at times, they always have our backs."

Dylan snorted. "It's like we're not even standing here."

I flipped him off before Eddy and I hugged again. She held me tightly for a minute, then wiping at her eyes, she straightened. "Okay, I'm ready to deal with the police. Let's do this."

Jasper bopped her on the head. "You'll stand at the back and keep your mouth shut, Edith. The last thing we need is anyone looking at you when it comes to this shit. You stay under the radar."

She saluted him with a sarcastic wiggle of her head. "Yes, sir."

"Smartass," Jasper muttered, but he didn't push anything else.

I drifted closer to Beck, and he wrapped an arm around me, holding me against his side. We would not show the police any of the chinks in our armor. Not today. Today we were a formidable team that could take on any fucking thing.

We took the stairs to the main lobby level, assuming that was where the police waited for us. The security on the front desk remained where they were, blocking the elevator, eyeing the half dozen officers that stood before them. Some in uniform. Some plain clothed.

"No one gets through," George, the giant security man that I was pretty sure was bulletproof, was saying to the cops. I had no idea how old George was; his dark skin was smooth except for a few laugh lines, but the few sprinkles of gray in his black hair told me he was older than I thought.

However old he was, he was scary and formidable, and the police officers were not pushing forward on him at all.

"Thank you, George," Beck drawled, nudging us past one of the uniformed cops and hitting the elevator button. "We've got it from here." Barely even bothering to look over his shoulder, he addressed our guests. "I assume you'd like to speak with us?"

One of the guys in a suit, as opposed to a uniform, cleared his throat and stepped forward. "Mr. Beckett," he said, flicking a cautious glance over me, then a quicker one at the rest of our crew. "We need to speak with Miss Deboise as a matter of urgency."

A sneering sort of smile crossed Beck's lips. "You mean you need to speak with *me*. If there is a police matter concerning *Miss Deboise*, then it's me you need to be informing."

As much as I knew he was playing his role—the arrogant, entitled heir to a multi-billion dollar corporation—the misogynistic tone rubbed me the wrong way. Scowling up at Beck, I dislodged his arm from my shoulders and stepped closer to the cop.

"What Beck meant," I said in a sickly sweet tone, knowing Beck was glaring death at my back, "is that I'm Riley Deboise, and you're quite welcome to speak with me directly. After all, this isn't the eighteenth century." Calling myself a Deboise turned my stomach, but Wells' point had stuck with me. I was a Deboise, like it or not. There were many bigger things to concern myself about than a stupid surname.

The suited man shook my hand and gave me a tight smile. "Thank you. I'm Detective Shepherd, this is my partner, Detective Riggs. May we speak with you somewhere more private?" He shot a look at George, who gave a sassy brow lift, and I needed to swallow back a laugh.

"We can speak upstairs," Dylan offered, stepping in before Beck did something dumb. Like beat me over the head with a club then drag me back to his cave. "Just you two, though." He nodded to the detectives. "Our apartments are a bit tight on space. Your officers can wait here in the lobby."

I turned to the elevators, trying to hide the hard eye roll I'd just given Dylan. Just when I thought he was being the reasonable one. Nonetheless, the two plain clothes detectives joined us for a tense, silent ride up to the top floor then gave Dylan a narrow-eyed glare as we stepped into my expansive, open plan apartment.

"Yes, such cramped confines," the partner—Detective Riggs—muttered under his breath. He looked younger than his partner, maybe in his early thirties, with a dark shadow over his jaw where he'd not shaved.

Half amused, half frustrated by the boys' behavior, I indicated for the cops to take a seat.

"Can we get you coffee?" I offered, "Beck will make it." I speared my boyfriend with a sharp glare, and he narrowed his eyes back at me. "Dylan, you'd better help."

"I'll take one, thanks boys." Jasper smirked at Beck and Dylan, flopping down in my dusky gray armchair.

Evan nodded, perching on the arm of the couch I sat on. "Same."

The alpha male dickheads of our group scowled sourly, but did as they were told. They damn well knew they were throwing their weight around unnecessarily. Detective Shephard had specifically said they were here to speak about something, not *question* or *detain* or anything like that.

"Sorry about them," I apologized when I could hear the two of them clattering around my kitchen.

Eddy snickered, taking the seat beside me. "The Delta boys have a bit of caveman syndrome where Riley is concerned."

"Probably a good thing," Shephard murmured, then cleared his throat again. "Miss Deboise—"

"Riley," I corrected him, and he nodded.

"Riley. You received a vase of roses recently, correct?" His gaze was even on me, but a chill ran down my spine at the reminder. But he didn't know about the rose left at Carl's murder scene, only the ones left on my doorstep.

"Should we be waiting for legal counsel?" Evan asked, speaking up before I could respond myself. "I understand they're en route."

Shephard gave a small shrug, even as his partner looked annoyed and generally irritated. "If you'd feel more comfortable, then by all means. But we aren't here to question you on anything, Riley." He raised his brows at me, silently asking if he should continue or wait for our lawyers to arrive. But really, I didn't trust Delta paid lawyers as far as I could throw them—which wasn't far.

"Go ahead," I responded with a nod. Beck and Dylan had just slapped together the quickest coffee in recorded history and were already rejoining us so there was no sense in stalling any further. "Yes, the roses were left on my doorstep. I take it you tested the, uh, blood?" I swallowed hard, my mind flashing to Carl's blood dripping from the rose under his wipers.

Shephard nodded. "The blood was nothing exciting, just store-bought pig's blood."

"Can't understand why that's even an option to purchase," Detective Riggs muttered, scratching his stubbled cheek. "Just asking for stupid high school kids to pull dumb pranks on each other." He shot me a pointed look, and I frowned.

"Are you implying this was a *joke?*" I demanded. "You brought six uniformed officers with you to tell me that you have dismissed this threat as a high school *prank?*"

Riggs was getting under my skin.

"No," Shephard replied in a firm, no-nonsense tone. The look he shot his partner was a clear *shut up, you asshole.*

I squinted at him suspiciously. "No? So... what did you find out? I'm assuming it's something to warrant this downright weird visit?"

"The black rose triggered in our database as being linked to an open investigation," Shephard explained. "The specific variety is rare, called Osiria. It's native to a remote region of Turkey, so not something readily available at florists. We're worried that this links you to another victim. We've brought uniformed officers with us because until we can verify more information, we think it best you keep a police guard around the clock."

My brows shot up, and I licked my suddenly dry lips. The guys all seemed fine letting me take the lead on this conversation—and rightly so—but I could practically feel the tension vibrating from all four of them. Eddy was the only normal one in the room, looking as pale and worried as, I'm sure, I was.

"When you say, another *victim*, I take it you don't mean someone else who is being stalked?" My voice was husky, and I knew the answer before Shephard shook his head.

"Miss Deboi—uh, Riley. These roses are involved in an open murder investigation. A young oil family heiress in Texas was recently stabbed to death in her bed. The only clue left was a black Osiria rose drenched in her blood." Detective Shephard looked grim as he shared this information. "Obviously, we ask you don't share these details outside this room, but I need to impress on you the seriousness of your situation. That young lady had been stalked too. Gifts left in her bedroom, roses in her locker at school, things like that. Her family didn't take it seriously, and she died for it. Please don't make the same mistake."

I stared at him for a long moment, searching for the right words. Eventually, Eddy spoke for me. "Thank you for letting us know," she said with flawless politeness. Of course, she was a Langham heir, too, even if she wasn't *the* heir. "I'm sure Riley would appreciate having your officers watching over the apartment building, but we do have our own security for school."

I cleared my throat, coughing out the lump of shock and fear that had formed with the news of a murdered heiress who'd been getting the same roses as me. "Yes, what Eddy said. Thank you."

Detective Shephard frowned at me, looking more like a concerned parent than a police officer in that moment. "Any other roses, or just anything remotely out of place, please be sure to call us. Okay?"

I nodded, biting my lip and trying to erase Carl from my brain. "Thank you for letting us know. Was there anything else?"

The lead detective shook his head and stood up. "That was all for now. Thank you for being amenable to our protections, I'm starting to think the rumors about the Delta heirs is unfounded." He shook hands with me, then with everyone else, and headed to the door with his partner following.

Just as they were about to step out of my apartment, Riggs paused and looked back, scanning his eyes over all six of us. "You know, you'd all be a hell of a lot safer if you moved back home with your moms and dads. Militant Delta Estate is better guarded than the local prison."

I gave Riggs—that prick—a sarcastic smile. "I appreciate your suggestion, but I'd rather run my chances with a serial killer than sleep under Catherine Deboise's roof again. Have a great evening!" I slammed the door in his face before he could respond then turned back to the guys with a glower. "What?" I snapped, watching the Delta masks slipping off their faces, and Evan wrinkled his nose at me.

"You know he probably works for Catherine? The whole Jefferson PD is on Delta's database." Evan wandered over to my floor-to-ceiling window and peered down at the street, presumably where tonight's officers were stationed.

I sighed, flopping down onto the couch and kicking my feet up onto Eddy's lap. "I know. Catherine can kiss my ass."

"But also, that's why I figured it was easier to just accept their cops," Eddy piped up. "If they're being paid by Delta anyway, what difference does it make if it's them or someone else? I figure Beck has his own guys out of sight anyway."

Beck grunted a noise but didn't disagree.

Jasper sighed heavily and stood up, grabbing his jacket from where he'd tossed it. "All right, wish me luck. If I'm not back before school, then maybe report me missing."

He headed out the door, and I shot a confused look at Evan, who grinned wickedly.

"He's going to see Layla," he filled me in. "This new development sort of pushes more urgency on checking Huntley's files, don't you think?"

Fear coursed through me, and I clenched my fists to stop them trembling. "You think Katelyn might have been killed by this same guy?"

"I'm getting a feeling," Beck said with a grimace. "This psycho likes heiresses. We need to be more careful. I'll make some calls." He disappeared into the outside hall, presumably to make those mysterious calls within his own apartment, which I doubt he'd even slept one full night inside since "moving in" the other week.

Dylan sat down on the couch beside where I had my head propped on a pillow. "You need some food, Riles," he commented, stroking my messy hair with his fingers. "You barely ate at lunch time."

Evan snorted a laugh. "She ate plenty... of Beck's tongue."

"Shut up," I growled, throwing a spare cushion at him and missing.

"How about we order Chinese?" Dylan suggested, and my stomach groaned its agreement in unison with Eddy's enthusiastic approval. "I take that as a yes." Dylan laughed and pulled out his phone. He didn't stop stroking his fingers through my hair, instead just using his other hand to find the delivery app and select our favorite foods.

Some time later, Beck returned and took Dylan's seat, but I was already dozing. A little nap before the food arrived wouldn't hurt, and the stress of everything was weighing down my eyelids like they were made of lead. Despite the fact I was being stalked by a murderer, plotting a mutiny for my bio-parents' empire, and working to free my best friend from jail, I couldn't help but soak in the peace and security of that moment. Lying there, surrounded by my chosen family, the people who I loved and trusted, I could push the bad shit aside.

Chapter 15

I had no idea what woke me, but one minute I was deep asleep and the next my heart was racing and my eyes were wide open. Fear coursed through me like electricity, and I didn't move for the longest time. I simply lay there, holding my breath and listening for what had woken me. My bedroom was silent, the only sound coming from Beck's deep breathing as he slept beside me.

That was what finally allowed me to relax. If Beck was still asleep, then it had to have been a bad dream that'd woken me. Still, my heart was pumping, and I doubted I'd be getting back to sleep any time soon. Beck's arm was heavy around my waist, and when I tried to slide out of bed, he tightened his grip, pulling me back into his body.

"Where are you going?" he mumbled without opening his eyes. His voice was so thick, I doubted he was even really awake.

"To pee," I whispered back with a smile. "Let me go, caveman."

Beck mumbled something incoherent but kissed my bare shoulder and released me from his grip so I could scramble out. By the time I'd grabbed his t-shirt from the floor and tugged it over my head, his breathing had evened back out into sleep, and I took extra care not to make any sound as I crept into the bathroom.

When I was done, I decided not to get back into bed straight away. I was still wide awake and would only end up tossing and turning, then eventually waking Beck up. Still, it wasn't until I headed back into the living room that I remembered the folder Sami had given me in the bathroom at school.

I grabbed it out of my bag then tossed it on the coffee table. Whatever Wells had sent me would need some brain power to process, so I padded around in the kitchen and made coffee in my awesome Queen mug. Not wanting to turn on too many lights and wake Beck, I just flicked on the little table lamp beside the couch and settled against the pillows to tear open the sealed packet.

"I probably should have opened this sooner," I murmured to myself, flipping through what looked to be a case file. One that catalogued all the grisly details of the heiress murdered in Texas two months ago. Wells must have somehow intercepted the information before the cops came to see me, which made me a little bit impressed at his reach and resources.

A thorough read of the papers showed nothing drastically different from what Shephard had told us, just offered a whole lot more detail. Including crime scene photos that turned my stomach and set my heart racing with fear. I was so engrossed reading a diary photocopy from the victim—sixteen year old Cordelia June—that I didn't hear anyone creeping up on me until a hand touched my shoulder.

Needless to say, I screamed, and the papers I'd been holding scattered everywhere while I scrambled away from my attacker ... only to find Beck in a fit of laughter on the floor behind the couch.

"You asshole!" I shrieked, throwing a pillow at his head. Hard. "You scared the crap out of me!"

"Aw, I'm sorry, Butterfly," he snickered, pulling himself up and climbing onto the couch with me. "I couldn't resist. What had you concentrating so hard at three in the morning, huh?" He peeled my arms away from my face—which I'd been hiding to stop him seeing just how badly he'd scared me—and kissed my neck.

I considered telling him all the crap I'd just read, especially the part where Cordelia had thought the roses were being sent by a secret admirer. She'd journaled about which boy at school she thought might be responsible and talked about how flattering and exciting it all was. This was a month before her murder. The gifts had steadily deteriorated from there, roses turning up covered in blood and her cat being left dead on her bedroom floor, until finally—while her parents were away on some business trip—the stalker had broken in, tied her up, tortured, and raped her before stabbing her to death. A single black Osiria rose was left tossed on her body, the signature of her killer. I worried about the fact that my first "gift" was the bloody roses. Did that mean he was lessening his timeline with me? Or had there been other gifts before the roses?

"What sort of shit did Delta intercept for me?" I asked Beck, and all humor died from his face. "Have there been other gifts? Or just threats?"

His face was suddenly alert, not a single sign that it was three in the morning and he had only had a few hours sleep. "Three written threats, two bunches of flowers, some stuffed animals, and a diamond necklace which was traced to an oil heir currently living in South Africa."

I blinked at him, while attempting to smile. "Well, where's my necklace? I love diamonds." I joked to hide my discomfort about people sending me stuff. Especially when those flowers and stuffed animals—similar to what Cordelia got—probably came from the crazy serial killer.

Beck's hand wrapped gently around my throat, and my body clenched. His voice at my ear was a whisper. "No one puts jewelry on this perfect body except me."

I snorted, but didn't disagree. There was a beat of silence, and I sighed. "I think those first flowers and the stuffed animals were from the Osiria killer," I said softly.

Beck stilled, face unreadable. "What makes you think that?"

I turned fully toward him, suddenly desperate not to think about my fucking stalker and this messed up Delta world. I needed to stop seeing those crime scene photos. "I'll tell you soon," I breathed, moving my face closer to his. My heart stuttered out of rhythm for a moment as I stared at Beck. He was fucking gorgeous. Too gorgeous for his own good.

"First though ... why are you awake?" I asked softly. His eyes darkened, going stormy at my change of subject. But he indulged me, letting the heavy shit go for a moment.

"Couldn't sleep without you," he admitted, brushing a thumb across my cheek. Beck leaned in close, wrapping his arm around my shoulders and touching his lips ever so softly against mine. "I can't seem to get enough of you, baby. I think I'm addicted."

I smiled into his kiss, embracing the rush of butterflies erupting inside me at his words. All the bad thoughts disappeared, and I was back to my happy place. The potency of Beck confessing his feelings never seemed to dissipate, and it was fast becoming my kryptonite.

"If that's true," I murmured back, sighing with pleasure as he kissed down the side of my neck, "then I'm just as addicted. I can't seem to keep my hands off you, Sebastian." Demonstrating my point, I ran my hands down the hard planes of his bare chest, skimming across his abs and settling at his waist.

He let out a small, manly groan as my fingernails trailed over the lines of his lower abs, those delicious ones that created the V shape right above his junk. "I have an idea how we can handle this," he informed me, between scorching kisses.

"Hmm?" I replied, fuzzy headed with lust and fascinated as to how I'd just ended up straddling Beck when a moment ago I'd been sitting beside him. He was smooth. Real smooth. "How to handle our mutual addiction to each other?"

"Uh huh," he confirmed, pushing his t-shirt that I'd borrowed up and tossing it aside. I'd been sleeping naked, so without his shirt, my whole body was bare to his touch. "Normally I would just do it, but something told me I should actually *ask*. You know. Make it official?"

I froze, even as his warm hands cupped my breasts and toyed with my hard nipples. "Make what official?" I asked in a breathy whisper, scarcely daring to breathe. What the fuck was he asking me?

Beck took his time, kissing me long and deep—prolonging the anticipation—before replying. "Butterfly? I was wondering..." he trailed off, dropping scalding kisses against my skin until he reached my breast and captured a nipple between his lips.

I let out a low groan when he sucked, threading my fingers into his hair. Whatever the fuck he wanted to ask, he was seriously making sure I'd say yes. "Wondering what?" I pressed, even while I shifted my weight up on my knees and tugged his boxers off. When he didn't immediately respond, I took his hard shaft in my fist and gave him a few teasing strokes. "What were you wondering, Sebastian?"

"Fuck," he groaned, his fingers finding my wet heat and dipping inside. "I was wondering if you..." he broke off again, gripping me by my waist and pulling me closer so that his cock was lined up with my aching pussy. "If you'd be cool with me moving in. Permanently." He punctuated his request by thrusting inside me, tightening his arms around my body to pull me down until we were totally joined.

The air all rushed out of my lungs, and my fingernails bit into Beck's muscled back. Whether it was in response to his suggestion or the sheer delirious ecstasy of having him inside me, I wasn't totally sure.

He only gave me a hot second to adjust before starting to move, holding me still as he pumped his hips up, grinding into me deep and possessive as he always was. Except, unlike all our anger fueled fucks lately, this time it was pure, unfiltered love that he screwed me with.

"Holy shit," I moaned as his pelvic bone ground against my clit with every thrust, "Sebastian... you're playing dirty."

A dark chuckle bubbled out of him, and he laid a hot, open mouthed kiss against my throat. "You're damn right, I am. So?"

I laughed back, relishing in the exquisite pleasure radiating from my core. "And if I say no?"

A low, dangerous sound rumbled from Beck's chest and he flipped us, landing us with my back on the couch and him firmly entrenched between my thighs. "You're not going to say no, Butterfly," he informed me with utter confidence.

The deadly little twist he put into his hips as he fucked me had me panting with need, and when he slipped a hand down to toy with my clit, I almost screamed. Still...

"What makes you so sure?" I pushed, enjoying making him wait for my answer. Power play was *always* going to be our thing, no matter how comfortable we got with each other.

His lips brushed mine ever so softly, his tongue tracing the curve of my lower lip carefully, *teasingly*. "Because you're just as in love with me as I am with you, Butterfly."

I groaned, totally unable to deny it and also totally unable to fight the orgasm that was building with every push of his hips, every flick of his fingers, every delicious word from his lips.

"Fuck you, Sebastian," I moaned, locking my heels together behind him and holding on for dear life as he pushed me over the ledge into a toe-curling, earth-fucking-shattering climax.

"I guess it's okay, then." My voice was husky from the screaming and panting of my finale, but he still heard me. His grin was wicked and totally smug, and seconds later, he came with a grunt.

"Thank fuck for that," he mumbled into my sweaty neck when he collapsed on top of me. He was heavy enough that I was totally trapped... but in a good way. "I already arranged to move my stuff in today while we're at school."

Typical. Fucking. Beck.

I started laughing then, but it was one of those exhausted, totally relaxed sort of laughs, and Beck vibrated against me with a silent laugh of his own. Fucker.

"I'm just glad you were asking that and not something more serious," I admitted, feeling a bit silly for that initial spike of panic—and excitement—that I'd experienced when he mentioned making things *official*.

Raising his head, Beck gave me a bemused smile. "Butterfly," he practically purred, "did you think I was going to *propose* to you? Like this? With my cock buried inside your sweet cunt and a serial killer lurking somewhere in the night?" His tone was slightly joking, but there was a darker thread to it that made me shiver.

"It would be your style," I muttered back, defensive. "Not that I'm in *any* way considering marriage to you. So we're clear. We are way too freaking young for that shit."

Beck just hummed a noise in response and crawled backward down my body, hooking my legs over his shoulders. His warm breath feathered over my throbbing, swollen pussy, and my breathing stuttered.

"Sebastian," I growled in warning, "you *do* agree, don't you?"

He hummed his response again, using his fingers to part my lower lips and dragging the tip of his tongue down my pulsing clit. I gasped in response, a shuddering sound that ended in a pathetic sort of whimper. Damn him for playing my body like a seasoned pro.

"Agree to disagree, Butterfly," he murmured, his voice muffled as he kissed my inner thigh, "but I promise I won't propose." Two fingers entered me, and his mouth closed over my sensitive clit, drawing a cry from my throat. Just when I thought that we'd put the matter to rest, I caught his whisper of, "*this week*."

Sneaky fuck.

Chapter 16

Beck and I had finally made it back to bed around the same time the sun was coming up, and couldn't have been asleep long when someone started hammering on the door.

"I've got it," I told Beck, sitting up and hunting for clothes. Where the fuck were all the clothes?

Beck made a growling noise of frustration as he rolled out of bed and sauntered into the living room totally naked and unashamed. "No, Butterfly, you don't. Did you forget you're being stalked by a murderer?" He leveled a warning glare at me, and I dropped back into the fluffy bed with a deflated sigh.

Honestly? Yeah, I had forgotten for a hot second there. Being with Beck made me feel so safe, and this whole fucking relationship felt like such a dream that every now and then the real world just faded away.

"What?" Beck snapped, yanking my front door open and not even trying to cover his nudity.

A little bit scandalized, I raised my head from the pile of pillows just enough to see who was getting an eye-full before breakfast. My bed was in just the right position to view the front door from where I lay.

"It's done," Jasper snapped, totally devoid of his usual cheery disposition. "Katelyn was getting the roses too. If we can convince Huntley to hand over their black files, Dante should be free by the end of the day."

Hearing this, I let out a squeak of excitement, shooting upright on the bed and totally forgetting to cover myself. "Jasper! That's fantastic news!" I paused, frowning. "I mean, not that she was being stalked by the same guy... but there's no way they can let the case against Dante stand now, right?"

Jasper gave a shrug, running his hand through his messed up blond hair. A gesture he looked like he'd done a lot before coming here. "Right. If we can find out why Huntley hasn't already come forward with the info. Anyway, it's been a hard night, I'm going to catch some sleep. I'll be at Ducis by lunch or something."

His voice was totally flat, and he didn't even give my naked tits a second glance before leaving.

"Uh, what the fuck was that?" I demanded of Beck when he closed the door again.

"What was what?" he replied, coming over to me and pushing me back into the pillows. "Other than you giving Jasper spank bank material for the next thirty years. How many times do I have to tell you that *these* are mine, Butterfly?" He was teasing, but the possessive way he cupped my breasts made me groan.

"That's exactly what I'm talking about," I said, keeping the conversation on track before he distracted me with another orgasm. "Jas didn't even *glance* at my tits. No jokes, no sly grins, nothing. He was like a robot. Not to mention the fact that he didn't so much as flinch seeing you open my door in the nude."

"Ah, that." Beck let out a sigh, rolling off me and propping his head up on his hand. "I suspect whatever he did to get Layla's help isn't sitting comfortably on his conscience."

My brows shot up. "Jasper has a conscience when it comes to women? Color me shocked."

Beck gave me a quick grin. "You know he does. The thing with Layla last year was over before we really knew much about it, but I know she messed him up a bit. I even thought he was a bit heartbroken for a while there."

I shook my head, confused. "So what changed?"

"Nothing, Jasper just went back to being Jasper. We haven't really talked about her since then, until we came up against this hacking issue. That's what put her on his radar, you know? She hacked his computer and tried to blackmail him with all the naked selfies he had saved. Clearly, she didn't realize how widely distributed those pictures already were." Beck laughed lightly at the memory, and I smiled.

Still, it made me feel awful for our friend. This chick must have been someone pretty special to have such a profound effect on Jasper.

"I feel bad," I confessed, sighing. "I never want to put you guys in awkward situations to help me."

Beck snaked a hand around the back of my neck, pulling me toward him and kissing me firmly. "Jasper would happily walk through broken glass to help you, Butterfly. We all would. Don't act like you're forcing us to do shit we don't want to do."

I grumbled, but knew he was telling the truth. I might only be sleeping with Beck, but all the guys—and even Eddy—had found places in my heart. And me in theirs.

"Come on, get dressed and we can stop for donuts on the way to Ducis," Beck suggested, and I eagerly bounded out of bed.

"Fuck yes!" I yelled back at him as I entered the bathroom and started the shower running. "Gimme ten minutes."

THE FIRST HALF OF MY day went by pretty uneventfully. I'd become pretty used to having one of the boys shadowing me, and Evan was good company so I wasn't complaining. Better yet, Eddy didn't seem to have the same desire to fight with him that she had with Jasper, Dylan, or really even Beck. So it was a peaceful sort of day.

"Is this weird for you?" I asked my best girl friend as we put our books away in our lockers after Chem. "I know when I arrived here you didn't really hang out with the guys at school. Now you're queen of Ducis." I was teasing but also kind of serious.

She snorted a laugh. "Princess, at best. And only because I'm friends with the real queen." She poked me in the side, and I laughed. "But yeah, it is kind of weird. Our whole lives, Jasper has been my brother in private and a stranger in public. The other four were even worse than that. Ever since Oscar—the oldest of the heirs—turned thirteen and the board took more interest in the boys lives, none of them had really even acknowledged my existence outside of the Delta estate."

"You know that wasn't our choice," Evan commented, and Eddy whirled around to scowl at him.

"Private conversation, dickhead. At least pretend you're not listening." She propped her hands on her hips and narrowed her eyes in challenge, to which Evan raised his hands in surrender.

"I'm just saying," he forged on, risking Eddy's ire, "We were just doing what we thought was best. No one ever accused teenage boys of being the sharpest tools in the shed, right?"

Eddy folded her arms and huffed. "You're not a teenager, Evan."

"I was then," he countered, rolling his eyes. "We all were. By the time we realized that wasn't the only way to play it, you seemed to hate us all. It took this walking tornado to shake shit up and blow away the past." He shrugged and jerked his head in my direction.

I gasped with mock outrage. "I resent being called a tornado," I muttered.

"Whatever," Eddy replied, dismissing Evan with a wave of her hand. Like he wasn't just going to keep walking with us, regardless. "Anyway, it's kind of nice." This was said back to me, answering my original question. "Not the whole thing where everyone treats us like we could crush them if they cross us ... but it's nice being close to Jasper again. I missed him."

Evan made a loud fake cough, and Eddy rolled her eyes.

"I guess the others aren't as bad as I thought too." She paused, looking wicked. "Except Evan. That guy is a total prick, right?"

"Hey!" Evan yelled, "Little shit." He tried to grab her, but she danced out of his reach with a peel of mocking laughter.

I snickered a laugh as he chased her into the lunchroom, eventually catching her around the waist and tickling her until she apologized. It was such a cute *normal* moment, I could almost see the two of them as a couple. Almost.

I started to follow them when a red-haired girl stepped into my path. Her chin was tilted up with determination, but I was quick to notice the tremble in her hands, clenched at her sides.

"Can I help you?" I drawled, narrowing my eyes in a threatening sort of way. Sure, it wasn't the friendliest thing to do given I didn't know this chick from Barbie. But I was pretty confident she wasn't about to invite me for a sleepover.

"You think you're so much better than us," she spat, but her voice quivered. With fear? I hoped so.

My brows shot up. "Do I?"

"You should be ashamed of yourself," she waged on, like I hadn't spoken. "You're nothing but a loose-legged homewrecking *murderer*. Beck will use you up and throw you aside and the rest of us will be there to laugh when it happens."

This chick clearly had a screw loose. Didn't she hear that I punched a girl in the face yesterday?

I took a step closer to her, feeling a thread of satisfaction when she flinched. "Listen ... whatever your name is. You all seem to be under some delusion that I'm one of you. I'm not. I'm one of *them*." I indicated to the lunchroom where my guys were all at our usual table, and Beck was glaring menacingly over at us. "As for whose home I supposedly wrecked, you can't seriously be talking about Brittley?" I scoffed a laugh. "She was never dating him, except inside her own head. Grow up, stop tearing other women down to make yourselves feel better." I flicked a glance down the hall where her friends watched with rapt concentration. "It's not classy, and it's certainly not going to get you ahead in life. So, just back the fuck off. Got it?"

The redhead looked uncertain, then steeled herself. Her nostrils flared and her fists tightened at her sides. "What if I don't? What are you going to do about it? Hit me, like you did Sarah-Jane? She's probably going to need a nose job, thanks to you."

Sick of the dramatics, I took another step closer to her, and she flinched back again as predicted. "Maybe I will." She paled to almost gray, and I rolled my eyes. "Have a great day." I brushed past her with a deliberate shoulder check and continued into the lunchroom to join my guys.

For all my independence and preaching about being bigger than petty high school games, I still went straight to Beck, sat in his lap, and kissed him for *way* longer than was acceptable in a public forum. So sue me, I was human. Those crazy bitches needed to learn that Beck and I were solid, and I wasn't going *anywhere*.

"Everything okay?" he asked me in a husky whisper when I released his lips. His eyes shot across the lunchroom, indicating to red-haired Barbie.

I gave him a smug smile. "Totally fine, I just needed to mark my territory."

His brows shot up, and a small smile played across his lips. "Butterfly, did you just piss on me?"

"You're damn right I did," I replied with a wicked grin.

Chapter 17

"**O**h, bingo!" I announced, checking my phone. "He agreed to meet tonight, even invited us to dinner." I grinned broadly at Beck across the dining table from me and waved my phone.

"Seriously?" he muttered, sounding a bit shocked. He reached for my phone, and I handed it to him to see for himself. "Huh. Technically, he invited *you* to dinner, but even so..." His brow furrowed, and I groaned.

"What? You've got that look. What's wrong?"

He gave a small shrug, handing my phone back. "Just seems suspicious that he agreed to meet so easily. Everything we hear about Graeme Huntley is that he holds his privacy of utmost importance. Now he's inviting a Delta heir into his home? Seems... odd."

I huffed, disappointed that he wasn't congratulating me. "Maybe he's just curious about what I want to discuss? I mean, I'm still his niece."

Beck nodded, but didn't lose the tension in his jaw.

"What does it matter?" Dylan commented. "It's not like Riley is going alone, and Huntley wouldn't dare hurt her so close to the vote. They need Catherine to hold her seat and she can't do that without a living heir."

"True that," Jasper agreed. "Hey, can I come to dinner too? I really want to see the inside of Huntley Manor."

"No," Beck replied, throwing a scrunched up ball of paper at his friend across the table. We'd all been working on school assignments while eagerly waiting on a response from Graeme Huntley. We needed to know why he hadn't shown the cops his stalker files for Katelyn and decided the best way to find out... was to ask.

Beck was done now though, leaned back in his chair, gaze on me. "What?" I finally said, my lips tilting up before I could stop them.

"We never finished our conversation last night, Butterfly," he said softly, and I realized that I hadn't given him the folder yet. I'd packed up the papers and slipped it in the drawer before we went to bed, and then promptly forgot all the scary horrible shit.

"You said that you thought the gifts were from the stalker, the flowers, maybe."

Beck had actually let it go longer than I expected, but he'd clearly had enough of waiting.

Leaning over to my side table, I pulled out the file. "Wells sent me this. Apparently, he found out about the police investigation and wanted to give me the heads up."

Beck took the papers, his face hard and unreadable. Dylan leaned over to read on one side and Jasper on the other. The three of them were silent, and when Evan lifted his eyebrows at me, I just shrugged. He eventually got up and stood behind the couch to see as well.

A tic started high in Beck's jaw. Dylan's too, if I was being honest. Jasper looked sick, and Evan was pale, his eyes wide as he stared down.

"You should have given this to me straight away," Beck said softly, that menace in his undertone his scary one. "I figured the papers you threw were to do with school or something unimportant. Not a fucking dossier on this rose killer."

I shrugged. "Sorry. I just … the nightmares."

I'd needed a break from the nightmares, and Beck had given me that.

A knock at the door sounded, and we all startled. Our whole crew, Eddy included, was already inside my apartment … so who was knocking on the door? No one should have been able to even get to our floor without the appropriate access keys, Evan had ordered the elevators rewired to block access from the rest of the building.

"I'll get it?" Eddy yelled, moving out of the kitchen where she'd been making a snack, missing all the drama.

Dylan was on his feet in an instant. "Sit down," he snapped as he stalked over to the door. He took a moment to peer out the peephole then swung it open to reveal … no one. A chill of fear ran down my spine, which quickly turned to ice when he bent to collect something from the doorstep.

That act had all three other boys bursting out of their seats and doing all kinds of shit that I barely even noticed. Beck pulled a gun from God knew where and darted out into the hall with Evan tight behind him, Dylan tossed the package to Jasper then slammed the door shut and flicked all my deadbolts. He then disappeared with a gun of his own in hand, checking all through the apartment then winding up at the huge living room window. He stood there for a while, peering down at the street below before giving a faint nod and tucking his gun away in the back of his jeans.

"Here." He held his hand out for the package, and Jasper handed it back over as he came over to where I still sat. Totally frozen.

"Riles, you okay?" Jasper asked, touching my hand where I clutched the edge of the table. My grip was so tight my knuckles were white, nails biting into the wood varnish.

I blinked a couple of times, trying to shake myself out of the shock I'd sunk into. "Yeah," I replied in a hoarse whisper. "Yeah, just open it." I nodded to Dylan, who held the small package in his hands.

He gave me a nod, lifted the lid of the shiny gift box, then frowned.

"What is it?" I asked, trying so freaking hard to hide the panic in my voice. "Is it…?" Any number of horrible things crossed my mind, fueled by the crime scene photos of Cordelia June's murder.

Dylan didn't reply, just held up a flash drive then tossed the box—and the rose—onto the table. "Jasper, pass over your laptop," he said.

"What if it's a virus?" Eddy suggested, right as Dylan was about to plug it in. "What if this is some, I dunno, Huntley ploy to hack your computers? Even if it doesn't immediately do anything, it could be a Trojan horse designed to lurk and gather info every time you use your laptop."

Both boys paused, then Jasper rushed out of my apartment, returning a few tense moments later with a brand new, still in its box, tablet. "Smart thinking, sis," he complimented Eddy as he ripped the packaging open and powered up the device. Dylan passed him the flash drive and he plugged it in, propping the screen on the table for all four of us to see.

"Video file," Dylan murmured, and Jasper tapped the icon to open it.

When the file began playing, I was too shocked and dumbfounded to do anything but stare in horror.

"Whoa," Eddy murmured, but even that didn't cut through my stunned disbelief. "Girl, is that…" On the screen Beck flipped me over, pressing me into the couch as my legs circled his waist and—

"Turn it off!" I shrieked, finally breaking out of the trance and slapping my hand over the screen. "Oh my god. Oh my god. He has a camera in here." Nausea twisted my stomach, and I swallowed hard.

Jasper and Dylan were already scouring my living room, searching for the hidden camera while breath rushed in and out of me with increasing speed.

"Hey, come on, girl," Eddy said, rubbing my back, "you're okay, just put your head between your knees for a minute. You're about to pass out." Helpless to do anything else, I did what she said.

Thankfully, it only took a few seconds for the fuzziness to fade and my breathing to slow, because the slamming door almost startled me into a heart attack.

"What's going on?" Beck demanded.

"Got it!" Dylan announced, pulling the tiniest little speck of technology from the decorative light fixture over my kitchen island.

Beck's whole body turned to stone, and his eyes fixed on the *thing* on the end of Dylan's finger. "Is that what I think it is?"

His friend gave him a tight smile, then walked over to the table and dropped the micro camera into Evan's beer.

"Show me," Beck demanded, his voice like the crack of a whip. Even I flinched a little.

Jasper handed him the tablet, and I watched as Beck hit play. This time, without the distraction of watching my very first sex tape, I could hear the audio. Except that wasn't audio of Beck and me fucking on the couch. That was—

"Is that someone jerking off?" I exclaimed, totally horrified.

Eddy screwed up her nose and made a gagging sound. "Pretty sure it is."

Beck stared at the screen, watching the clip and not saying a damn word. The look on his face, though…

"Turn it off," I snapped at him, and his gaze rose to meet mine. "Please, Sebastian. Turn it off."

He shook his head. "I need to see if there is any message here, other than the fact that this sicko filmed us and then beat off over it."

I clenched my jaw, angry at him for refusing my request and fucking *furious* at this psycho who'd placed a camera inside my apartment. He was *inside* my apartment! Was that what had woken me that night? Then how the hell had Beck slept through it?

A deep shudder ran through me.

"I can't stay here," I muttered, standing up and grabbing my bag. But, if he got inside my apartment, who was to say he hadn't bugged everyone else's? "Where do I go?"

For a moment, no one replied. Beck was still watching that fucking video, so it was Evan who spoke up.

"Grab some clothes and go change in my apartment," he suggested. "I seriously doubt this creeper put cameras in there, too, and you still have dinner with Graeme tonight."

I groaned, rubbing my eyes and probably smudging my makeup. "Fucking hell. Doesn't this *psychopath* understand how many other things I'm dealing with? As if I need to be stalked by a serial killer right now!" I said it with a bitter laugh, but it was only to stop myself from crying.

I started toward my bedroom, then paused. "Can someone please check the bedroom for cameras? I can't..." I shook my head, the words sticking in my throat.

I can't fucking deal with the idea of him watching me right now.

"Any trace?" Dylan asked Evan quietly, while Jasper hurried into my bedroom and started turning over every item of movable furniture.

From the corner of my eye, I saw Evan give a grim headshake. "This prick is good. Trained. The officers didn't see *anyone* come in or leave. Not even the other building residents."

Hearing this, I shuddered again. Just evading some lazy cops who were probably napping or eating, that didn't shock me. But if my guys couldn't find a trace of him or work out how he was getting in and out ... that scared the shit out of me.

Once Jasper cleared my bedroom—or as much as he could without any detection technology—I grabbed a change of clothes and my makeup bag. Regardless of stalker gifts and sex tapes, I still needed to free Dante from prison. That meant I needed to bring my A-game to this dinner with Graeme.

"Beck," I snapped, returning to the living room where he *still* stared at the fucking tablet, even though the video must have ended already. Using his nickname seemed to break his train of thought, though, and he narrowed his eyes at me.

"Yes, Riley?"

I pursed my lips, getting a handle on all my out of control emotions. "I assume you're coming to dinner with me?" He gave a short nod. "I'll be ready in fifteen. We can deal with this later." I gave a pointed look to the tablet in his hand then followed Evan down the hall to his apartment.

Chapter 18

Graeme Huntley answered his own door and I was surprised enough by that, that I almost stepped back into Beck. I managed to catch myself though, plastering on a polite smile. Graeme stared down at me, a smug sort of look on his face. There was silence for a minute, and I realized that this was my first time seeing him since I'd caught him making out with his sister, and it took actual effort to control the way my smile wanted to twist into something more like disgust.

"Welcome Ms. Deboise and Mr. Beckett," he said, the epitome of politeness. He wore a dove gray suit, with an open white dress shirt. Looking rich and business casual. "Please come in."

Said the spider to the fly.

We stepped in together following Graeme. Beck had barely spoken a word to me since the folder and "gift" incident back at my apartment. The simmering fury in his eyes did not abate, and I wondered if Graeme would think Beck was here to attack him or something. Because right now, he looked capable of anything.

Graeme's house was flawless and apparently brand new. Considering they had only been living here for a month or two, I wondered if it had been built for them in anticipation of the vote. Or if it was a lucky coincidence that a brand-new mansion was just available for them to purchase.

We entered a large, formal living area first, dressed mostly in gold and sky blue styling. "Please, have a seat," he said, gesturing toward a gold tinged leather couch. The sort of couch that looked fancy and uncomfortable. "The staff will be by shortly to take a drink order."

Beck and I both sat, and I decided there was no way I was eating or drinking anything here tonight. I remembered all too well how my father drugged me. Graeme I trusted even less than Richard, and that was saying something.

Graeme took a seat across from us, crossed his legs, looking the picture of elegance as he tilted his head in my direction. It was such a direct contrast to Beck, who was all broad and relaxed, leaned back in the seat. Legs spread slightly, arms to the side, expression one of coiled lethality.

"I was surprised to receive your message," Graeme said softly, eyes glittering in the low light. "But I'm glad to have this opportunity to get to know my niece."

I focused on keeping my breathing nice and even, so as not to let him catch a glimpse of my nerves.

"Thank you for the dinner invitation," I returned, playing his game. "I figured there has been too much hostility between our families and it was time to break that cycle."

Plus, I know you're fucking your sister.

His grin broadened. "Something tells me there's more to this visit than just breaking the cycle of hatred between our companies. Tell me, Riley, what is the real reason you're here tonight. Maybe if we get that out of the way first, the rest of the meal will be more pleasant."

I seriously doubted that, but it was worth a shot. "I need you to release the black files."

He didn't speak, but his expression conveyed his shock.

"Not all of them," I hurried on. "The ones for Katelyn only should suffice."

He shook his head, and for the briefest moment, grief crushed his face. He'd loved his daughter. I hadn't been sure, but it was there.

"You have a lot of nerve," he said softly, "coming into my house and bringing up my murdered daughter."

Our polite conversation was now over.

"Dante didn't kill her," I said just as bluntly. "It's a killer already being hunted by the police, a killer that is now targeting me. By withholding that file, you're withholding evidence that might help catch the actual killer."

Graeme crossed his arms, face again emotionless. "There is nothing in that file you need to concern yourself about. That fucking gangbanger killed my daughter, and he will pay for his crime."

I turned to Beck, unsure where he wanted me to go now. Should I threaten him? Tell him that I saw him and Catherine and threaten to expose them? One way or another, I was leaving here with that file released to police.

"I will vote for you," Beck said shortly, and I sucked in a deep breath.

Both because I was shocked he'd just come out and said that, while also realizing that Graeme would expect me to be shocked.

"In the Delta vote for a new member of the board," Beck continued, "I will cast mine in favor of Huntley taking the sixth seat."

Graeme looked between both of us, like he was unsure what to believe.

"Beck, no," I said shaking my head, deciding to push my "shock" a little further. "I really want to save Dante, too, but there has to be another way."

He reached over and pushed some of my hair behind my ears. "It's only one vote, Butterfly. Graeme has to secure two more to actually get his seat. It's not that huge of a sacrifice on my part."

Beck acted supremely confident that there was still no way that Graeme would take the sixth seat, which again, was all part of the game we played. Beck had told me the other night that he was almost certain Graeme had two secured votes already: Catherine and someone else on the board who they'd managed to bribe or threaten to his side. Which was why Katelyn had been working so hard to get Beck's vote. The third and final they needed.

"Will you confirm this in writing?" Graeme asked.

Beck nodded. "I will, but you will need to keep that hidden until the vote. If my father hears about it, he will try and revert the vote back to him."

Graeme tented his fingers in front of him, regarding us both for a moment. "Why do you want to free the gangbanger?" he asked, still clearly suspicious about why Beck would offer something so huge for someone like Dante.

My eyes burned, as they did every single time I thought about my best friend. "Dante is my family," I said simply. I had the heirs now, they were the most important people to me ever, but that didn't make Dante less of a part of my family.

"And Riley is mine," Beck growled.

Graeme's expression brightened, and he straightened in his chair. "In that case, consider the file yours. I will have it couriered over to your house, and also the separate files sent to both your private network and the police investigating the Osiria Killer."

I straightened then too. *Osiria killer?* We hadn't told him that. "You knew," I said breathlessly, fury simmering in my gut. "You knew and you were still willing to let Dante pay for a crime he didn't commit."

His eyes shuttered. "Ah, yes, well ... that was a favor for someone. But I consider that favor repaid, and now I'm looking out for the future of Huntley and Delta. We will be stronger together."

Beck and I didn't bother to answer; I was too busy trying to figure out who the favor was for. Catherine? It had to be Catherine. She was the only one who wanted Dante out of the way so he couldn't cause her more trouble.

That bitch needed killing more and more every day.

"You only have one vote," Beck reminded him. "Unless of course you have something to tell us about the rest of Delta board."

Graeme shook his head. "You let me worry about that. You just need to enjoy the fabulous meal."

He clapped his hands and three waitstaff entered the room, clearly having waited for his signal. "Drinks for everyone," Graeme said, sounding jovial. Bastard thought he'd gotten exactly what he wanted.

Beck ordered a scotch, and I shook my head, wanting nothing. "What if it's drugged," I said to Beck from the corner of my mouth.

He shook his head. "He won't risk upsetting us. It will be fine."

With a sigh, I asked for some water, trusting that Beck—the most suspicious person I knew—would tell me if I needed to worry.

Once we had our drinks, we made idle small talk until dinner was announced. I wondered if Graeme's wife was going to join us, but she never appeared. When Beck commented on this, Graeme's eyes lowered.

"She hasn't taken Katelyn's death well."

I wondered if that was actually true. These wives of billionaires all seemed the same: beautiful, deadly, and fucking broken beyond repair. No doubt Mrs. Huntley had an addiction to pain pills, plastic surgery, and alcohol. At minimum. She probably didn't even notice her daughter was dead.

Cynic of the year goes to...

Beck steered the conversation back to more pleasant topics, mostly about business and shares and stocks and bullshit I did not care about. I picked at my tiny little bird that was supposed to be food, but mostly freaked me out, all the while wishing we could escape.

Just when I was pretty sure I was about to lose my mind, a suited man entered the room and leaned down to hand Graeme a folder. There was an exchange of words I couldn't hear, and then the man left.

Graeme rose to his feet. "Here's your folder," he said simply. "My manager felt it was safer than courier, so he had it delivered here."

Beck and I were on our feet, too, moving around the long table toward him. I held my hand out, but Graeme didn't give me the folder. "First thing," he said, lifting his other hand. There was a single piece of paper on it—Beck took it from him.

He read through quickly before taking the proffered pen and signed his name at the bottom. Simple transaction that could net Graeme billions in money and incalculable power.

Only he'd be in jail and unable to reap any benefits, of course.

This had to fucking work. It had to, because otherwise, we were in big trouble.

Graeme handed the folder to Beck, and I tried very hard not to sucker punch him. Of course the misogynistic asshole would think that Beck needed to handle the "black files" because a silly little woman would not be capable. Beck must have seen the look on my face because he flashed me a slow smile and handed the folder over. I opened it to confirm we had the right information, flicking through until I found the flower images. She had been sent three bouquets, as far as I could tell, starting from innocent to one dripping in blood. I flicked over one more page and gasped. It was an image of Katelyn's body, with a single black, bloodied rose on top of it.

"You have a photo of your dead daughter?" I asked horrified as I stared at the man across from us. "Why? How? There was no rose on her body; I would have remembered that."

Graeme nodded. "It arrived the night she died. I wasn't … here at the time, and the letter sat unopened on my desk for a few days. It came in an official looking envelope, with a return address that was traced to some abandoned lot in New York City. I did my due diligence in following it up, but there were no leads, so it simply went into the folder."

I bared my teeth, hissing out words through them. "This should have gone to the fucking police!"

Graeme shook his head at me like I was an annoying brat. "The police have a tenth of the resources that I do. Besides, my daughter is already dead and nothing can bring her back. Taking this to the police would have only stirred up more trouble that we didn't need on the eve of the vote."

So callous. No thoughts about others being killed by this same person. Or about bringing his daughter's killer to justice. He'd rather protect the Huntley name and not drag it through the mud any more than it already was.

With a huff, I swung around and marched toward the front door. Beck stayed behind for a few minutes, and I wondered what he was saying to Graeme. It really didn't matter. We got what we were waiting for.

By the time Beck got out of the house, I was standing at the driver's side of the car. "I need to drive," I told him. It had been too long since I'd raced, and right now, my body was literally shaking at all the pent-up anger and fear inside.

He eyed me for a moment before nodding and unlocking the car. I slid into the Bugatti and Beck took the folder from me while I adjusted my seat. My eyes closed for a moment as I caressed the soft leather, breathing in the car scent. When I started her up, the throaty hum of the engine settled me even more, and a somewhat genuine smile crossed my face.

"We did it," I said to Beck, turning so I could see him.

He nodded. "We got the folder, and set the vote in motion, but something about Graeme is bothering me."

I snorted, shifting into gear. "Is it the fact he fucks his sister? Because that shit bothers me."

Beck's lips quirked into a smile. "I've been thinking about Oscar's body."

My foot pressed harder on the accelerator as we wound down the path, heading toward the large imposing gates of Graeme's estate. "You think Graeme was the one who took it?" I asked. We hadn't spent a lot of time focusing on the fact that my brother's body was literally stolen from his grave.

"It could all be connected," I said, really considering it. "Maybe Catherine and Graeme dug it up to make sure no one ever discovered that Oscar was the product of an incestuous relationship."

Beck's hands clenched on his thighs. "Despite what Richard said, we still don't really know if he was Graeme's child with her or Huntley Senior. Could be either."

I swallowed, trying not to gag.

The gate slowly opened, and I was thankful that I could finally get the hell away from this place.

"Do you have any thoughts on how to find out about Oscar's body?" I asked.

Beck shook his head. "Only the dumbest fuck alive would keep the body close to them. Unless we can get one of them to confess, I don't think we'll ever figure it out."

For a brief moment, I wondered if I could torture Catherine for information. Even though I hated her more than anyone else in this world, I doubted I could ever inflict pain like that on anyone. Something she'd no doubt view as a weakness, but for me, it was a hard line I had to draw. I mean, I did punch someone, so maybe I wasn't exactly a pacifist. But systematic torture was a whole other sociopath game.

Graeme's estate was on the opposite side of Jefferson to where the Delta estates were. It was very natural out here, lots of forest and trees lining the road. It was really dark out, and that was the main reason I didn't notice the car behind me until it was basically up my ass.

"What the fuck?" I said, flicking my eyes to the rear view mirror and back to the road multiple times. "No lights…"

Its engine roared, and it was coming at us so fast then that I knew it was going to hit us. Luckily, this wasn't my first high speed chase, and I managed to swerve to the side and miss the direct hit, thereby saving my baby Bugatti any damage. These bastards better not hurt her, or I would reevaluate the torture thing.

Beck was on high alert then, his head turned to watch the car as it dropped back, and I picked up the speed. "It tried to hit us," I said quickly, my foot pushing harder and the engine really opening up.

A warning flashed up at me, and I eyed the small indicator. "Tires…" I said slowly before my attention was taken by the car behind again.

It was crossing two lanes in an attempt to come up beside me and smash me off the road. Not willing to give it that chance, I pushed my foot harder, and we jumped ahead.

"Graeme or the serial killer?" I asked Beck between gritted teeth, my focus almost completely on keeping us alive.

Beck didn't answer, just withdrew his gun and lowered the window, cold air whipping around us.

I caught a glimpse of the other car in our taillights, only noting that it was black and sleek before it zipped up the side again. Beck opened fire, aiming right for the front windshield. It swerved and backed off, giving us some breathing room. I let out a sigh of relief when I saw the lights of Jefferson up ahead. Once we were back in the main population, surely this other car would back right off.

The Bugatti beeped at me again, and I remembered the tire warning which had come up before. "Beck…" I said slowly, just as I felt the car start to slide. At this speed, any loss of control was deadly, and I immediately lifted my foot from the accelerator.

"Beck, get the fuck back in the car," I screamed reaching out for him. At the same time there was a huge bang from the back of the car, and I knew immediately that the tire had blown. *Motherfucker!* Someone had messed with the tires. A slow leak or something so I didn't notice immediately. Then the high speeds would have heated them and if the pressure was low…

With both hands on the steering wheel, I struggled to control the car, sliding down an embankment. The moment we hit the edge, the Bugatti flipped over and over, my arms coming up to cover my face as I screamed. Flashbacks from my last crash filled my head, and I wondered if this time my luck would run out. *Beck…*

"Riley!" Beck roared, and that was the last thing I heard before my head slammed into the side of the car and everything went dark.

Chapter 19

BECK

The moment our tires blew I knew we had been sabotaged by Graeme Huntley. That fucker wanted his files back; the accident was designed to incapacitate us but not kill. Only he hadn't anticipated the speed Butterfly would drive at, delaminating those tires faster, and sending us out of control and tumbling down an embankment.

Bracing myself against the door, I managed to keep my head from smashing into anything, while holding Riley back as well.

Fear was not an emotion I felt often, generally I was uncaring about living or dying. I just did my fucking job and got on with the bullshit. But now that I had Riley, I had a lot to lose, and we were in the midst of a dangerous game.

When the car came to a stop, I shook off the pain, reaching across to check on my fucking soul who was in the seat beside me. Her pulse thrummed strongly in her neck, and I let out a relieved breath. She was unconscious, a cut on her temple and another on her arm, but I couldn't see anything too life threatening in my quick examination. Reaching for my phone, I dialed Dylan.

"We've got a fucking problem," I said immediately, and I knew I had his complete attention. "Someone sabotaged the Bugatti, and we crashed." I gave him our location and told him to get the paramedics out here straight away.

I was desperate to get Riley out of her seat, but not knowing the extent of any neck injuries, I decided not to move her just yet.

Tires sounded on the asphalt above our ditch, and my head snapped in that direction. *One car. Two sets of footsteps.*

They were coming to finish the job, which was to either grab the file or kill us. Depending on who had orchestrated this and what their end game was.

My gun was lodged into the side panel—I'd been determined not to lose it when we rolled—so I reached down and grabbed it, determining there were three rounds left. My door was crushed, and I had no way to open it, and there was no time to crawl out the window, so I dropped my head back, feigning unconsciousness.

Riley stirred slightly beside me, a pained moan leaving her, and I silently asked her to stay still for just another minute.

They were almost on us.

I always knew when someone was watching me, this unease trickling over my skin as the pair paused near my window.

"Both out cold," one man said, his voice not known to me.

"Get the fucking files," the other added, "before someone comes."

My finger twitched on the gun, and I gave them two more steps before my eyes flew open and I blasted the first one-point blank in the head. He dropped, and his friend did the same, clearly trained to avoid fire. He was gone along the ground, and I tumbled out of the too small window, managing to be up and after him in less than a minute.

I was injured. and he was fast, but still, I caught him just before he reached the dark SUV parked on the edge of the road. I could have easily shot him, but then I would have been with no one to torture for information.

He glanced over his shoulder and went pale as fuck as he saw me right on his ass. He fumbled for his gun, but it was too late. I wrapped my hand around his throat and jerked him to a stop before spinning and slamming him against a nearby tree.

"Who sent you?" I asked, my voice deathly quiet as I fought the rage inside of me. It would be a twitch of my hand to break his neck, and I was almost desperate to do it. They hurt Riley. They could have killed her.

No fucking mercy.

He couldn't speak so I loosened my grip just a fraction. "Fuck you," he spluttered out, face red.

My lips twisted into a smile, the sort of smile which was usually the last thing he would see in this world, but there was so much more fun for him to come. Another car screeched up, stopping right in the middle of the road like they gave no fucks about traffic. Jasper slid out of the passenger side and practically threw himself across the road.

"Riley!" he yelled, looking pissed and frantic.

"Alive," I bit out, "but hurt. She's still in the Bugatti. I was afraid to move her in case of neck injury."

Dylan was there as well, in his silent way. "I'll check her out."

"Deal with this guy," I said to Jasper and Evan. "I'm going with Dylan."

"You want us to kill him?" Evan asked, looking like he would love nothing more.

I shook my head. "No, he has a lot to tell us about his role in this. Would be a shame to end his misery so soon."

When I released him, he dropped to the ground, falling in a heap. Choking and gasping for air. Evan and Jasper moved in on either side of him, their expressions dark and hard.

"Come on," I said to Dylan, needing to get back to Riley.

"You're hurt," Dylan said as I slid down the embankment, my shirt riding up to reveal some scrapes and cuts.

I shook him off. "It's nothing. I've had worse. Let's focus on Butterfly."

Because if she wasn't okay, I would fucking destroy the world in my rage, and no one wanted that to happen.

In the distance, I heard a car engine roar to life, and I paused because that wasn't the same engine as the SUV or the car that had run us off the road. There were no houses around here either.

Was there a third player?

My feet moved faster as I raced to the crashed Bugatti. "Riley!" I shouted, fear tearing through me as fast as I was tearing through the bushy undergrowth.

I hit my door hard, and when I saw the empty seat where she had been, rage like I'd never known tore through me.

The next few minutes were nothing more than flashes of red and black across my vision, and Dylan calling for Evan and Jasper to try and stop me from tearing the door off the fucking car.

"Beck!" Dylan shouted in my face. "You're not helping Riley by losing it.

We need to figure out who the fuck took her, and then we need to kill them. But we won't do either of those things without a clear head."

My fists clenched as my blood pumped through my body, everything burning. Dylan was right, though, I needed to get my shit together because my Butterfly needed me. "A car started up," I managed to get out, "about half a mile that way."

I pointed through the trees, already moving in that direction.

"It was a stock standard straight six-cylinder. A regular old piece of shit."

There had been something familiar about its engine, but I couldn't put my finger on it.

"I heard it too," Dylan said. "Caught a glimpse of it down the road when we stopped, but I was too worried about Riley to pay it much attention."

I locked my focus on him, even as we tore up the road to where the car had been. "What did you notice?" I bit out. "Surely your computer of a fucking brain remembers something."

Dylan could catalog a scene and draw it play by play without any fucking effort. It was how his brain was wired.

He paused, giving himself a moment to think. "White sedan with blue markings on the side. Dark windows. No one in the driver or passenger seat. Straight six-cylinder."

Another pause. "It almost sounded like a—"

"Cop car," I said, cutting him off as the familiarity of that noise finally registered. The police in Jefferson all drove the same nondescript white sedan.

Dylan nodded. "But why the fuck would the police have taken her?"

A rumble rocked my chest as my teeth clenched. "Not the police, but someone close enough to lift one of their cars. Or … someone that works for them."

The rose killer.

It made perfect sense. That's how he remained out of jail—he worked for the police. Probably destroying evidence before it got close to incriminating him.

Dylan almost looked pale, despite his darker skin tone. "You think the serial killer has been that close all along. Like … at the police station while we were going in there with Riles?"

He'd reached the same conclusion as me.

I nodded. "Yeah, those bastards like to stay close. Keep an eye on things."

We reached the spot, but the car was long gone. I saw the indent from the tires, and seeing they were the exact tread of the police vehicles, I figured that was the first place we needed to go.

"Tell Evan and Jasper to clean up the scene before the ambulance gets here and get whatever information they can out of that fucker before disposing of him," I bit out. "I need to head to the police station."

Before I left, I grabbed the Huntley folder and then called for one of our cars to come and pick us up. Dylan ended up joining me, while Evan and Jasper took our guest to one of the safehouses for some one-on-one time. They'd get whatever information out of him, and hopefully we would find Riley before it was too late.

Chapter 20

A scratching sound filtered into my head, disturbing the unconsciousness I was existing in. A groan escaped from me as I gently shook my head. Opening my eyes proved to be more difficult than it normally would be, my head aching like I had the worst hangover of my life. It also seemed very bright behind my eyelids, but not warm. I wasn't in the sun…

Wiggling forward, I paused because I was propped upright, but my hands were tied behind my back.

What the fuck?

I managed to pry one eye open, wincing at the sudden shock of light. A beam was shining directly at me, and I couldn't see anything except dancing dots in front of my vision. When my other eye finally opened, I forced myself to look around, even though my eyeballs were watering so badly I was basically crying.

Where the hell was I? I tried to remember what had happened, but everything in my memory was dark. Shaking my head again, I worked at the bindings on my hands, trying my best to loosen them enough to free my arms. My legs were bound, too, one to each leg of the chair I was on, but I'd worry about that once my hands were free.

Rope cut into my skin, but I didn't let that stop me. My head continued to pound away while I tried desperately to find my last memories.

Eventually some of it came back … the hard drive, the video in my apartment … dinner at *Graeme Huntley's*.

I'd gone to Graeme's with Beck. Had he done this? Kidnapped me.

A low screech from nearby as a door opened triggered me. *Tires.*

Jesus fucking Christ. The tires had exploded, and the Bugatti rolled.

Beck! Where the fuck was Beck?

Footsteps drew my attention, and I worked my wrists harder, ignoring the pain—at this stage it felt like I was completely rubbing my skin off, but if it got me free.

Because the lights were in my eyes, I couldn't see anything except shadows. "Y-you're making a h-huge mistake," I stuttered, trying my best to death glare the shadow cloaked figure in front of me. I'd been so focused on my restraints that I hadn't noticed my chattering teeth or the freezing cold seeping into my bones. Where the hell was I? Siberia? "Delta w-won't take this lying down, and y-you know it. They'll f-find m-me and then you'll p-pay."

"They won't find you before I'm done," the man replied, and I was shocked that it *wasn't* Graeme's voice. I was so sure he was responsible … then again, he wouldn't have been getting his hands dirty with this sort of shit. It was probably some paid muscle he'd hired to intimidate me.

He shifted into the light and showed me his face.

"You!" I sucked in a startled gasp, recognizing the man in front of me. But finding myself even more confused than ever. "You work for Huntley? I don't get it. Were you at the police station to plant evidence or something?"

The good looking, dark skinned man—James? Johnson!—smiled a disturbingly charming smile at me, shaking his head like I was a damn moron.

"Quite the opposite, Miss *Deboise*. I was there to destroy evidence. Couldn't have everyone screaming serial killer too soon, now could I? That would have ruined all my carefully laid plans." He tilted his head to the side as he said this, like he was fascinated by what my reaction would be.

Thankfully, I'd been working really freaking hard on my Delta-face. While internally I was shaking and screaming, I kept my face blank and empty. If this fucker got off on seeing his victims afraid, he was shit out of luck with me.

So far.

"The rose," I spat. "The one from Katelyn's body. You got rid of it before the evidence was processed, so they wouldn't link the crime to Cordelia June's."

Johnson nodded, smug as a cat in cream. "Yep, took a photo for her parents of course, and my own records, but then I ditched the rose. Didn't want to tip you off too early." He changed topics in a flash. "I could have killed you that night, you know? I was *this* close." He held up his thumb and forefinger about a quarter inch apart, and I noticed he was wearing black leather gloves. In his other hand, a twelve-inch hunting knife gleamed as it caught the light. Of course he wore gloves. This guy was proving to be even more skilled than my guys and all their Delta training.

"So why didn't you?" I asked. I had zero clue how I'd save myself from this situation which only seemed to be getting worse. Maybe if I could just *stay alive* then Beck...

That idea broke off as fast as it came, and I swallowed back a cry of anguish. Where was Beck? Had he survived the crash?

Regardless. Dylan, Evan and Jasper were still out there, and they'd become suspicious if we didn't get home soon. Surely, they would find me. Us.

"Your constant bodyguard made things more complicated," Johnson admitted. "None of my other ... the other girls didn't have a boyfriend to work around. When I heard him saying he was moving in permanently, I saw my window closing and escalated things."

I licked my lips and tasted blood. "So you object to killing men? I'm sure there's some psychology there."

Johnson gave me a sly grin, like I was being funny. "It doesn't get my rocks off, if that's what you're implying but no, I have no issues killing anyone that gets in my way. Except Beck..." He trailed off with a shrug, and I knew what he meant.

"Except you don't know that you'd win against Beck," I finished for him. "You know he's better than you."

Johnson—surprisingly—nodded. "He is. Or he would be, any other day of the week. Since he met *you*, though, well he's all kinds of distracted. If he hadn't been too busy with his face buried between your legs, I never would have gotten close enough to deliver even the first bouquet."

"So you tampered with his car. Too scared to take him on yourself, huh?" I was well aware that it wasn't smart to taunt the killer with a knife, but I was pissed right the fuck off and it slipped through the cracks.

Johnson laughed. "Actually, that wasn't me. I just took advantage of the opportunity it presented." He casually placed the tip of his blade against my throat, then dragged it down my chest until he reached the neckline of my dress. He hadn't pressed hard enough to cut, but I flinched nonetheless, then mentally kicked myself at the flare of excitement in his face.

"What do you mean?" I demanded, trying to keep him talking and not slicing me up. "You didn't fuck with our car?"

"Nope," he replied, angling the blade to the dead center of my chest and adjusting his grip. "If I was a betting man, I'd say Huntley saw a prime opportunity to open two extra seats on the Delta board. Wasn't there some draconian rule about needing an heir to hold their position?" He said it like he didn't care, but he'd clearly done his research.

Before I could reply, his hand tightened on the knife, his arm flexing.

My tenuous hold over my fear slipped, and I let out an involuntary scream before realizing he hadn't stabbed me. He'd just sliced through the front of the navy dress I'd worn to dinner, leaving it open down to my waist and showing off the sexy lace bra I'd put on for Beck.

"Fear is such a pretty thing, don't you think?" he purred, using his other gloved hand to stroke the pulse in my throat which must have been visibly pounding. My breath was coming in short, panicked gasps and it took every ounce of my willpower to force it slower and not give Johnson the satisfaction of my terror.

"I think we have different definitions of pretty," I snapped back at him and really considered spitting like I had at Catherine on that first day. "What's your deal anyway? Some heiress stand you up on prom night and you decided to start stalking and murdering chicks to make up for it? Ever consider therapy instead?"

A brief flicker of anger in his eyes was the only reaction I got, but it was enough to know I'd hit a nerve. Then again, the way he sliced his blade across my thigh would have told me I'd pissed him off too.

"Fuck!" I shouted before biting my tongue. The hot burn of pain lanced through me, and I ground my teeth together hard, trying so freaking hard not to cry.

I was going to die. Just like Katelyn, with dozens of stab wounds in my body. Never knowing if Beck was okay. Never knowing if we would beat Delta at their fucked up games.

"Why haven't you just killed me?" I sobbed, the pain lancing through my nerve endings.

Johnson chuckled again, the anger gone from his face. Psycho.

"Where is the fun in that? I was fucking Katelyn for weeks before I ended her. She never had a clue about the person she invited into her bed, thinking herself all clever because she was fucking the police for inside information. Little did she know..."

Jesus. "You're going to keep me for weeks?"

The blade was back on my skin, the blunt side dragging across my breasts. "That really depends on how good you are, doesn't it, princess."

He leaned in closer and pressed his lips to mine, the blade between us, and I fought my gag reflex because I wanted to vomit in his mouth. But I had to try and stay alive—at least give the guys a little time to try and find me.

So I did nothing. I let him press his lips to mine, and I didn't bite them off like I wanted.

When Johnson pulled back, his face was lit up, pupils dilated. "That's more like it," he said softly. "I love my women, you have to understand. An obsessive love for a person who can't love back because they're too rich to even see those beneath them."

His words were weird and disjointed, and it was very clear that he was insane. In a sane sort of way. He rose, turning to switch the massive spotlight off, and I could have groaned at the relief of not having a high beam in my face. My head ached, eyes watering as I let my head fall forward.

My eyes locked onto my thigh, blood pooling out of the wound and dripping to the floor. A slow plop, plop, plop as it oozed out.

Johnson was back in my face again, and I stifled the scream. "Now," he said slowly, lifting his blade again, "where were we?"

Chapter 21

BECK

It was nearing 1:00 a.m. when I entered the station. Stopping at the front desk, the woman looked up from her papers, and as she focused on my face, hers twisted, terror widening her eyes.

"I— Can I h-h-help you?"

I wasted no time on pleasantries. "I need the detectives in charge of the Osiria killer case."

Dylan remained just behind me, and when her eyes flicked up to him, she visibly gulped. Neither of us were doing a very good job of hiding ourselves today. Right now, the world could see us in our true form, and it scared the fuck out of them.

She lifted the phone and called through, speaking only a few words.

"They've gone home for the night," she told us breathlessly.

I leaned in closer. "Get them the fuck back. Now."

She blinked before speaking into the phone again. When she dropped it down, she nodded to the seats behind us. "They'll be here in fifteen minutes. Please take a seat."

Ignoring her, I leaned even closer so my forehead was almost pressed against the bottom of the glass panel. "I need you to give me files of all the staff and their dates of employment."

She was already shaking her head. "I'm sorry, but that is all classified information—"

I slammed my hand on the desk, and she jumped in the air.

"Do as you're fucking told. It's not the night to piss me off, trust me."

A tiny amount of fire entered her face, as she jumped back, clutching a folder to her body. She was in her forties, mousy brown hair, and large black-framed glasses. She was like a little mouse defying a fucking anaconda. "Don't talk to me like that," she said, soft but firm. "Threatening me will land you in jail."

I laughed darkly. "Yeah, I don't think so, love. See, I basically own this fucking station, and I will not hesitate to tear it to the ground if I don't get what I need. Now."

"Beck."

I turned to the rumbly voice, seeing Captain Decker stride through the security door.

"Thought I heard your dulcet tones out here. What seems to be the problem?"

Decker went way back with my father—I didn't trust him at all, but I knew he could get me what I want.

"I need all personnel files, with their start dates, and any vacation time and so on."

I knew the killer had been out of town when that heiress was killed, and it would be easy to see if anyone had vacation days. Or if it was a new employee.

Decker watched me for a minute, and Dylan stepped closer to my back, ready for whatever was about to happen.

"Give him whatever he needs, Francine," he said, turning to the woman.

She sucked in a deep breath but didn't argue.

Smart move.

I drummed my fingertips on the counter, glaring down at her while she frantically bashed away at her computer to pull up the files I'd so politely requested. Decker cleared his throat in a pointed way, and I took my sweet ass time shifting my attention to him.

"Can I ask what this is all about, Sebastian?" he said it as politely as he could, but there was that edge of condescension that said he didn't take me anywhere near as seriously as my father. That was an issue I needed to fix and couldn't think of any better time like the present.

"It's Mr. Beckett to you, Decker," I snarled, channeling my father like I'd never done before. "Let's not forget who pays that healthy second salary for you."

From the corner of my eye, I saw Francine's cheeks flush and her eyes bug out, but she was smart enough to keep her head down and mouth shut.

Captain Decker, on the other hand, didn't look like he was handling the power dynamic well. I couldn't blame him too much. Until now, none of us heirs had shown any interest in personally dealing with the hundreds, if not thousands, of employees on Delta's less than above board payroll.

"Now see here—" the Captain started, his face an unattractive shade of red as sweat formed on his shiny forehead.

"I wouldn't, if I were you," Dylan commented, cutting him off. "In case you forgot, Beck turns twenty-one in a couple of months. We all know Rome has pretty much handed over the keys to the kingdom already, though." His voice was quiet, conversational even, but the threat was clear.

Captain Decker took a few very visible breaths, his nostrils flaring and his face still pink with indignation as he looked between Dylan and myself. Finally, he turned his attention back to Francine—the safe option. "Are you finished printing those files yet?" he demanded, and the woman hurried to collect a stack from the printer and hand them across the counter. "Mr. Beckett, Mr. Grant, if you'd care to join me in my office? I'm sure I can help you navigate these documents a lot quicker if we can understand what you're looking for?"

I gave Dylan a small head jerk and followed Decker through to his office with me bringing up the rear.

"There was a murder in Texas a couple of months ago," I started when the door was closed behind us. "A young heiress stabbed to death by the killer dubbed the 'Osiria killer,' due to the rare roses he leaves behind."

Decker nodded. "I'm aware of this, we suspect that the gifts being left for Miss Deboise are from the same killer. Detectives Shephard and Riggs said they spoke with you and left a protection detail?"

"Some protection," Dylan muttered under his breath, and Decker scowled. I could tell how badly he wanted to call Dylan out and demand an explanation, but he bit his tongue at the last second. Wise.

"We think the killer is one of your cops," I announced with zero emotions. It was safer that way, for everyone involved. "Riley was taken tonight by someone driving a police car. So we need your records to show new recruits and also who might have taken leave over the time Cordelia June was murdered. They'd also have had access to Riley's so-called protection detail. This bastard was following us tonight."

Decker had paled so much he looked almost gray. "You don't need to check these." He tossed the stack of papers onto his desk then circled around to boot up his computer. A few quick seconds of tapping and he turned the screen toward us.

"Six weeks ago we took on seventeen transfers from out of state. Three of those came from Texas. All of them checked out, though. Clean as whistles."

I sucked in a deep breath, staring at the screen where three officers' mugshots were displayed alongside their basic details. "Shit."

"Is that—" Dylan frowned at the screen then shot a look at me. "Did you know Johnson was back in town?"

"Fuck!" I shouted, spinning around and slamming my fist into the wall beside the door. The cheap drywall crumbled, and my hand went right through to the hollow interior, sending up a cloud of dust.

When I shook the shit off my hand and spun back around, Decker was looking at me with a stunned expression. "I take it you recognize Officer Johnson?"

"He transferred from Texas? From the same town as Cordelia?" I demanded, double checking what he'd just said. What my gut was telling me was true.

Decker nodded, and I needed to take a calming breath.

Of course, it could have been a coincidence. But only fools and dreamers believed in coincidences, and I was neither. This fucker ... he fit. Not only had he been in the right place at the right time, he'd been on Riley's protection detail today. He *had* been following us, and we'd *known*. Worse yet, he was trained. Not in the ordinary police force kind of way, either. Delta wasn't the only mega-power that wanted its future leaders to be *trained* and there were actual camps dedicated to providing that service.

That was where we'd first met Johnson, before we started at Ducis. He'd been heir to his own family's immense fortune—albeit new money—until his father's secret love child showed up. The details were hazy, but our spies told us that she somehow orchestrated for Johnson to be legally disowned. Tossed out on his ass.

"Explains how he was getting past us," Dylan commented softly, and I shook my head in disbelief. Johnson was good. Crazy good. And totally, certifiably insane, even before the shit with his dad.

"Where does he live?" I demanded of Decker. The captain quickly scribbled down an address on a scrap of paper and handed it over.

"This is the address we have for him," he said, "but something tells me he won't be somewhere so obvious."

I wracked my brain for a beat, trying to remember anything I knew about him.

"He said he had grandparents in Jefferson, right?" I said to Dylan. "He mentioned it as soon as we told him where we'd come from."

Dylan nodded, face serious. "Yes. I remember him saying that."

"Find that address!" I said to Decker.

The captain nodded. "Will do. You head out, and I'll send through the address and backup asap."

He was already reaching for the radio on his desk, but Dylan stopped him by snatching the handset out of his hand and smashing it against the deck.

"No need," Dylan snarled. "This is Delta business. Just get the address."

I shoved my way out of the police station with a deathly scowl on my face, Johnson's "address on file" clutched in my hand. We would start by checking it out, but something told me the grandparents' place was our winner. Decker better find that property straight away.

Then Johnson was going to pay for every scrape on Riley, a thousand times over.

Chapter 22

The steady pitter patter of my blood splashing against the concrete floor was the only sound keeping me awake. My head was fuzzy and thick from blood loss, but as far as I could tell, he was yet to hit anything debilitating. So long as I didn't pass out from all the little cuts he'd made, then I should be fine to run. It was all surface wounds, and so far I'd escaped anything worse than some slimy kisses and rough boob grabbing.

Johnson had been gone for a while, long enough that I almost started to panic. Had he gotten bored and decided to leave me here until I was unconscious? Or was this the opportunity I'd been waiting for?

Biting the side of my cheek in an attempt to focus my thoughts, I raised my heavy head and tried to shake the stringy, blood crusted hair from my face. I must have taken a head injury in the crash because Johnson had been focusing his attacks on my body.

I took a few deep breaths then strained to hear.

Silence.

Surely this was as good an opportunity as I'd ever get. I'd been Johnsons prisoner for too long to just keep waiting for a rescue. It felt like I'd been in that dark room for days, but it was probably only a couple of hours. Still way too long for my liking.

Thankfully, my attacker had left the glaring spotlights off when he'd run out of here some time earlier, and my eyes had grown more accustomed to the dark. Enough that I could make out my shadowy surroundings.

As far as I could tell, I was in some kind of shed. He'd placed my chair in the dead center—well away from the equipment—and set up an industrial looking spotlight directly in front of me.

A grim smile crept across my pained and cracked lips, and I swallowed back a smug laugh. This prick had severely underestimated my desire to live, and my newfound spine of steel. One thing that being sucked into Delta's world had taught me was that I was much stronger than I ever thought. If I could survive my parents' death, being in a plane crash and being forced to shoot a man in the head ... then I could damn well get out of this mess.

Spotting my target, I sucked a deep breath in then held it for what I was about to do. Because it was gonna hurt.

As hard as I could, I threw my weight to the side of the chair, trying to tip it over.

Nothing happened.

"Fuck," I cursed under my breath. My arms tied behind the chair back were preventing me from leaning far enough to topple the chair. I bit my cheek again, clearing the spinning fog from my brain before using every damn ounce of effort to lift my arms *up*. It wasn't a particularly high backed chair, so it only took a moment of excruciating, tearing pain in my shoulder sockets before I managed to slip over the chair back.

"Fuck yes," I congratulated myself, turning to jelly and taking a moment to rest before the next step. My arms were still bound behind me but at least now I could shift my weight over far enough to—

Gravity took over exactly as I wanted, and I braced myself just a fraction of a second before hitting the damp concrete floor. My anticipation of how much it was going to hurt was understated. Every stab and slice Johnson had inflicted on me, along with my wounds from the car crash, all *screamed* with pain and for a moment my whole world went black as I slipped into unconsciousness.

Thankfully, my body was in too much pain to leave me knocked out for long, and I blinked my way back into consciousness while panting through the agony.

Thank fuck for small mercies, I'd landed in the direction I'd been aiming. Just a few feet away from a pair of garden shears that had been kicked under a work table. Johnson had them out while trimming his fucking black roses earlier. Taunting me. Well, the joke was going to be on him. I would use his fucked up sheers to free myself.

Hopefully.

A few feet sounded so damn close, but when tied to a chair, bruised and bleeding ... it may as well have been on another planet. But I'd come this far, and I'd be damned if Johnson came back to find me *halfway* through an escape attempt. That'd just be damn stupid, so there was nothing else for it. I had to reach those shears, free myself, and get the hell out before he returned.

Easy, right?

Right. Keep telling yourself that, Riley.

Gritting my teeth, I started wriggling my way in the direction of the equipment. Through a mixture of frantic thrashing, and digging the bare toes of my bottom leg into the concrete, I was making progress. For the first time since realizing Johnson intended to kill me, I grabbed hold of hope. I could do this. I *could* do this!

It took a while, and I needed to stop to rest every couple of inches, but eventually my head brushed the leg of the work bench and my heart soared. Fuck. Yes. Who said you needed special Delta training to be a total badass?

Another extended session of wriggling, grunting, panting and straining, and I had the handle of the shears between my teeth. Backing out from under the workbench took a little more effort, given I couldn't drop the death grip my teeth held on the shears.

After a minute of struggling, I gave myself a rest and lay there panting. My whole body was screaming with pain, and the room spun with dangerous speeds before my eyes, but it was just a reminder that I needed to push through.

"Come on, Riley," I muttered to myself, hoping the pep talk would help focus my energy. "Come on, you can do this. You're not the weak, defenseless heiress he's mistaken you for. You can save yourself."

Whether I really believed that, it didn't matter. It was either try ... or die.

Groaning with the effort, I picked the shears back up in my teeth. I was still on my side, my hands bound between my back and the chair, and my legs tied to each chair leg. But I just needed my hands free. Once I managed that, the rest should be cake.

My neck muscles howled as I lifted the shears from the ground with my teeth, turning my face to the ceiling then over my shoulder. I sucked a couple of rasping breaths, then sort of *threw* the shears with my mouth, aiming to drop them into the gap where my hands were bound.

There was a *thunk* as they hit the wooden chair back, then ... nothing. I waggled my fingers and only just brushed the side of the fucking things, which seemed to have gotten hooked between the slats of the chairback.

"For the love of *fuck*," I groaned, peering at the sheers hooked in the most infuriating location *just* out of reach of my fingers. For lack of any better ideas, I gave my body a quick shake, rattling the chair against the floor.

To my amazement, they dislodged from the chairback and dropped neatly into my hand. I was so stunned, I almost burst into tears but bit it back. There would be plenty of time to cry—or laugh—after Johnson was dead.

It took me multiple tries, and several agonizing cuts to my fingers, but I finally managed to snip the cable ties holding my wrists together. The second they were free, I wanted to scream and howl my satisfaction, but a noise held my tongue.

I froze.

There it was again! Someone was coming, heavy boots crunching on gravel, and I was willing to put money on it being Johnson.

Frantic, I cut my legs free and staggered to my feet, searching for a weapon in the darkness. The shears were great, and I wasn't losing them, but I wanted something big to smash over his head. I had one chance to debilitate him.

Moments later, I positioned myself beside the locked door, clutching a shovel to my chest, and leaning into the wall for support. The second that psychotic asshole walked through the door, I was getting the hell out.

Keys jingled outside, and I held my breath.

The distinctive *snick* of a padlock opening reached my ears, then the clank of the bolt and the creak of the door. For a second, he paused in the doorway, his long shadow cast by the moon at his back stretching across the floor. Then he stepped into the room, and I struck.

My shovel hit home, smacking him in the side of the head with all the force I could muster up. While weak from my injuries and the mission to cut myself free, I still held enough strength that he dropped to the ground, and in that moment, I grabbed my shears and fucking *ran*...

...Straight into the arms of a second person.

Arms like steel wrapped around me, knocking the heavy garden utensil to the ground, and I screamed. Fuck hiding my fear, I had nothing left. Maybe if I was loud enough, a neighbor would hear. Either way, I wasn't going down without a fight.

I screamed and thrashed, kicking and hitting my captor with everything I had. It wasn't until his hand closed over my mouth—cutting off my hollering—that I heard what he was saying. Ah shit.

"Riley! Riles, babe, cut it out!" Jasper yelled at me, keeping one hand over my mouth while his other wrapped around me like a straight jacket, keeping me from hurting *myself*. Not that I needed it anymore. The second my mind cleared enough to realize this was my rescue party rather than my murderer, I was like a puppet with cut strings. My whole body sagged, and a whimpering sob worked its way free of my throat.

"Hey, hey, babe we got you," he soothed, turning me around in his arms so I could cling on like he was a life raft in a storm. "We got you, Riles. You're safe."

He sank to the ground with me still glued to him, sobbing into his shirt as all the fear and desperation of the night flooded through me, battling with the realization that I was *safe*. They'd come for me, just like I knew they would.

"Oh shit," I gasped, pulling away from Jasper and wiping my eyes on the back of a grimy hand. "Who did I hit?"

"Me," Dylan replied, coming out of the shed with his shirt off. He held it wadded up in a ball against his bleeding head where my shovel had connected, and I gasped.

"Oh my god, Dylan. I'm so sorry." I looked up at him, horrified that I'd tried to kill my friend, but not physically able to let go of Jasper yet. "I thought you were..." I swallowed hard, unable to say the words *I thought you were coming back to rape me or kill me or both.*

He shook his head dismissively, his eyes soft as he looked me over. "No apologies necessary, Riles. You did exactly what you should have. It's my own dumb fault for charging in there unannounced."

I looked around, then frowned when I didn't see anyone else. "Where's Beck? And Evan? Are they..." I didn't even know what. The last time I'd seen Beck was as I crashed his beautiful Bugatti into an embankment. What if he had never made it out? What if his neck had been broken on impact?

"Dealing with Johnson back down at his house," Jasper informed me. "They've still got him alive, though."

The relief would have knocked me down, if I wasn't already on my ass. I arched a brow, even though tears were still running down my face. I couldn't seem to stop them. "So I could finish Johnson off myself?" I asked, and shocked myself at the cold cruelty to my voice.

"We kept him alive in case we couldn't find you," Dylan corrected. "But if you want to kill him yourself, you're more than welcome to. Not even Beck will argue with you on that point."

I nodded slowly then took Dylan's hand when he offered it to me. As badly as I wanted to stand on my own two feet when I faced my attempted murderer, I just didn't have anything left. The second I stood up my knees turned to jelly, and I would have collapsed in a heap if weren't for Dylan scooping me up.

"It's a decent walk down the hill," he told me, "I'll put you back down before we get there."

I gave him a weak smile, appreciative that he knew where my head was at. But that was what made us all such a formidable team, wasn't it? We were all so tuned in to each other. The old, corrupt bastards at Delta and Huntley didn't have a fucking clue what they were in for with us five.

They'd learn, though. Just as soon as I dispensed a bit of justice for my own sake.

Chapter 23

It was no wonder it'd taken the guys so long to find me. Johnson's property backed onto an expansive stretch of forest, and the shed he'd taken me to must have been an easy mile and a half from his house.

"I see why you kept him alive," I murmured to Dylan as he subtly supported me with a hand on my waist.

He grunted a noise as we entered the house to find a badly beaten Johnson, Beck and Evan standing over him. "It could have taken days to search that area if his information was bad and we hadn't found his path."

I nodded, then took a few steps closer to the famed *Osiria Killer*. Hardly the terror inspiring figure that had toyed with me earlier in the evening, he was now a pathetic, bloodied lump just staring up at me with dead eyes.

"Come to finish the job?" he asked me, his voice thick with pain but totally devoid of apology.

Beck's gaze was locked on me from behind Johnson's body, the intensity so fierce I could almost feel the heat, and it made me shiver. I couldn't look at him yet. Not unless I wanted to crumple into a sobbing mess ten times worse than I'd done to Jasper.

Respecting my need for strength, Beck silently held out his pistol for me. His blood smeared hand brushed mine as I took the weapon from him, and I flinched slightly at the heat of his skin. He was a fucking furnace, like his body temperature was reflecting his fury.

The gun was heavy in my hand. Solid and unwieldy, unlike the small handgun Beck had gifted to me in those early days. This was a tool for killing, plain and simple.

I clicked the safety off, just like I'd been taught, and aimed the barrel at Johnson's head. How easy it'd be to just ... shoot him. He wouldn't be my first kill but by god he'd be the most justified.

"What are you waiting for?" Johnson spat at me. "Just do it. I deserve it. I would have happily tortured you for days, making it as agonizingly painful as possible before I took what was mine ... your sweet cunt." He smiled. "Then I would have stabbed you to death. Just like Cordelia. Just like Katelyn. Just like the four other girls in other states that have incompetent police departments and never connected the dots." He started laughing then, but it was a bubbling, blood filled laugh that resulted in his coughing and hacking.

I pursed my lips, staring at him down the barrel of Beck's gun. He wanted this. He *wanted* the easy death at my hands.

Well, fuck that.

I flicked the safety back on and handed the gun over to Beck. "No, I think we will let the legal system handle you, Johnson." I crouched down and pretended like the pain of my injuries didn't make me want to pass the fuck out. "Won't that be fun? Getting your picture splashed all over the news? Being dragged up in front of a jury so the whole world can see what a pathetic, inadequate, cowardly sack of shit you are?" His beaten face paled, and I knew I'd hit the mark. He had thought he'd do all this terrorizing and murdering and then just take the easy route out. Never need to answer for his crimes.

"Are you sure?" Evan asked me from where he stood, his arms folded and more than a few smears of blood on his clothing. "The legal system doesn't always mete out the punishment that fits the crime. Knowing this piece of shit, he'll plead insanity…"

This caught my resolve for a moment, the possibility of Johnson actually being free to walk the streets again one day a possibility I couldn't consider.

"If that happens," I said softly, "we'll track him down and make sure he never has a chance to touch another woman."

Johnson snorted a pained sound. "It was pure fucking unlucky that you all caught me tonight." His eyes lifted to Dylan and Beck, looking between them. "These two with their eidetic memories and knowledge of cars. They told me they tracked me through the police vehicle. I was supposed to be following Riley tonight as protection duty. But … the opportunity to grab her was too good to pass up."

I smirked. "You got greedy, asshole, and now you'll pay."

He didn't look that worried, and I hoped I was making the right decision. Sirens cut through the early morning stillness.

"Looks like Decker decided to send out the troops," Dylan said.

Beck still hadn't spoken, and I still couldn't bring myself to look at him. Not when SWAT and armed police stormed in the room. Not when I gave my statement and the photographers took pictures of the room I was held in. Not when the greenhouse of Osiria flowers were found out near his torture house. And not even when some preliminary photos of my injuries were taken, the ones on my arms and throat mainly. The others they would get at the station.

"Johnson has had this place on lockdown for a long time," Decker said, swaggering around like he'd single handedly solved a serial killer case. "We found the records of how long it belonged to his grandparents. They died in odd circumstances and left it to Johnson. It was the only thing he ever inherited after his family disowned him."

He turned to the psycho in question, who had just finished having his rights read to him and was being led out to the police car, and asked, "You never really tried to hide this address … why?"

Johnson smiled, teeth bloody. "It's my original killing grounds. Sentimental reasons."

Beck finally spoke up, his voice graveled and deeper than I'd ever heard. "He's lying. The Johnson I knew was not sloppy like this. Multiple times tonight he left a bread trail to him. Which leads me to only one conclusion. He wanted to be caught. This is his swan song. Go out with a bang taking down the biggest heiress in the world."

Beck was looking at me, I knew it, and I swallowed the burning lump in my throat.

Johnson was still smiling but it was strained. "You got here just a little too soon, unfortunately," he said. "The crumbs should have been picked up after I was done with our beautiful Riley. You overachieving fucks were always two steps ahead."

Beck was killing him in his head. I could see that.

"We'll make sure there is no fame for you, asshole," Dylan said, his expression as deadly as Beck's. "By the time we're done, not a fucking person on this planet will know your name."

Now that really upset Johnson, but he was already out the door, and we didn't get to enjoy his unhappiness for long. At this point, my body started to shake.

"Miss Deboise," a woman I didn't know interrupted my breakdown. "Your ambulance is here."

I shook my head. "No. I don't need an ambulance. I wasn't raped or sexually assaulted in any way you need to test. I just have some minor wounds that a Band-Aid will fix." A large Band-Aid.

She opened her mouth to protest but didn't get far before Beck and Dylan stepped in front of me, blocking me from her view. "She said no," Beck rumbled.

For the first time since all of this happened, Beck was close to me, and as his scent washed over me, my legs crumpled. He must have been waiting for it, because he spun so fast, his arms around me as he lifted me gently into his arms.

A sob escaped before I could stop it, followed by another. Beck's stormy eyes bored into mine as he leaned over and kissed me, just a brush of his lips.

"Butterfly," he breathed, and my heart started to go all out of sync as my pulse and breath raced. "I thought I fucking lost you."

Another sob. And another. The sobs kept ripping from me with force and agonizing emotion.

Beck turned and strode from the room, like he was shielding me from everyone and everything best he could.

"Tomorrow, Beck," Decker called. "All of you need to be at the station tomorrow to give your statements."

Beck didn't bother to reply.

Chapter 24

Dylan ended up driving us home because Beck refused to let me go. Or I refused to let him go. Either way, we were not separating for any fucking reason, and no one argued about it.

When we reached our apartments, we went straight up to mine, the five of us silent. Eddy screamed when we opened the door, her face red and tear-stained.

"You found her!" she cried, and I held out a hand to squeeze hers, needing to reassure her the best I could that I was alive. Beck still held me, and in the back of my head I knew I should demand my independence and walk, but this whole thing had fucked me up too badly. I just couldn't do anything but hold on to my rock: Beck.

"I'm going to clean Riley up," Beck said shortly, already heading for the bathroom.

"I'll get my medical kit," Dylan replied.

Beck just strode forward, into the tiled room, letting the door close behind him. I'd stopped crying and was now exhausted, draped across him. He gently lowered me to the floor, his hands tracing up my arms and across my neck to cup my face.

"You scared the fuck out of me today, Riley."

Serious eyes drilled into mine, and I shook my head. "Thank you for saving me."

A flicker of amusement crossed Beck's face. "Judging by Dylan's bleeding head, it looked like you kind of had it handled, Butterfly. Something which doesn't surprise me at all."

There was no way to tell if I would have gotten out on my own. But fuck knows, I would have given it a red hot try. Beck kissed me suddenly, and I pressed myself into him, needing new memories to erase the last twelve hours. I needed memories, and I needed Beck, because for twelve hours, I hadn't known if he lived or not in the crash. I hadn't known if I would see him ever again.

This was a gift.

Just as the kiss started to get heated and I moved to wrap my legs around him, my body screamed at me for being so rough with all of my injuries. Beck drew back at my gasp, his worried gaze tracing along me.

"Time to get naked, baby," he said softly, already stripping my once fancy outfit from me. He didn't say anything else as he removed clothing, but his gaze darkened with each new injury he uncovered. There were dozens of shallow cuts across my thighs and a few on my stomach. None of them were bleeding now, but they cast a macabre sort of artwork across my skin, and it was hard to look at them, knowing how close I came to being murdered. There was bruising on my breasts, and no doubt other places I couldn't see from my angle.

Beck was breathing heavily by the time I was completely naked, and not in the usual way he would be. His fury spilled over as he turned and smashed his hand into the towel rack, ripping it completely from the wall.

"Fuck!" he shouted, and I remained where I was, completely unafraid even though Beck was losing it worse than I'd ever seen before.

He braced both hands on the sink, sucking in deep breaths, staring down into nothing as he struggled to get himself together.

"Beck," I said softly. No response. "Sebastian Roman Beckett."

His shoulders tensed before I saw him squeeze his eyes shut, and then eventually stand. "I'm alive," I reminded him. "These injuries…" I waved across my body, "they're fucking nothing compared to what he would have done. We both stopped him in time. Don't beat yourself up."

He shook his head, dark hair tumbling across his forehead. "I should never have let you out of my sight in the first place. Chasing down that asshole after the crash almost cost me my life."

I stilled, wide eyed staring at him, not even able to blink. "He almost killed you?"

Beck stepped the two steps back to me, stopping right in front of me. "*You* are my life, Riley. My fucking life, heart, and soul." His hand slammed against his chest. "Without you, there is no fucking me, so yes, he almost killed me."

Dylan chose that moment to step into the bathroom, closing the door behind him as well. Beck growled and in a split-second had stepped in front of my nakedness.

The pair of them faced off, two alpha males, both of them acting pissed and territorial.

"Guys," I said, after a minute of posturing and rumbling chests. "Can we maybe do this later? I'm pretty dead on my feet."

Beck jerked his head to me, and I tilted my face back. "I'd really like a shower first before anyone patches me up."

With a deep breath, he nodded, stepping aside to turn the water on. He knew the exact just-below-scalding temperature I loved, and I tried not to laugh at the way Dylan was staring at anything other than the naked chick in the room.

"They're just tits," I said, trying to joke about it. "I'm sure you've seen two or three ... hundred of them in your life."

Dylan's eyes were dark when they met mine. "Not just tits when they're yours, Riley."

He whispered those words, and I wasn't sure Beck heard, but I sure as fuck did. It made my heart ache at the pain and sadness on Dylan's face.

"Shower's ready," Beck said, breaking the tension.

When I stepped inside, I had to bite my lip to stop from crying out. The water washing over all the shallow cuts felt a lot like someone pouring acid on them but there was no other choice. I had to be clean. I needed to get the filth from that place off me. Like I could wash the memories away at the same time.

Beck stayed right with me. Dylan never left either, and I felt their silent support. When I couldn't reach parts of my back, Beck took the cloth and stroked across my skin, until finally, the water was no longer filled with blood and dirt. Running clean.

When I stepped out, I dried off, and Beck disappeared into my walk in to find me some clothes.

Dylan stepped closer, armed with shit that looked like it was going to hurt me. "Surprised he left you alone with me," he started conversationally. "All naked and shit."

I snorted. "Why do you think he's grabbing clothes. He's going to get the important bits covered."

Dylan's eyes darkened, but he didn't comment. Instead, he reached out for my arm, hesitating slightly before I nodded my permission. Beck strode in then, black bra and panties in hand, and I was getting dressed first whether I wanted to or not. After that, Dylan went back to work.

Disinfectant was brushed across every wound, my body tense and teeth clenched as I hissed through them whenever a particularly painful one was found. Beck stayed close, brushing a hand reassuringly across my back, offering comfort.

"These three probably need stitches," Dylan said, stroking across my thigh. Those wounds had started weeping again after the shower. "But I can just butterfly tape them now, and they should be fine."

I nodded. "Yeah, I don't care if they leave scars or whatever. I'm not allowing strangers to touch me."

Beck pressed his lips into the side of my head, basically holding me up now as my body crashed. By the time Dylan was done, handing me a couple of painkillers, which I swallowed down in a gulp, everything was fuzzy around the edges.

I managed to walk myself into the bedroom.

"None of us will leave you tonight," Dylan told me from the doorway.

"You're safe."

I blew him a kiss, aware I was always safe with my boys, and slipped under the covers. Beck and Dylan spoke for a few minutes, but I was already drifting off. When Beck slid in beside me, he wrapped me up in his arms, and I pressed my face into his chest.

"I love you," I murmured, because there was a point I never thought I'd get to say that to him. "I fucking love you."

Beck chuckled. "I love you too, Butterfly." There was a pause and darkness pressed in around me, my body going heavy and content as sleep stole me.

"I'm never letting you out of my sight again."

I thought I heard Beck murmur those words, but it was all dark before I could grasp onto that thought.

THE PAIN WOKE ME IN the early afternoon, the wounds and patches on my body reminding me that I'd been hurt. Again. When I opened my eyes, gingerly shifting around to get more comfortable, I turned to find Beck's eyes focused on me. The thick dark lashes framing light gray eyes. He had himself propped on one arm, and it was clear he'd been watching me for a while.

"Hey," I rasped out, voice hoarse.

He didn't say anything, just leaned over and pressed his lips to mine. The kiss was slow, Beck's full lips pressing against mine, moving tenderly. A low moan left my mouth as I opened and darted my tongue out, to caress across his.

"Baby, fuck," Beck murmured. "You're killing me here. You're hurt. We can't do this."

I'd like to say I'd temporarily forgotten about my pain, but my body was actually hurting me quite a fuckload, and I knew Beck was right.

I still pouted.

"Should have shot Johnson," I said, unhappily. "Bastard continues to ruin things even behind bars."

We both sobered at that thought. "We should head to the police station first," Beck finally said. "Get it out of the way."

I almost jerked up then as a thought occurred to me. Of course, almost jerking had a cry bursting from my lips, as my entire body shouted at me. "Ouch. Fuck."

Beck lifted me then, helping the rest of the way. "You okay?" he asked, looking me over.

I nodded, not sure that I actually was. Something felt like it might be bleeding again, but that was a worry for later.

"Have you heard anything about Dante? Did you get that file to the police?"

A fuzzy memory was tugging at the back of my mind, but it was from my time held by that asshole, and I wasn't ready to think about it just yet.

"Johnson confessed to Katelyn's murder," Beck reminded me. "We don't need the file any longer. I wouldn't be surprised if Dante is out right now." He paused with a grimace. "Which is good, considering we don't *have* the file anymore."

This sparked at that same fuzzy memory. "Wait, what? Where is it?"

Beck huffed an annoyed sigh. "Safely back on Graeme Huntley's desk, I suspect. He was the one who tampered with the car, not Johnson. That prick just took advantage of the situation when it presented too tempting to pass up."

I gasped as the memory of Johnson telling me the same thing clicked back into place, and I shuddered. "My uncle and I are going to have some stern words about the needless destruction of beautiful cars," I said with a thick coating of anger. "And about his casual disregard for our lives."

Beck gave me a half smile, stroking a finger down the side of my bruised face ever so gently. "Fuck, you're sexy when you're mad, Butterfly. Remind me to piss you off again when those cuts are healed up." His gaze was hot and full of promise, tempting me to jump back into his arms. But the trickle of blood running down my thigh had other plans.

"I think I ruined the sheets," I commented, looking down at the gash on my outer thigh which had started seeping from between the butterfly clips. Smears of bright red decorated the crisp white sheets, and I wrinkled my nose. "We might need bleach."

"You need stitches," Beck corrected, scowling down at the bloody mess.

The idea of any stranger, even a medic, touching me right now made my skin crawl. Nope. Not happening.

"Can't Dylan fix it for me?" I suggested. "Maybe use that glue stuff they put on head wounds?"

Beck gave me a long look, but must have seen how badly I didn't want to visit a medic and finally nodded. "Stay here, I'll go grab him."

"I'm not paralyzed, Sebastian, I can walk over to his apartment." I rolled my eyes at him, but he gently pushed me back into the pillows.

"I know you can," he replied, dropping a quick, gentle kiss on my forehead. "But you don't *have* to. Stay here and I'll even get you coffee."

My belly fluttered with excitement at the mention of coffee, and I relaxed into my bed. "Fine. You win."

Beck flashed me a triumphant grin then sauntered into my living area wearing nothing but his boxers. Fucking hell, where did he get off looking so damn incredible after a car crash and full night of serial killer hunting?

It became clear why he'd said I didn't need to walk over to Dylan's apartment. Beck paused beside my sofa and spoke a few quiet words. Moments later, a sleepy looking Dylan popped his head up and peered over at me still in bed.

"Give me five minutes, Riles," he called out to me. "I've got the stuff over at my place."

I just waved a hand back, like I wasn't bothered. Like I wasn't acutely aware of the pain without Beck's distraction and just barely clinging to composure. Because *holy fuck* my entire body was in agony.

Thankfully, Dylan was back faster than Beck could even make my coffee, and he brought pain pills.

"You rock," I groaned, taking the pills from him and washing them back with the water he offered. "Thank you."

Dylan peered at my seeping cuts for a moment then glanced up at me through his thick black lashes. "Anything for you, Riles."

Something in his tone immediately sent my mind back to this morning, when he'd watched me shower and I hadn't even attempted to hide my nakedness from him. Shit. I needed to rein it in before I gave him the wrong idea about us... because as much as I loved him, I was *in* love with Beck. And Beck had some serious issues with jealousy.

Clearing my throat, I averted my gaze away from Dylan's smooth, dark skin and rippling muscles. Holy shit, these Delta boys looked like they should be on a firefighter calendar holding kittens and shit. Only their calendar would be dark and scary, and they'd have knives and guns.

Was there a calendar for billionaire sociopaths? I'd buy it.

While Dylan worked on my injuries, I dropped my head back and rested against the pillow. Exhaustion came and went, in such huge waves, and right now I felt like I could sleep again, even though I'd only just woken.

A familiar voice at the doorway caught my attention.

"Let me in!" Eddy demanded again.

"Sorry, sis. Orders from the big man himself. Riley needs to rest."

Eddy snorted. "What, God told you not to let me in?"

Jasper howled with laughter before he turned to peer through the bedroom door. "Hear that, Beck, Eddy thinks you're God."

Beck, who was stretched out beside me, just smirked. Arrogant bastard.

"Let her in," I said to Jasper, shooting Beck a narrow-eyed glare. "I'm not dying. I'm perfectly fine."

Eddy basically hip checked her brother to get past him, hurrying straight over to me. She climbed across Dylan, uncaring about stomping on him, and snuggled down on the side that Beck wasn't dominating. I winced as she wrapped her arms around me, but when she gasped and tried to pull away, I shook my head and held her close.

"I'm fine," I said against her protests. "Don't worry about it at all."

We remained like that for ten or more minutes while Dylan fussed, Beck stroked my hair, and Eddy held me like I might float away if she didn't keep hold of me.

"Dante is out," she whispered out of nowhere.

I jerked my head up on the pillow. "He's out?"

She nodded. "Yep. All charges were dropped before a judge this morning, and he sent me a text straight away asking if I knew where you were."

My throat suddenly felt thick and scratchy. I couldn't swallow and breathe properly.

"What did you tell him?" Beck asked, hiding his emotions fairly well, even though I could hear the pissed off in his tone.

Eddy lifted her eyebrows. "What do you think I told him? I said that I'd check with you all and let him know if he had any Riley privileges left."

I waited for Beck to go caveman and start cursing Dante out and telling me I could never see him again. Then I'd have to bitch back and tell him he didn't own me and I would be friends with whoever the fuck I wanted.

It was kind of our thing. Even though I felt a little too tired and fragile right now to really give it my all. Turning to Beck, I waited … and waited some more.

But all he did was smile. "Choice is yours, baby," he said, and I was pretty sure my mouth dropped open.

"Wh—What?"

Beck's grin grew, those perfect white teeth stealing my attention for a second before I remembered that we were having an actual conversation. "You're not going to carry on about Dante?" I asked, not sure I believed a fucking word coming out of his gorgeous mouth.

Dylan snorted, but didn't comment. I paid attention to him again for a moment, realizing that he was spending an awfully long amount of time fixing my leg up, his huge hands wrapped around my thigh. In fact, if he moved his hands just an inch higher…

"Dylan," I said in warning. He just lifted his head, winking, and if I didn't have Beck to compare him to, his breathtakingly handsome face would have knocked me over. But I did have Beck, and Dylan was going to have to take a small step back.

Just for now. Until we worked this dynamic out.

Because Dylan had been almost possessive since they got me back from Johnson, the fucking psycho. And I got it, but the lines were blurring. Not in my heart, but … maybe in the physical world.

"Move that hand any higher, Dyl, and you're going to lose it," Beck said. He never missed a thing.

Dylan lifted both hands in the air in surrender. "All fixed up. You can go back to discussing Dante."

Yeah, anything to take the heat off him.

He wasn't wrong, though, and I turned back to Beck. "You're not going to fight me on Dante?" I asked again.

Beck shook his head. "No, Butterfly. I can't fucking deny you anything. If you want Dante in your life, then I won't stand in your way. But I will stand at your back and make sure that fucker doesn't put a knife in it again."

A smile burst across my face. "You're so sweet," I said, leaning over to kiss him, forcing myself to ignore the pain.

Eddy cracked up then. "Only Riley would think that was sweet. You're both as fucked as each other."

She wasn't wrong.

Chapter 25

It took Dante three days to find me. Three days where I did not make it easy for him. Eddy wasn't allowed to message him. No one was allowed to talk to him at all … he needed to fucking prove himself to me. Now that no one was paying—or blackmailing—him to be in my life, did he really want to be in there? I needed to know.

Bang.

The door practically rattled on the third day, and I exchanged a glance with Beck and Dylan, both of them on their feet before me, stalking toward the door. We knew Jasper and Evan were at Delta meetings with their parents and shouldn't be back for at least three hours. Eddy was with her mom shopping or some shit. Apparently when she moved out, Mrs. Langham decided she missed having a daughter.

Which left…

I moved slower, still recovering, but I was right behind them when they swung the door open, guns in hand.

"Dante," I said, breathless all of a sudden.

He didn't seem remotely fazed by the guns pointed at him, if anything he barely even noticed them.

"Riles," he said, and in that one word there were a thousand memories. Dante had said my name so many times over the years in so many different circumstances. He'd been the first guy to steal my heart—as a best friend.

As my family.

"Let him in," I said to Beck and Dylan, and they shot him one more long stare before both stepped back.

Dante leaned over to get through the doorway, and I wondered if he'd gotten even taller in prison. I didn't remember him being so *huge*. His head was freshly shaved, black hair less than an inch thick. He had new ink too, it was visible right across the top of his chest, shiny, red in places, with some scabs already showing.

It was my butterfly. The car gleaming and blue, with a dark-haired chick driving it … no, not a chick. Me. He'd marked me on his skin again. In the most prominent place that existed. The only more obvious skin would be his face, and I was grateful I hadn't ended up there.

"Riles," he said again, his voice breaking as his eyes locked with mine. "Please."

My hands were shaking; I tucked them in at my sides to hide the tremor. From the corner of my eye I could see Beck—he looked fucking furious. But he didn't block Dante as he took another step to me.

I could count on one hand the amount of times I'd seen Dante cry, and those very rare times were mostly when we were children. But there were tears in his eyes right now. He might have been all bad boy with his black clothing, tatts, and masculine features, but there was no hiding the depth of sadness in his green eyes.

He looked broken.

Finally I stepped forward, freeing my hands, and reaching out to take his. The hand he'd held out since he stepped in the door.

"Hey," I rasped out before clearing my throat.

Dante squeezed his eyes closed, head dropping down as he held my hand like it was the only thing tethering him to this world. "Fuck," he sobbed.

Just one sob, but I knew he was about to lose it. Something he would hate to do in front of Beck and Dylan.

I turned to them. "Will you give us a few minutes, please?"

Beck's jaw tensed, and if I looked down, I knew his fists would be clenched. He examined my face, searching for … *something*. Finally, he gave a single nod, and my heart swelled at that small gift from Beck. His trust. It had been a fucking long hard road to get here, but this was another step forward in our relationship.

"We'll be next door, baby," he said, brushing a hand over my back as he walked out the front door. Dylan did the same thing, a silent gesture of support, and then he was gone too.

As the door closed with a thud, Dante's arms came around me in one sweep of movement. He crushed me to him, and I managed not to cry out, even though most of my injuries were still painful. But if I cried, I would bring Beck back, and right now, I needed this moment with Dante.

We both fucking needed it.

"I deserve to die," Dante said into my shoulder, his voice a husky mess of emotions. "You should take Beck's gun and shoot me."

My heart ached at those words. At the thought of Dante not being in my world. "I have my own gun," I joked, trying to ease the heavy in the room.

Dante pulled back, still holding me up, examining my face with his red-rimmed eyes.

"I wouldn't blame you," he said simply. And I could tell he meant that.

Narrowing my eyes on him, I roughly shoved him, not moving him an inch. "Don't ever fucking talk like that again. You screwed up big time, don't get me wrong, but you are not allowed to die. Not. Ever."

Dante's lips twitched, and I cleared my throat and wiggled for him to let me down. I stepped back. The air was heavy, filled with an ass ton of emotions, and after the last few days, I wasn't really able to stay afloat in all the heavy.

"So, did you hear I was kidnapped?"

Way to break the tension, Riley. For fuck's sake.

Dante's entire demeanor changed, his face dark and scary, and there was the guy who managed to be part of one of the largest gangs in our area. Who managed to live in the world of Delta and not get completely annihilated. He was tough. Not Beck or Dylan level, but still up there. I'd always thought he could have fit in with the heirs, only now they would probably never trust him.

"Who do I need to kill?" he said, the words barely audible but the fury clear as fuck. Only someone that had lived our life, especially recently, would take my statement as truth and not laugh. Somehow, Dante knew I wasn't joking around.

"It's a long story," I said as I moved toward the couch. Dante followed, his eyes assessing me closer this time, no doubt noticing the way I was moving quite gingerly.

"Tell me everything, Riles," he said when we were seated, a few inches between us.

I turned to him. "I will, as long as you tell me absolutely everything that Catherine has done and manipulated in my life."

He paled, skin resembling the white curtains behind me. "You got the files and the phone?"

I nodded. "Yes. But I want to hear it all from you. I want to know how you fought her."

I had faith in him.

Dante nodded, and then he started his story. Beck and Dylan returned a few minutes after Dante started talking, and the three of us were silent, giving him his chance to explain. His chance for confession and redemption.

It was fucking painful for me at times, when he spoke about her manipulation, which was much further spread than I'd expected. One example was Dante destroying all of my college applications—except those in this state—to ensure I would never be able to go far from Catherine.

Beck's chest was rumbling as he pulled me back into him, but I couldn't look away from Dante.

"I did what I could though, Riles," he said, his eyes pleading with me to understand. "Wherever I could lie to her and get away with it, I did, and I tried to stop your parents' accident. I warned your father. But he did the fucking opposite of what I asked."

He palmed the top of his head, rubbing a hand across the short strands when he closed his eyes. "It was a fucking mess, and I was saving money to try and get us all out, but…" he paused, and I almost held my breath waiting for him to finish. "There was a kid before me," he said in a quiet, pained voice, "and I will never forget how she took her out."

What?

"Who?" I said, body trembling.

He squeezed his eyes closed again. "Fuck. Riles. I hate being the one who has to tell you this."

"Dante," I snapped, fear making me mad. "I need to know. I need to know everything. You didn't protect me from keeping me in the dark, you made me weak. I'm not fucking weak any longer."

Beck stroked his hand down my side, and I felt a tiny bit better.

That seemed to strike a chord with Dante, because he stopped hesitating. "Your friend from elementary school, Scarlett … she didn't just move away in the fourth grade."

I paused. "What happened to her?"

He snorted but there was nothing remotely amused about it. "Her entire family was killed in an explosion. Final ruling was a faulty electrical board that caught fire and blew the car up. But I knew it was Catherine."

My head spun as I tried to reconcile what he was saying with what I remembered. Scarlett and I were inseparable for years, but then she was just gone, and she'd never kept in touch.

"Her parents worked for Catherine," Dante whispered, "and they used their daughter to keep track of you. But when they got scared and ran, Catherine had them killed."

A choked cry escaped from my throat. My entire fucking life was a lie.

Dante reached out for me. "She never knew, though." He was rushing to say this, trying to pull me from the dizzying spin I was in. "I didn't have much time to know her before she ran—Catherine was bringing me in because they had expressed interest in getting out—but it was clear she never had a clue. She loved you, Riles."

I held a hand up, unable to speak. Standing, I rushed into the bathroom, slamming the door behind me. Stepping farther into the brightly lit room, I let my gaze linger on my reflection. I looked pale, and small, with a mess of dark hair floating around me.

Catherine had reduced me to this. To a shell of the former person I was. A shell of the fucking person I could have been.

A scream ripped from me before I could stop it. An angry, pissed off, rage filled scream. Reaching forward, I smashed my hands through all the shit around the sink, sending it flying before I turned and moved for the cupboard nearby.

Strong hands caught me before I sent the rest of my makeup and toiletries flying.

I struggled for a beat, but common sense kicked in quickly. I was never going to shake Beck. He didn't say anything, he just held me, tight enough that it … actually helped. After a minute, I no longer felt like I was going to shake into a million pieces, my fury and pain so strong that my cells could no longer contain it.

"Who the fuck am I?" I asked Beck, hating the broken in my voice. "Catherine has been controlling me since birth. Nothing was real. I'm not even sure my mom and dad were real at this point."

They were too dead to tell me, but I had my suspicions that they might have worked for Delta too. Why else would my father freak out like that and try and run? A normal person would have gone to the police.

"Are you even fucking real?" I said, lifting my tear-filled eyes to meet his. The next words caught in my throat at the tumult in those stormy gray depths. *Holy fuck.*

"I'm going to say this one time, Butterfly," he said in that quietly menacing voice. "This is the realest fucking thing that will ever be in your life."

My body reacted involuntarily, pushing into Beck, needing to feel his hard body against mine. For some messed up reason, the madder he got, the scarier he became, the more I wanted to climb him like a fucking tree.

"The past doesn't fucking matter, because after this vote, you'll never have to worry about Catherine again. She's going to pay. She's going to have everything she loves and desires in this world stripped from her. I will make sure of that."

"How long until the vote?" I said, needing this shit done in my life. I needed one normal day. Just one.

"Eight days."

Eight more days until this was all over. Eight more days until I took my fucking life back.

Debitch was going down.

Chapter 26

Dante didn't go far from me; Beck let him stay in his old apartment, because we were now ... living together. Something that should have freaked me the hell out, but it didn't. Having Beck around was my comfort in life, and the officialness of "living together" didn't diminish that at all. While I was still recovering, we spent the next few days at home, eating, sleeping, and Beck loving the fuck out of my body until I could barely walk. But this time it was completely okay with me. I hadn't had many happy days since my parents' deaths, but this week, it actually kind of felt like I was being given a gift.

If only it wasn't the last hurrah before we were all destroyed. With the vote closing in, my nerves were completely shot. I alternated between relieved and terrified, because I had no idea if this was all going to go our way.

Either way, it would all be over soon.

THREE DAYS BEFORE THE VOTE, I was leaving the bathroom, still drying my hair.

"Riley, what the fuck is this in the sink?" Beck yelled, and I pranced across, dressed in just a bra and panties, peering over his shoulder.

"Huh, guess I forgot to wash my bowl," I said with a shrug, pressing my breasts to his arm because it felt good and I was somewhat addicted to Beck. "Who knew we could actually grow something green. I'll tell that to the dead plants in the bathroom and on the balcony."

A smile actually worked its way across his lips, and I shrugged again. This was one of our first little snags in living together. Beck was meticulously clean, and I was kind of a slob. Neither of us were working on making that mesh better either, and probably we'd need to get a cleaner in at some point— when we weren't so suspicious of strangers—because cleaning was never going to be my thing. But for now, we were all "odd couple bickering" which generally turned into the best kind of foreplay.

My nipples ached as I brushed them across his arm again. "Are you trying to distract me, Butterfly?" Beck asked, and he was the one distracting me, because I liked that rumble in his voice.

The towel from my wet hair hit the floor, and Beck's hands were on my ass as he lifted me to the bench.

"Is it working?" I asked, breathless as he parted my knees and settled between them. He'd just jumped out of the shower before me, so he was only wearing a pair of boxers and nothing else. Boxers which were strained far too tight over his erection.

Beck chuckled a dark, sexy sound as he captured my lips with his own, coaxing my mouth to open so he could explore with his tongue. Large, rough hands skimmed over my sides, reaching behind me to flick the clasp of my bra open and discard the garment somewhere across the kitchen.

His palms cupped my breasts, and I moaned into his kiss.

"I'd say it's working pretty well," he told me, his voice a husky promise of *all* the orgasms. Hell yes.

I looped my arms around his neck, pulling him closer as I sealed my lips to his, drinking him in like a fine wine and groaning when he ground against my core. If this was what living with Beck was like, I could safely chalk it up as one of the best decisions I'd ever made.

Seriously, it was like we couldn't get enough of each other. Any time the opportunity presented we were clawing at each other, desperate to be closer...

The cold touch of metal at my hip made me pull back with a gasp, only to find Beck with a fucking butcher knife in his hand.

"Um…" I squinted at the blade, then quickly clued in when he swapped it to his other hand and sliced the other side of my panties open. Smart man, using the tools available.

He grinned at me, tossing my destroyed underwear over his shoulder then sliding the blade back into the big wooden knife block behind me.

"That's better," he murmured, trailing his fingers over my bare pussy. "We should just make a no clothing rule inside the apartment."

His index finger slid inside me, and I gasped. "I'm okay with this rule. It's a good rule." A small whimper escaped my throat as he added his middle finger and delved deeper. "It's also a rule you're already breaking, Sebastian Roman Beckett."

He gave me a wicked grin and seconds later his boxers had joined my ruined panties somewhere across the kitchen. Good riddance, I say.

"Fuck me," I groaned, taking his hard cock in my hand and caressing his velvet smooth skin.

"That was the plan," he joked, gently biting the flesh of my shoulder then kissing the side of my neck.

I gasped as he grabbed my earlobe between his teeth, sucking at it and sending all kinds of tingles shooting straight back down to my aching core. It was official. My brain had turned into a sex induced mush pile.

Wrapping my legs tighter around his waist, I pulled Beck closer, guiding him into the right position then pushing my hips forward impatiently. "Please, Sebastian," I begged, desperate to feel him inside me. "I need you. Please, baby, fuck me."

For a second, he had that evil look in his eye that suggested he wanted to tease me more, but another wiggle of my hips saw his resolve crumble, and he thrust deep.

The force of his hips meeting mine pushed me back a little on the countertop and I needed to release my grip on Beck's neck. Instead I dropped my hands to grip the edge of the polished marble counter as I spread my knees wider and let him in farther.

"Holy shit, Butterfly," he panted, pausing with his forehead against mine for a second then kissing me hard enough to leave my lips swollen and tingling. "Hold on, baby."

It was all the warning I got as he gripped my ass in his hands, yanking me right to the edge of the counter and then fucking me hard and fast. *Exactly* how I needed it.

"Oh my god, yes," I cried out at some stage when he did *something* with his hips and an orgasm crashed over me without any freaking warning at all. It took me so much by surprise that my grip on the counter slipped and we both would have probably ended up on the floor if I hadn't flailed and grabbed back on fast.

Still, the back of my hand clipped the coffee pot and it hit the ground with a loud smash.

Fuck it. Who needed coffee when you could wake up with multiple orgasms from Beck's magic dick?

He snickered as I screamed my way through two more orgasms and muttered some smart-ass remark about how he'd warned me to hold on. I don't know. I'd lost all sense of sight and sound at some point when he'd found my G-spot and clit simultaneously.

Eventually—in time with maybe my fourth orgasm—he found his own release, grunting and panting as he pumped into me.

For a long damn time, the only sounds in the kitchen were our intertwined heavy breathing and the pounding of my own pulse inside my head.

Head back against the high cabinets in the kitchen, I sucked in air as fast I could, trying to get my breath back. "You're going to kill me," I said, wheezing between each word. "Like ... I swear to fucking god one day my heart will stop mid-orgasm."

Leaning forward, Beck buried his head into my shoulder and neck, breathing me in, his body still hard inside of mine. He'd come, but I knew Beck could go again almost instantly. Was his superpower, for sure.

A knock on the door had a low rumble escaping from him, and he straightened. I groaned as he stepped back. My body was aching in a dozen delicious places, but apparently, we needed to answer the door first before any more fucking was to occur.

"In the bathroom, Butterfly," Beck said, leaving the kitchen for a minute to grab sweats before striding back out. I watched his bare, retreating back, and my pussy clenched again. Fucker was too goddamn sexy. Pants riding low, Vee visible, bronze muscles everywhere.

Knowing he was commando under those sweats had me desperate to rip them off, but he was already moving to the door.

I sighed, and wiggled to get down, closing the bathroom door just as Beck opened ours. "What?" I heard him say.

I cleaned up the best I could, actually remembering this time to throw the towel in the hamper. As I passed the mirror, I caught sight of the marks across my skin. I was healing, but it was slow. At least most of the pain was gone now.

I went to leave, pausing at Beck propped in the doorway. He was watching me, an expression I couldn't read on his face. "Who was at the door?" I asked.

A few more steps and I was in front of him. "Dylan."

He leaned forward and pressed his lips to my shoulder before more kisses across my neck and along my jaw. He finished with my lips. Long, soul-destroying kisses, that had me forgetting everything.

"Don't let her take this from us," I all but begged, melancholy hitting me unexpectedly. "We need to fight to the death to keep this, Sebastian."

His hug was immediate. "We will fight, baby. We will fight and fucking win."

His confidence fueled my own, and when he released me, I strolled past into my closet. Second attempt at getting dressed today.

"You didn't say what Dylan wanted?" I called. We usually all had breakfast together, so it was probably that, but I liked to check. My anxiety at receiving bad news was at its peak.

Beck followed me. "Delta meeting. This is a pre-vote meeting and all current board members and heirs have to be there."

Something cold trailed down my spine. I hadn't seen Catherine since I caught her making out with her brother. Since all of the horrible shit I'd found out about her. I didn't think I'd have to see her again until the vote … but here we were. "Is this a good idea?" I said softly. "What if … we fuck up and they somehow know what we're planning."

Beck's grin was not nice. "We won't fuck up. This is a game we've been playing for years."

I shook my head in frantic motions. "Not me, though. I barely have a Delta face. What if I fuck it up?"

He cupped my face, slowing my agitated head movements. "You won't," he said simply. "It's going to be okay, and soon, it will all be over."

Over. That might have been my new favorite word.

Chapter 27

BECK

When Riley stepped out of her room, I fought the urge to wrap my hands around her body and drag her back in there. She wore a power suit, one I'd never seen on her before. Black, with a deep red dress shirt, that cut low across her cleavage with the tiniest hint of lacy bra visible.

Fuck. I needed all my focus and concentration today, because this was where the mind games and power plays started, but with Riley dressed like that, her tight skirt skimming over her curves, black heels making her long legs look even longer...

"Trying to kill me, Butterfly?" I asked, stepping closer, needing to touch her.

She was the best and worst kind of drug. Completely addicting and intoxicating, and when I'd thought that I'd lost her for a short time, I knew I would not survive without her.

"You need to stop looking at me like that, Sebastian," she said, her voice husky with need, "or we won't be making a meeting."

An annoyed grumble shot from me, "I'm not sure that's a bad thing at this point." I kissed her softly. "I have something for you," I said when I managed to stop kissing her fucking perfect mouth.

Her eyes lit up. "Oh, I love things. What did you get me?"

I just stared. She was breathtaking, and I knew how fucked I was, but it was too late to change it now. This woman owned every part of me.

"Thought you might like a vest to match mine," I said, trying to focus, which was not helped by Riley's hands running in under my suit jacket and up over the black vest. "I got them for all of us—it's an heir uniform. It also has a holster in it for your gun, which makes it useful as well." And I would not let her go in there unarmed.

Her face lit up. "Fuck yes! Okay, hang on while I put it on."

I handed her the light-weight vest, which was black to match her suit. She hurried off, reappearing a moment later, her gun in hand. After making sure the safety was on, I showed her how to holster it and then made sure the vest was securely fitted. "Perfect." Just as I was leaning down to capture her lips, there was a heavy thud on the door.

On instinct, I shifted Riley behind me and had my gun in hand as I strode forward.

Jasper and Evan didn't even blink at the barrel facing them. "Time to go, our ride is here."

I nodded, slipping my gun back into the holster under my own black jacket.

"I fucking hate that these assholes want to control every aspect of their meetings," I said, holding the door open for Riley, who strolled out.

Jasper ran his eyes down her body, starting at the tip of her shiny black hair before he let out a whistle. "Damn, girl. You look sexy as fuck!"

Like he just remembered himself, his gaze shot up to me, and he gave me a sheepish smile. I didn't return his smile with anything other than a single curl of my lip. Jasper, Evan, and even Dylan—my fucking pathetically in love best friend—were the only guys I could tolerate around Riley. And only to a certain point.

Dylan thinking he was in love with her was starting to push my buttons. But I fucking got it. I really did. Riley was without a doubt the most beautiful, brave, strong, smartass, perfect woman in the world.

But she was mine. And I didn't share.

Not even with my best friends ... my brothers.

Dylan would just have to find his own.

"I'm nervous," Riley confessed just as Dylan exited his apartment, wearing a dark blue suit. "I don't have a good feeling about this."

Jasper slung his arm around her, almost knocking her off her heels.

"Jas," I said warningly.

He winked at me. "I'm just comforting her." He turned to face Riley. "Don't stress that pretty little head about this. It's all standard ... or so we've heard. Prelims for the vote. They want to make sure everyone is on the same page."

Riley didn't look convinced, but before she said anything about that, the door to my old apartment slammed open and a giggling Eddy stumbled out, Dante's arms around her, keeping her steady.

Jasper's face was awash with anger as he stepped forward. "What the fuck?"

This development didn't surprise me. I knew Eddy had visited Dante in prison. I knew she was fucking hung up on him. And I knew she would take none of our warnings about not trusting him.

"Edith," Jasper snarled. "Are you out of your fucking mind?"

She swung around, eyes wide as she realized we were all standing in the hall between our apartments. "Shit. You fucking s-scared me."

She pressed a hand to her chest, but didn't move away from Dante. Who still had his arms around her, only this time it was protective.

"You know he was accused of hurting a woman before Katelyn, right?" Jasper continued, pushing forward, concern for his sister clouding his normal judgement. "What the fuck was her name, Riles?"

"Hailey," she whispered.

Jasper nodded. "Right. Do you want to be his next victim?"

Dante was looking at Riley now, and even I could see the fucking hurt on his face. "You believe I could do something like that, Riles?" he asked softly, and I was about half a second from stepping in between them so he stopped staring at her like that.

Riley shook her head. "Why do you think I never bothered to ask you about her? I know you'd never hurt any woman, and especially not one you loved."

My Butterfly was way too fucking trusting. Dante had deceived her for most of their lives. Sure, he'd done so to protect his family, but it showed that he wasn't above looking out for himself and his interests over Riley's. Or Eddy's.

"What happened?" Eddy asked, turning toward Dante.

He lowered his gaze to meet hers, and I liked the fact that there was definitely something there between them. Made it less likely I would have to kill Riley's friend because he couldn't keep his fucking hands off her.

"Catherine got to her," he said simply. "She didn't want me distracted, and she knew Hailey meant something to me, so she paid her off. It was a not very subtle warning to me that she owned me. My life. Every single part of it, and if I ever strayed, she would destroy my world."

I knew this game. Delta played it a lot. "Catherine made the charges go away too?"

Dante snorted cynically. "Yeah, because I fell back in line."

We were all just good fucking soldiers. Well, no more.

Jasper looked slightly placated, the red fading from his cheeks. "If you so much as break her nail. Or fucking cause her to cry, I will come for you, asshole," he said, pointing a finger at Dante. "I can kill you and get rid of your body before anyone even notices you're missing."

Eddy glared, but surprisingly, Riley didn't. She was fast acclimatizing to our life.

Glancing at my watch, I schooled my face. "We've got to go. The car is here."

"Where are you going?" Dante called after us.

Nosy fucker.

"Delta business," I said, and then I wrapped Riley in under my arm, keeping her close. I pressed my lips to her head, and breathed her in, calming myself down. It worked in one way, but in the other—the light floral scent of her skin cream had my dick hard and ready to fuck her right here.

If only we were alone.

"Delta faces on, boys," Jasper said, already having forgotten about his sister. "We're about to walk right into the lion's den."

"Everyone armed?" Dylan asked, and I could see that he was armed to the fucking hilt. Three guns, multiple blades, and at least one heavy duty taser. None of the weapons would be obvious to most people, but I was trained to assess my targets.

"Right now, Dylan was a one-man killing machine.

Scary motherfucker.

"Yep, got my babies," Jasper said patting his long wool coat.

"Me too," Evan added.

"You know I am," I said.

"Yes!" Riley said, sounding excited.

Dylan's smile was a touch too fucking familiar as he watched her, but now wasn't the time for this conversation again. It could wait. Today we needed to be a seamless team. And it definitely made me feel better to know she wasn't walking around in this world unarmed. We would be there for her as much as possible, but as recent situations proved, sometimes the enemy got around us.

Not today though. I knew exactly who the enemy was, and I would not let my guard down for a second.

The mental war had already begun. And knowing Delta, the physical war wouldn't be far behind.

Chapter 28

I was surrounded by four tall, gorgeous, suit clad dudes. The sort of guys that were scary and lethal, but also sweet and kind. This should have been the start of some wicked fantasy, instead we were walking into a nightmare.

My gut would not calm down, not for the entire elevator ride, or for the twenty minutes in the black car with its blacked-out window, or even when Beck's hand dropped to my bare thigh, caressing it up and down in a soothing and arousing manner.

I couldn't shake the darkness.

At one point, I actually wondered if I was going to throw up, but when I got the window down and some fresh air filtered around my face, the sensation subsided.

Beck didn't say anything comforting, maybe he didn't want to actually lie because none of us knew how this was going to go, but he did keep his arm around me, occasionally pressing his lips to my head.

When the car finally pulled to a halt, the five of us remained where we were for a minute.

"We stay close," Beck warned, his voice low. "No matter what they do, don't let them separate us. Especially not Riley."

"None of us!" I bit right back. "If we're going down, I'm going down with all of you."

Jasper nodded. "Family."

"Always," Evan added.

Beck's lips smashed into mine for a moment, and I gasped into the kiss. It was rough and perfect, and there was a scary feel of goodbye to it.

"I love you," I whispered. Before he could say anything, I turned to the others. "I love you all. Don't do anything stupid. Promise me."

Whole fucking lot of them thought they were invincible.

For once, no one joked around, they just nodded. "We promise, Riles," Dylan said, and then he opened the door.

They clearly had this planned, because Beck caught my arm, making sure he exited first. Then he shut the door in my face.

I swung around to Evan and Jasper. "What the fuck is happening? Are they going in alone?"

Evan patted my shoulder. "Calm yourself, Bulma. Vegeta just wants to play the hero and make sure everything is safe before you walk into danger."

I narrowed my eyes on them. "Are you fucking kidding me? Right after I told them not to do anything stupid."

Jasper laughed, like the hyena fuck he was. "Yeah, did you notice that Beck agreed to nothing. Asshole is sneaky."

Asshole was sleeping on the couch the moment we got back home.

The door opened before I could say anything else, and I glared daggers at Beck as I slid across to get out, ignoring the hand he held out for me.

Smug bastard just laughed. I really should shoot him with my gun, but unfortunately, I had grown quite fond of him.

"So … give it to me straight … are we expecting trouble today?" I asked quietly, taking Dylan's arm when he offered it and not missing the smug look he shot Beck. Whoops, maybe I should use Jasper if I want to annoy my brooding boyfriend. Less chance of anyone getting killed.

"Not necessarily," Dylan answered, walking with me into the shiny polished marble lobby of Delta's Jefferson building. "But this close to the vote, and with everything else that's happened lately…" he trailed off with a shrug, and I nodded.

"Better safe than sorry," I murmured, agreeing.

"Always be prepared," Jasper added, throwing me a playful wink. "I learned that at Boy Scouts."

I wrinkled my nose at him. "You went to Boy Scouts?"

"No, but I hear great things," he replied with a smirk.

I shook my head and rolled my eyes. "Dick."

The five of us blew past the lobby security desk, setting metal detectors blaring with alarms and not even pausing a beat. The uniformed officer there looked more interested in avoiding our gaze than stopping us, anyway, so we stepped into the elevator unhindered.

As the doors slid shut and the box started moving, Evan started humming a tune under his breath. At first, I didn't give it much thought, but there was a thread of familiarity to it.

Glancing at him, I frowned in confusion. He just kept humming, but gave me an amused, brow raise.

It wasn't until we were stepping out onto the conference room floor that it clicked what the song was, and I burst out laughing.

"How very appropriate," I told him, snickering while he broke off the tune and grinned back. "*Never smile at a Crocodile.* Couldn't be any more fitting for a meeting with Catherine Deboise."

"I don't get it," Beck commented with a small frown.

Evan sang the lyrics under his breath as we walked across the plush carpet with the conference room ahead of us putting emphasis on the part about the crocodile imagining how well the object of its attention would fit inside it's skin. Essentially implying Catherine was plotting to kill us all.

With the joke explained, we were all chuckling as we entered the board room, and I don't think we could have disturbed the Delta council more if we'd walked in wearing eight-foot-tall Teletubby suits.

"Something funny, daughter?" Catherine asked, her voice tart and her blue eyes narrowed. "I wasn't aware that this was a comedic meeting."

Unable to pass up an opportunity to get under her skin, I just gave a blasé shrug. "Just discussing plans for your retirement home, Catherine. You've been looking so stressed lately, it's showing around the eyes." I indicated to the crow's feet which were *barely* visible, but to a woman of Catherine's vanity level it was a scathing insult.

Her mouth tightened, pursing into something that vaguely resembled a cat's asshole, and I tried really hard not to laugh.

"Thank you for joining us," Mr. Langham addressed us, cutting off whatever Catherine was about to respond with. "Please take a seat and we can begin."

He indicated to the vacant side of the table where five seats were in a row, facing the older generation.

"We can't begin," Catherine snapped, shooting a glare at Mr. Langham. "Rome hasn't arrived yet. We can't start until all members are present and accounted for."

"Rome couldn't make it today," Jasper's father smoothly replied, and the dismissive glance he gave Catherine said he didn't care much for her attitude either. "And given that he's already signed over his vote to Sebastian, there seems no need to inconvenience him with the preliminary discussions."

Catherine balked and looked a little pale. Frightened? No, not Debitch. Just annoyed, I was pretty sure.

"Yes, but Sebastian isn't a sitting board member yet," she argued back, not even trying to hide the irritation in her voice, "and it's in the *bylaws* that all members attend this meeting."

Dylan's dad—prick that he was—just scoffed a laugh and leaned back in his chair. "Bylaws also don't permit *women* a position on the board. Yet here *you* are, and with your whore of a daughter sitting as your heir, no less."

Beck had just sat down in the seat beside me, and I spotted the tension zap through him at Grant senior's misogynistic statement. Beck's hands tightened on the arms of the chair, and it took *every* ounce of my control not to reach out and soothe him. Such a gesture would only fuel Dylan's dad's claims.

Besides. This was Catherine's fight, not mine.

"How *dare* you speak to me like that?" Catherine hissed at the older gentleman, who just sneered back at her. Every time I was around them, I understood more and more why they all had such an issue with the bond the guys and I shared. The older Delta generation straight up hated each other and must be constantly watching for knives in their backs.

"That's enough," Mr. Rothwell snapped, interrupting the pissing match between Catherine and Mr. Grant. "Rome doesn't need to be here, so let's just get on with it. Greg?" He nodded to Mr. Langham—Greg—who nodded back and clasped his hands in front of him.

"Delta council meeting is now in session."

Those words seemed so damn innocent, but they must have been the trigger for what happened next. Before anyone could speak another word, a loud explosion sounded from the base of the building and the room shook. As far as I knew, Jefferson wasn't on a fault line, so that was no earthquake.

We all glanced around, confused, until Catherine acted.

Faster than I thought I'd ever seen her move—faster than she'd slapped me that first day I'd arrived—she pulled a knife from inside her Dolce and Gabbana jacket and stabbed Mr. Grant through the side of his neck.

Frozen in shock, I watched as she wrenched the knife back out again, sending a massive arc of blood spraying across the table and splattering her own face in the process.

Chaos was breaking out all around me, and all I could do was *stare*. Catherine grinned at me from across the table, blood dripping from her face and her white teeth flashing and right then I knew. Catherine was the one responsible for Oscar's death. The look in her eyes as she grinned at me was so cold, so ruthless, so totally removed from sanity... she had zero issues murdering her children to get ahead in life.

And yet. There I sat. Fucking *frozen*.

Until a hard body slammed into me and knocked me to the ground.

"Butterfly!" Beck boomed from above me, "Snap out of it! We're under attack!"

Dazed, I peered around me. Beck was hovering over me in a crouch, popping off shots from his Glock 19 every few seconds as shadowy figures appeared in his line of sight. The glass walls to the conference room were totally shattered and shit was going crazy.

"Sorry," I gasped, scrambling out from under him and reaching for my own gun. "Catherine set this up. She murdered Dylan's dad." I was in shock, and repeating things we already knew.

Beck just grunted and shot another attacker dressed in black who tried to get close. The lights were flickering, probably damaged by that initial blast, and it was allowing our assailants the cover of shadows as they closed in on us.

"No wonder she was so pissed that my dad didn't show up," he replied to me, popping the empty clip from his gun and slamming a fresh one home. "She wanted to eliminate the entire board and heirs in one fell swoop. Ballsy bitch."

From under the table, I could see bodies scattered around the room. Judging by the expensive wristwatches and signet rings visible, all three Delta board members were dead, along with several of our anonymous attackers. Huntley mercenaries, I'd be willing to bet.

"Are we okay here?" I asked Beck, pulling my own gun from the specially designed vest halter. "You guys can kick their asses, right?"

Beck grunted again, and a cold chill of fear ran through me.

"Watch out!" Dylan yelled from somewhere, and Beck covered me with his body just moments before another—smaller—explosion rocked the room. Dust from an obliterated wall kicked up in a storm cloud, and I needed to cover my nose and mouth with my blazer to keep from breathing it all in and choking.

"What the fuck?" I croaked, coughing and flapping a hand in front of my face to clear the air. "Did someone just throw a fucking grenade?"

Beck paused a moment, looking around before answering. "Yep."

I spluttered. "I was joking! Fucking hell." I shoved him off me again so that I could see more than just a pile of bodies and the back of Beck's suit, but he put out an arm to hold me in place.

"Stay here," he ordered, his voice all business. "Get under the table and stay out of sight. I need to help Jasper." He shot me a serious look over his shoulder. "I mean it, Butterfly. Stay hidden. I'll be straight back."

I nodded. With grenades being thrown, bullets flying everywhere and Debitch knifing people in the neck, I really didn't think it was the best time to be practicing my female empowerment and independence. I was easily the least capable fighter in the room, so yeah, there was no shame in doing exactly what Beck told me to.

In saying that, I wasn't totally cowed into hiding. When I heard shouts and rapid gunfire not far from me, I poked my head out just in time to see Jasper break a guy's neck, right before he got shot three times in the chest by another masked assailant. Beck popped out of nowhere and slammed his fist into the shooters face before dropping him with a headshot.

It was too late, though. Jasper's body hit the ground with a sickening thump, and a horrified scream tore from my throat.

Stupid, *stupid* Riley!

That scream pulled Beck's attention—because of course it did—and the next thing I knew, his head snapped back when the butt of an assault rifle slammed into his cheek.

"No!" I shouted, halfway clambering from under the table, my gun up and ready.

Without even fully comprehending what I was doing, my finger squeezed the trigger, and my bullet hit home in the forehead of the masked man who was about to shoot my boyfriend. The man dropped, dead, and Beck staggered back to his feet looking dazed and pissed right the fuck off.

"Riley, move!" Evan shouted from across the room, but I wasn't nearly fast enough.

The cold steel of a gun barrel pressed against my temple and Catherine's cloying, floral perfume invaded my nose like poisoned gas.

"I ought to thank you," my despicable birth mother hissed into my ear, "without you distracting these sociopathic pricks, none of this would have been possible."

I let out a bitter laugh, even as my stomach twisted with knots of guilt. I *was* a distraction, I knew that. "You're not making it out of this room alive, Catherine. Do yourself a favor and turn that gun around. It'll be a hell of a lot quicker than Beck will make your death."

"Oh, I don't know about that," she snickered, then raised her voice. "Drop your weapons or I'll shoot my stupid daughter in the kneecap."

I almost laughed at her ridiculous request, until I saw my guys—what was left of them—raise their weapons in surrender.

"What? Don't listen to her!" I yelled. "She's not going to shoot me. She clearly needs me alive."

"Alive, not unharmed," my bio-mom sneered. "Drop the guns, kick them away." This was a directive for Dylan and Evan. For Beck.

I shook my head, pleading with my eyes but Beck just stared back at me, totally impassive as he did what Catherine ordered.

His gaze didn't break from mine for a second. Not when Graeme Huntley stepped into the room flanked by a dozen more armed mercenaries. Not when someone grabbed me by the arms, wrenching my gun away and zip-tying my arms together. Not when Catherine and Graham started to drag me away, and all I could do was shout and fight to get back to my guys. I'd never seen Beck's face like that, completely without emotion, as he kept me locked in his gaze.

I struggled hard, but with my arms bound, they had the advantage. Catherine slapped me a few times, but that was the least of my problems. Just before I was completely clear of the room, I heard Beck growl my name, and I cried out when one of the black clad goons picked up a Browning Hi Power and started spraying bullets across my guys.

The last sight before I was wrenched into the stairwell, was the heirs falling, and then they were gone from me.

The only thing to comfort me now was my own screams.

Chapter 29

It was all a blur after that. After I watched the man I loved be shot not fifteen feet away from me ... something inside me just sort of snapped.

Soon the horrible screaming died off, my voice totally gone, and I slipped into a numb state of despair. They were dead. All of them. How? *How* had this happened? They were supposed to be the best of the best, totally unkillable. Weren't they?

Except, they were only human. And not even the most highly trained human really stood a chance when so severely outnumbered... and a loved one held at gunpoint.

It was my fault. Their deaths were on my hands, and I couldn't even escape the cold, endless pain of it all. Because Catherine needed me *alive*.

"We should have just killed her with the rest of them," Catherine had snarled as they shoved me into the back of a van and the driver peeled out of the parking lot. "Fuck the bylaws. Who's going to challenge me when they're all dead?" Her voice was cold enough to freeze lava, and despite my numb state, I shivered.

"Rome Beckett isn't dead yet," Graeme reminded her, "and neither is your *husband*." He spat that word like it was made of dog shit. "Your brilliant plan to wipe out the Delta council failed so you *need* your heir until the rules can be changed."

Catherine snorted an ugly sound as we bumped around a corner, and I almost toppled out of my seat. No one had bothered to strap me in, and my arms were bound so I just had to roll with it when I bumped into Catherine and she shoved me away again.

"I've taken out the elders in co-ordinated attacks," she said, "so now we just need to send someone to take care of Rome." Her face was creased in anger. "I should have known that bastard wouldn't show up for the meeting." Graeme huffed an annoyed sound. "And Richard? Why has no one *taken care* of him yet?"

"He's harmless," she bit back. "Nothing more than a senile, grieving old man. He wouldn't speak up against my new structure in the wake of his friends' tragic deaths. He *couldn't*. That man is barely capable of tying his own shoelaces, let alone challenging a hostile takeover."

Surprise zapped through me, almost enough to shake me free from the overwhelming agony of what I'd just seen happen. Catherine really didn't know Richard was faking? The van pulled up in front of what looked like a half-finished residential tower, and one of the armed, masked men who accompanied Graeme dragged me out onto the street, keeping his fingers banded around my upper arm.

"Take her up to the penthouse," Graeme ordered my jailer. "No one comes in until we get back."

Without even giving me a second glance, he and Catherine jumped into a sleek, silver Jaguar parked across the street and disappeared into the night. Presumably to turn up at the Jefferson Delta office and feign shock and horror at the tragic deaths of their "friends."

"Come on, kid," my guard ordered, sounding tired as shit when I resisted a moment. "I'm really not in the mood to knock you out and carry you."

Nor was I in the mood to *be* knocked out and carried. Wordlessly, I let him guide me into the open-sided building and into a cage that zipped us up the side. I lost track of what happened next because my eyes were covered. Probably so I wouldn't know how to access his "secret lair". The next thing I saw was the front door, which the masked guard unlocked and held it open for me to enter. Before I went more than two steps, he stopped me with a hand on my arm. From his pocket, he produced a switchblade and flicked it open.

For a moment, I thought... maybe he had other orders? Maybe he was going to slit my throat right here and leave my body for Graeme to find when he returned?

But instead he cut the cable ties restraining my hands, and I rubbed my wrists on reflex.

"Are you sure that's wise?" I asked, my voice hoarse and croaky from screaming.

The man looked me over, nothing past his cold blue eyes visible but they were enough to convey his pity and contempt. "You're not going anywhere, love. We both know that. At least this way I don't have to wipe your ass for you."

He jerked his head, indicating for me to get out of the way, then slammed the door in my face. The metallic clicking sound of locks turning seemed to echo through the empty, dark apartment, and I wrapped my arms around myself.

"Shit," I whispered to myself, taking a few more steps into the open living room. I'd lost my high heels somewhere and my tight skirt was crusted with blood. The deepest of my cuts from Johnson's murder attempt felt like they had reopened, because they burned under my clothes. Worse, my whole body was trembling like a damn leaf in the wind. No wonder that guard hadn't considered me a threat. I was just a pathetic, weak, little girl. No good for anything except *bait*.

My knees gave out and I collapsed right there on the floor.

SOME TIME LATER—I DON'T know how long—I peeled myself up from the floor. My tears had long since run dry and my emotions were drained.

All I knew was that I couldn't just give up. Not like this. I owed it to the guys, to Jasper, Evan, Dylan... to Beck. I owed it to them to get the fuck up and *do* something. Kill Catherine, expose her, or at least die trying.

Grasping onto that glimmer of determination, I started searching Graeme's penthouse for anything that might help me escape. Just the fact that he had a secret penthouse mere blocks from the local Delta offices told me how long he and Catherine must have been plotting this coup.

For the most part, everything about the apartment was standard rich-guy bullshit. Nothing personal, at all. Save one item.

An urn.

"Who are you, and why are you important to Graeme?" I murmured to the urn as I paused in front of it. The ornately carved golden object sat on a pedestal all on its own at the end of a corridor full of expensive artwork. A glass case covered it, and specially designed lights in the pedestal lit it up as an item of value.

Peering closer, I noticed something out of place. A necklace. Not the dainty, feminine sort, but a carved piece of bone or something in the shape of a turtle attached to a leather string. The sort of necklace guys wore if they'd been on a surf trip or something. The kind of necklace...

Oh shit.

That was exactly the kind of necklace Oscar had been wearing in that photo on Richard's computer!

"Oscar," I gasped, pressing a hand to my mouth in horror.

"Sick, isn't it?" A deep voice said from behind me, and I startled. So much that I almost bumped my brother's remains off the pedestal. If Richard hadn't darted forward and steadied the whole thing, we'd both be standing in ashes.

"Richard! How—what are you doing here?" I was starting to question my sanity. Maybe watching Beck get shot had spiraled me into a mental breakdown and I was now hallucinating things. "Wait, you mean this *is* Oscar?" I turned my gaze back to the urn and needed to swallow down the bile threatening to rise.

"I believe so," Richard replied, his face full of sorrow. "It's taken me months, but I think I finally got to the bottom of things." He held up a well-worn looking journal, but I wasn't following.

"Graeme killed Oscar? But why?"

Richard shook his head. "No, Catherine did."

I gasped, even though it really wasn't really that much of a shock. I'd had the exact same thought the moment she slit another man's throat right in front of me. Not to mention I had first-hand knowledge of how she treated her children. Catherine wasn't fucking sane. Not by a long shot.

"Oscar kept a daily journal," Richard explained, holding up the book again. "It was an exercise his therapist asked him to do, to help work through his anger after he found out about who really fathered him."

The pieces started clicking together in my head. "That's what was in the box inside his coffin? His diaries? Why keep them at all? Why didn't Catherine burn them or something?"

"Because Oscar knew the location of the Delta vault. My father—your grandfather—had been grooming him to take over the secret when he was old enough, but Oscar was always too smart for his own good and worked out the location on his own." Richard paused with a sad smile, looking down at the journal. "He's recorded it in here, but encoded it. Smart boy. When I saw Catherine with this just before the funeral, I forced her to put it in the coffin with—" His voice broke slightly. "With Oscar. She didn't get an opportunity to get them out again before he was buried, then I figured she just gave up because her read through didn't tell her anything."

"Is that why she dug him up?" I wondered. "To have another shot at decoding the diary?"

Richard shook his head, looking unsure. "If I know my wife at all, the reason she had Graeme dig Oscar up was to ensure that no one would ever find out her secret. Being a victim her entire life was her greatest shame... she would rather die before revealing that to anyone."

It was all starting to come together. Catherine had always seemed unstable and psycho, but the depth of her mental illness was so much more than I'd ever imagined. It literally dictated her entire life. Dictated to the point that she had planned some long-game scheme, twenty years in the making, to turn herself into the queen of the world. Delta had not even seen her coming. So secure in their power, they'd let the snake in the grass taken them down in one fell swoop.

She'd made my job of toppling them that much easier at least. Now I just had to finish the job.

Richard shook himself then, like he was shaking off bad memories. "We should go, Riley. They'll be back soon; they're following my trail to try and take me out like the rest of the board members. They got to Rome, so I'm all that is left."

The pain was so sharp. Biting. I stumbled as my knees threatened to collapse under me again, and Richard grabbed me. "Are they all dead?" I asked, staring up at him, praying he would unbreak my heart and soul. "Beck and the others definitely died?"

"I don't know," he returned. "I showed up just as the building exploded, and the emergency services were trying to evacuate."

"The first explosion?" I asked as Richard started to lead me through the huge penthouse. "Or the second one?"

"The third one," he replied grimly. "That one took out the entire top floor."

No! There was no way any of them survived.

Richard continued, not realizing that I was shattering into a million pieces in front of him. "I got there in time to see Graeme and Catherine throw you into the car and take off. It's only that I've been keeping tabs on her and her family over the years that I was even aware of this penthouse."

"If they want to kill you," I said woodenly, "why are you here, dropping yourself in their lap?"

I yanked my arm out of his. "You should just go. Leave me here, with your weapon, and I'll take care of it."

I might die in the process, but I was okay with that. With Beck and all the rest gone, all that was left for me to do, was to make sure Catherine and her fucked up family never hurt anyone again. It was the one focus in my head. The only reason I was still standing on two feet and breathing.

"Riley, no," Richard said. "Seriously. They're not good people. Trust me, I've known many bad humans in my life, and these two are topping that list."

Determination annihilated the pain for a second, and I grasped onto it. "That's why I need to take them down."

Before he could say another word, I lurched forward and pulled his gun from the back of his pants. I'd noticed it as soon as he walked in—Beck's training in observation was paying off.

I hadn't held this particular model before, it was thicker and heavier than my gun, but all of the normal parts were visible. I flicked the safety off.

"Go," I said, fury pounding through me, but I somehow managed to keep my hands from shaking. "Hide until I take them down. And if I don't, get to the vault and find footage to destroy Catherine. You can take Delta back."

Richard just lifted one eyebrow, not even looking concerned when I leveled his own gun on him. I think he knew I wasn't going to shoot him.

A scrape at the front door stole my attention, and I immediately jerked my hand behind me, telling Richard to hide.

He narrowed both eyes on me before melting off into the apartment, disappearing. I quickly dropped the gun into my empty holster … I still had Beck's vest on, even though they'd removed my gun from me.

Catherine flew into the room, Graeme right behind her.

"What the fuck did you do?" she screamed, getting right in my face, her hand swinging out to crack me across the cheek. "The footage is everywhere."

I blinked, managing to dodge her first hit before knocking her back with a little straight shot. Graeme remained back, watching the pair of us.

"I have no idea what you're talking about?" I said softly, looking between them, all the while my hand was inching to my side to grab the gun.

Graeme lifted a small device and hit a button, and a massive television started to lower out of the roof. Somehow it was already on, and the news was playing.

Catherine and Graeme's faces were flashing at me. And there was a banner running across the bottom of the screen. ATTACK AT DELTA OFFICES. TEN DEAD.

Graeme hit another button and there was sound: "*Catherine Deboise and Graeme Huntley are wanted for questioning in relation to ten murders and corporate espionage. They are considered armed and dangerous.*"

The report paused, giving out the police line to call. Then he crossed to another reporter who was on the scene at the office.

The dark-haired woman stared right at us as she spoke, her face serious. "Devastation here today, at this attack on the multi-billion-dollar Militant Delta corporation. The closely held family business has always had only five seats on its board, and we … at this stage, cannot confirm if any of the board members or their heirs are alive."

It crossed back to the original reporter.

"Can you tell us about the footage of Catherine Deboise and Graeme Huntley initiating the attack?"

The other reporter nodded a few times, like there was a delay in their information. "Yes, Sam, we can confirm that our news station received an anonymously sent file which shows Catherine Deboise allegedly murdering multiple board members. And she is joined by her brother, Graeme Huntley, another Fortune 500 member, to finish the attack."

There was a quick flash on the screen, showing Catherine, bloody knife in hand. They had blurred out most of the faces, and there was no obvious graphic violence in this clip, but there was no mistaking it was Catherine. The next clip was Graeme, his gun in hand as he fired a few rounds off.

I'd been watching the screen so intently that I had let my focus fall from the danger in this very room. Catherine's hand wrapped around my throat, and I let out a shriek, kicking myself for being so stupid. We went down, and I managed to claw at her face, and she released me briefly. I landed hard on my back, groaning as new pains hit me before I scrambled to grab the gun.

Only, before I could get my hand on the trigger, there was another gun pointed right at my face. "Say goodbye to your daughter, CC," Graeme said, death burning in his eyes. "If there are no witnesses left, then no one can really prove that footage wasn't doctored. We both have an alibi after all."

Catherine kicked me hard in the side; her pointed heels felt like they broke a rib. "This lowlife slut is no daughter of mine."

Graeme grinned, and I closed my eyes, knowing there was no way I could get my gun out in time. If only I'd left it with Richard, then we might have had a chance, but I'd wanted to finish this myself. Looked like all I was finishing was my time on Earth.

You'll see Beck soon. And Dylan, Jasper, Evan.

That was some comfort.

"Don't touch my fucking daughter," Richard roared, appearing from somewhere with a blade that he launched across the room and right into the side of Catherine's chest. Graeme swung around in a flash and four loud bangs sounded as he shot Richard in the chest. *No! No more.* In my head, I was sobbing and screaming, but my body had also gone into this robot survival mode. Without a thought, I whipped out my gun, and as Graeme turned around, I shot at him, landing at least one hit around his throat.

He dropped onto my legs, his gun spilling over to my side, and I snatched it up before managing to kick his gurgling and gasping ass off me, so I could lift myself up. I immediately searched for Catherine. Only there was nothing but a bit of a blood trail from where she'd dragged herself off somewhere.

Richard let out a groan, and I hurried to him, trying not to panic. My father was definitely an unknown entity, having been someone that appeared both trustworthy and also the absolute last person I should trust. But he had helped me a lot lately, and he'd just saved my life at great cost to his own.

When I reached his side, I let out a low cry; there was so much blood. It was everywhere, pooling under him.

"Phone?" I said, frantically patting his arm.

He groaned again, but I managed to find a slim cell in his pocket. I quickly dialed 911, screaming for an ambulance because my father had been shot. I also told them that I'd been kidnapped by Catherine Deboise and she was here. The person on the other end was frantic, and tried to get me to stay on the line, but I told her no. I stayed just long enough for them to trace the address from the cell, and then I hung up.

"They'll never find the entrance," Richard said, blood bubbling up in the corner of his lips. "Not in time."

He coughed weakly, and I held his hand tightly, refusing to leave him. I did keep an eye out for Debitch though, but she didn't show her ugly face.

"Riley," Richard said, his voice sounding weaker.

I leaned down closer to him.

"Give me my gun. Wipe it … clean."

I knew immediately what he was doing. Trying to take the wrap for killing Graeme, so that I didn't have to deal with that when I got out.

"No," I shook my head. "Catherine might come back."

He looked toward the other gun—Graeme's gun—and I relented, dropping Richard's into his hand. He managed to pull it to his chest, hugging it close.

His eyes found mine again. "I'm sorry for everything, Riley," he choked the words out. "So…" cough, "…sorry."

It hurt to breathe, and it wasn't just because Catherine had smashed my ribs. It hurt because I knew Richard was going to die, right here in front of me, and I'd already lost everything today. I'd lost my entire fucking family in one fell swoop.

I couldn't take another loss. I already had my hands pressed to his wounds, trying to stop the bleeding, but it still seeped out, so I shrugged off my jacket and used it like a makeshift bandage, trying to wrap it tightly across him.

"Stay with me Richard," I said, staring down as his eyelids fluttered. "Don't give up, Dad. Please don't give up."

The slightest smile tilted up his lips, and another sob ripped from me.

"D—d—daughter."

He managed to open his eyes and look right up at me then, but just as he did, horror replaced the pain on his face, and he tried to shove me aside, but he didn't have any strength left. I wasn't letting that bitch get the drop on me again, though, and with his slight warning, I dove to the side, and rolled a few feet away before jumping up. Catherine had a gun pointed at me, her other hand pressing to the knife wound in her chest.

She limped closer.

"It's all over," she said, and there were tears running down her cheeks. I wasn't even sure she realized she was crying. "The pain can finally stop," she whispered, staggering forward again.

I had my gun up as well, but she didn't care.

Finally, her eyes focused on me, and I wanted to just shoot her, but it was hard to kill someone. It hadn't gotten easier the few times I did it, and right now Catherine was an injured, broken woman.

So like a dumb fuck, I let her continue talking while I searched for the fortification to take another life.

"I thought that if I had all the power in the world, I would never be weak to anyone again," she told me, almost conversationally. "My father … he was a very bad man. Mean daddy," she added, in a little girl's voice. "Mean daddy always hurts me. Mean daddy loves me and hates me. Mean daddy hurts me."

Jesus fucking Christ.

She was gone, her mind existing somewhere back in the horrors of her childhood. She kept talking to her father, over and over, screaming for him to stop hurting her. I was briefly distracted from this when Richard's head lolled to the side, his eyes closed, and as my breathing turned ragged and harsh, Catherine seemed to snap back into herself.

"I killed Daddy, do you know that?" She was talking to me again. "He was my first kill, and I enjoyed it so much. That high of being the one in control. The one in power."

I shook my head. "Richard saved you first, and you know it. Without his strength, you would have been nothing."

Her face was red, black smeared around her eyes, hair in a dark tangle. She looked younger than usual, but also way more insane. "Richard was my angel, but then he was bad too. Always bad men. Always touching me."

Her sorrowful face turned to her brother. "Graeme was the only one who ever loved me. Loved everything about me. We could have ruled the world together."

I saw the moment her fury took over the sorrow. The moment the bad memories were replaced with the cold-hearted killer that she was.

Her gun kicked in her hand, and I pulled the trigger on mine in almost the same instant before I felt the slam of the bullet into my chest. Right above my heart.

She cried out as she fell, and I cried out too because the pain was so strong. My head slammed into the table that was behind me, and everything flashed in black and white at me while my chest screamed in agony.

As the darkness started to take me, I swore I heard the sound of sirens, of people storming into the apartment, but it might have all been a dream. Then, as I finally succumbed, I heard the one thing that brought light to my darkness.

"Butterfly!"

I was going home to Sebastian Roman Beckett. My heart.

Chapter 30

BECK

I managed to drag Jasper and Evan out before the third explosion. For a split second I thought Dylan hadn't gotten out, but then I saw him, a man over each shoulder, as he rescued a couple of Delta employees. Emergency service workers rushed at us, but I waved them off. "I'm fine," I snapped, "Evan and Jasper need some help though."

The woman hesitated, running her eyes along the blood trailing down my shoulder. One of the bullets clipped me, the other three ending up in my vest. I'd had multiple reasons for putting that vest on Riley earlier. One being a place for her gun, but two was the fact this was state of the art, top secret, developed exclusively by Delta's underground division, Kevlar.

It was basically designed to stop any bullet on the market, even armor piercing ones, and I made sure we all had them tonight. These vests saved our fucking lives.

Dylan strode over, rubbing his arm. "They took Riley, we have to find her."

I was so angry that it was starting to swell in my veins, my vision taking on something that resembled black and red. Death and blood.

"They won't kill her," I said, "Catherine needs her to take over Delta. We just have to figure out where she would lay low for a few days?"

We watched as our brothers were loaded into a van, both of them okay but knocked around. Jasper waved me over just before the door was shut. "Don't forget the footage," he wheezed. "Use the footage."

Fuck.

Dylan heard him too, and already he was on the phone, talking to our guys that we'd set up earlier to tap into the Delta offices. I'd had an idea that something big was going down here tonight, and I wondered if we might not get the footage we needed, to take them all the fuck down.

"They got it," Dylan said. "What do you want to do with it?"

I didn't even have to think. "Send it to Riley's lawyer. Make it anonymous. He'll know what to do with it."

Dylan nodded and barked out a few more commands on his phone. Police crowded in closer to us, asking questions, detaining people in the area, and I could not spend the next few hours locked in one of their interrogation rooms. I needed to find my girl.

Dylan and I took off, using whatever fucking skills we'd learned over the last two decades to run and jump and evade the police. This wouldn't work out well for us later, but right now, Riley was my priority.

"We should start with your father," Dylan said. "They're going to want a clean sweep. They think we're all dead and that only leaves Rome—and

Richard, but I doubt he's still alive."

Getting to my father in general was not easy. He was rarely at home, his suspicious nature caused him to trust very few people, including his wife. He had multiple safe houses and secret properties, and he never spent more than a few days at any of them. But there was one secret I knew, the very reason he'd decided to step down early and let me take a proxy position on the board—he had a serious girlfriend. One he cared about. One that wasn't just a fuck and leave. One that was taking up a lot of his time and he wanted to focus on her. I'd never seen him like that before and it had made him just a little bit lax in his security.

I just had to find the girlfriend.

My phone was up and to my ear in a flash as I dialed our contact in the police department. He answered in two rings. "Beck?"

"I need you to find someone."

He didn't fuck around. He got right to business. "Yep, ready."

I told him her name and the basic details I knew about her. She was a tiny, blonde-haired, blue-eyed woman, only twenty-five, and I was pretty sure she was a gymnast. My father thought he loved her, but no doubt he mostly loved her ability to put her foot over her head all the while sucking his dick.

"Give me five minutes."

I hung up the phone, and turned to the left, finding the closest car to steal. It took us about thirty seconds to get in and get her started, and then we were moving along the street, lights off.

When my phone rang, I answered it before the second buzz. "Yep."

"She was not exactly easy to find," he said quickly. "I had to search multiple databases, and she was only triggered in one. A national gymnastics league."

Dad probably didn't think that was worth hiding. Arrogant asshole.

I hit the speaker so Dylan and I could both hear. "Her place is in Jersey." *Fuck*. He quickly rattled off the address, and I hung up.

"They won't go to Jersey with everything happening. Chances are they've already sent someone to kill him anyway," I said before slamming my hand into the steering wheel. "Motherfucker!"

"Then let's check out Graeme's place," Dylan suggested.

I nodded, already swinging the wheel around and planting my foot. Times like these, I missed my Bugatti and her power.

Graeme's place looked abandoned when we got there, and even after smashing the door down and storming inside, there was not a single sign of life. Dylan and I checked every room, the basement, and the rest of the property. My phone started to ring after we'd finished, and I glanced down to find it was Jarrod Wells, Riley's lawyer.

I silenced it because, right now, I had to focus on finding my girl. I did not have time to worry about the video footage.

Only he rang again, and again, and again, and as I jumped back into the stolen car, grim-faced Dylan at my side, I finally snapped.

"What?" I growled. "I'm fucking busy."

"The footage is on the news channels," he said quickly. "The police are using it to flush them out, but I wanted you to know because this is going to make them desperate and scared. They'll be more dangerous."

My blood went cold, and I tried to count my breaths so that I didn't drive to New York and kill the lawyer. "They have Riley," I bit out each word. "You've just put a fucking death sentence on her head."

Catherine had no incentive to keep her alive, not when she was clearly going to jail no matter what happened. "Find me something," I said to Wells. "Find something that gives me an idea where to look for her. Graeme Huntley is a good place to start."

Dylan was already on the phone with every fucking contact we had, and I followed suit, both of us calling in the troops, while at the same time, checking every Delta safe house and any other Huntley properties we knew of. There was no one at any of them.

When Wells phoned me back, forty minutes later, I was just leaving our last possible location. "Give me something," I said as soon as I answered.

"Graeme Huntley purchased a property under one of his shell companies. Well, it's actually a shell of a shell of another entity, all hidden under a trust. But I fucking found it."

He sounded both proud and exhausted, like he'd been hunting down leads as hard as us. "If this pays off, you're getting the hugest fucking bonus," I told him.

Wells chuckled. "Just find her alive. Delta has already destroyed too many lives."

He then gave us an address.

A familiar address. Graeme's place was just up the road from our apartment building. One of the newest builds, I didn't think it was finished construction yet. Graeme must have somehow gotten them to fit out one of the apartments, but leave the others unfinished, to hide his safehouse.

"It's genius, really," Dylan said as I flew across the town in that direction. "Shame we'll have to kill the bastard."

Not a shame at all. I was going to fucking enjoy every second of it.

"I just need Riley to be okay," I said, my brother about the only person I'd ever admit my fear to. The only person I could show weakness around. "I can't fucking live without her."

"I know," he said, his eyes forward, expression grim. "All of us love her, Beck, and I have faith that she won't let them take her down easily. She's a fighter, our girl."

For once I didn't want to fucking pummel his face into the front dash for calling her *our* girl. Because she was ours. A Delta Heir. Our family.

My phone rang, but I ignored it. We'd put out a ton of feelers into our network and no doubt they were checking in, but I had a good feeling about the safe house. This was where we'd find them.

Dylan's phone started just after that, and he actually checked his screen. "It's Captain Decker," he said, and I took my eyes off the road for a split second to stare at him.

"Answer it," I said.

"Decker," Dylan said, his phone on speaker.

The Captain wasted no time on pleasantries. "Heard you were looking for your girl. We just got a call from a female, said her father was shot and Catherine Deboise was in the apartment somewhere. We're heading there now."

"Address?" I barked out.

He gave us the same street and number as the lawyer. "We're almost there," I said shortly.

Decker cleared his throat. "Don't do anything stup—"

Dylan cut him off before he could finish, the phone back in his pocket as I pressed my foot even harder to the floor. Ignoring stop signs and red lights, I flew toward the apartments, the sound of sirens in my ears.

I had a single-minded determination to get to Riley.

Tires screeching, I was out the door before the car even stopped. My body screamed, still fucked up from the last fight, but the pain was easy to ignore. Physical pain I was a fucking expert at handling. It was the emotional vise around my heart that was new. The thought that Riley might have been hurt ... possibly killed, in the time it had taken me to find her.

I was on the edge of losing my mind.

Dylan was at my back, always there when I needed him, as we stormed into the lower levels of the building. This bottom floor was not even fifty percent finished; the elevator was clearly not ready to take anyone up.

"How do we find their place in here?" Dylan bit out, gun in hand as he cased the area.

"We think like those fucking assholes," I snarled. "We figure out how we would make this safehouse work, and we'll know where they are."

At the end of the day, rich, arrogant bastards were all the same. We thought the same. Planned the same. And took the same risks.

Some of us were just better at it than others. Graeme was not one of those, so we should be able to figure him out.

"Service elevator," I said quickly, noticing it off to the side. This was how the construction crew got their stuff up to the higher levels.

Dodging around piles of wood, tiles, sheet board, and a fuckton of other building materials, I led Dylan to the cage which was attached to the side of the building. We had to step out through a makeshift door, but then we were inside, and I hit the button to take us almost to the top. Top floor was too obvious. Graeme would be just under that.

Police stormed in the building just as we started to move, and I shouted for them.

"Floor twelve," I bit out, as they raced toward us, but we were already shooting up the side. When we reached the floor, the metal cage door opened. My gun was in my hand, and I didn't move cautiously. There was no time for that.

It was dark up here. Tarps on the side blocked the last of the sunlight. At first, I thought I fucked up. Everything looked like a construction site—same as downstairs—but then Dylan spotted a single scuff mark in the dust. It was like God himself was on our side because somehow, a sliver of light hit that very spot creeping in through a gap in the drywall.

Staying silent, we followed that scuff, right to the back of the building. In the distance, I heard the elevator ding, and in front of us, the faint noise of screaming.

I was sprinting, and it took every ounce of my fucking skill to not land in a pile of power tools. Finally finished walls, a hallway, and nondescript door came into view.

Catherine was the one screaming as I hit the door with my shoulder, smashing it down. The entry led right to the formal living room, giving Dylan and me a front row seat to Catherine shooting Riley in the chest.

Panic and rage slammed into me, and I'd never moved so fast in my life, but it was still like slow motion as I watched Riley fall backward, smashing her head.

"Butterfly!" I roared, wanting her to know I was coming. Needing her to hold on.

I had no idea what her injuries were or if she had taken the vest off. I knew nothing except that I had to get to her.

My butterfly.

Chapter 31

An incessant beeping woke me, pulling me out from under the cloying darkness I'd been in. A sense of *déjà vu* swept over me and for a moment my heart seized in panic. Had everything been a dream? A coma hallucination after the crash with my parents?

Then a sharp, agonizing stab of hope hit me. If it had all been a dream, then maybe they were still alive.

A broad-shouldered man sat in the corner, his head in his hands and his body shrouded in shadows and I knew...

"Dante?" I croaked, knowing what would happen next. He'd look up, tears in his eyes and tell me that my mom and dad were—

"Butterfly?" It wasn't Dante who answered me, and it definitely wasn't Dante that raised his head and stared back at me with gray eyes full of love and sheer relief.

I blinked a couple of times, trying to clear the haze of pain medication. Slowly, the pieces all clicked back together, and my breath rushed out in a whoosh. Sadness pricked at my eyes, making them burn with impending tears.

"Sebastian," I replied, my voice breaking with a sob. As if my speaking his name had broken a spell, he rushed out of his chair and to my bedside. He reached out but hesitated just an inch away from touching my face.

"Butterfly, you gave us a nasty scare. What were you thinking, taking on Catherine alone?" His tone was scolding but only softly. He touched his hand lightly to my cheek.

"I don't know," I replied, narrowing my eyes at him. "I guess I was thinking that I *was* alone. That all of you guys were dead and I had nothing left to lose." I gave him an accusing frown, and he looked away with a guilty twist to his mouth. "What the fuck happened?" My voice was soft, broken with the fresh pain of thinking he was dead. "I saw you get shot. All of you." Another puzzle piece of memory clicked into place, and I gasped, bringing my hand to my chest. "Catherine shot me too! How—" I pulled down the neck of my hospital gown, expecting to find bandages over a bullet wound but there was just a mass of black and purple bruising instead. "Sebastian, how are we still alive? *Are* we still alive?"

It was a valid question. Maybe this was some fucked up afterlife where you carried your dying wounds and pain with you.

"Yes, Butterfly. And thank fuck we are. Our story is only just beginning; it'd be a tragedy for it to end now." His gaze returned to mine, and I glared back at him. As poetic and romantic as that statement was, it didn't answer the most important part.

"Start explaining," I ordered him in a menacing growl.

A sheepish grin tugged at his lips. "I had a bad feeling about the meeting. I don't even know why, it was just nagging at me. So I had those vests made..."

My eyes widened. "Those vests were bulletproof? You're kidding. They just felt like a rough cotton."

He shrugged. "New technology that Delta has been funding. Patent pending." He shot me a cheeky wink, and I scowled back.

"You prick," I said softly. "I thought you were dead. I thought you were all—" I broke off with a sob as tears blurred my vision and my throat tightened.

Beck's arms circled around me then, gentle over all my bruises as he hugged me into his chest and stroked my hair. "I'm so sorry, Butterfly. I'm so, so sorry. I should have told you."

We stayed like that for a long time, and at some stage he shifted to sit on the bed with me, so I could snuggle in tighter. I was crying not just for how I *thought* they were dead and they weren't, but for that glimmer of hope when I woke up and thought maybe, just maybe, my parents were still alive.

Eventually, my tears dried up, and I swiped an IV-connected hand over my face. "Catherine," I croaked. "Is she—"

"Dead," Beck replied before I even finished my question. "Same with Graeme Huntley, and all the other board members."

I strongly suspected it made me a terrible person, but a flutter of satisfaction traveled through me at this news. We didn't *need* to find the vault, after all. The empire was toppled, and somehow the five of us, the heirs, had survived. No doubt this was going to be a legal nightmare to sort out, but we'd figure it out. Together.

There was one loss that hurt though. "What happened to Richard?" I asked, taking the tissue Beck offered and blowing my nose. Crying always made my nose both runny and blocked up all at the same time.

"He made it," Beck told me, and I gasped, the tissue falling from my hand. "He flat-lined four times in the ambulance, but they managed to revive him, and four hours of surgery saw the bullets extracted. If you hadn't called 911 when you did, he would have been dead for sure."

I released the breath I hadn't realized I was holding. Holy shit. Richard was still alive. My last remaining family ... by blood, that was.

Something I'd learned since arriving in Jefferson was that family could be so much more than just blood relations. And mine? Well...

"Riles, you're awake!" Jasper blurted, coming into my hospital room with a large take-out tray of coffees in his hands. "What the fuck, dickhead?" This was aimed at Beck, who gave an unapologetic shrug.

"So much for calling us if she woke up, you prick," Evan added as he followed Jasper into the room. "You look good, Riley. Like a Disney princess just woken from a coma." His compliment fell flat when Jasper snickered and eyed my hair. No doubt I resembled a character from *The Walking Dead* more than *Sleeping Beauty*.

"Thanks, Evan," I muttered. "Nice to see you all alive too. Where's Dylan?"

The guys all seemed to exchange a *look*, and Beck just kissed my hair before peeling himself off my bed. "I'll go tell him you're awake," he said, totally evading my question. "Don't go anywhere, okay?" He cupped my face and peered into my eyes with total seriousness until I nodded.

"I'm not moving from this bed," I assured him. "I don't think I could, even if I wanted to." Because now that the drugs were fading out of my system, I could tell my whole body was just one massive bruise.

Beck pressed a gentle yet lingering kiss on my lips, then shot a warning look to both Evan and Jasper before slipping out of my room.

In his absence, I eyed up my two friends suspiciously.

"Which one of you is going to spill?" I prodded them. "What's with the weird looks when I asked about Dylan? Where is he, really?"

Jasper shook his head and pointed at Evan. Typical.

"Uh." Evan rubbed a hand over the back of his head, looking uncomfortable. "He didn't take everything so well. You were unconscious and got shot at way closer range than us... Or maybe just that you're more breakable..." He was rambling, but it answered the question of why I was in a hospital bed and they all weren't. Then again, both Jasper and Evan were wearing hospital ID bands so they couldn't have been discharged too long ago themselves. "So, yeah. He's in the chapel."

Evan paused, and I raised my brows at him.

"Praying," he explained, motioning to me in my hospital bed all hooked up to an IV drip, "that you wouldn't die."

Oh.

I didn't really know what to say to that.

"Not that we didn't care enough to pray," Jasper added, right as I was about to make a smart remark at him. "But you know how it is. Our belief in a higher power is a bit jaded, considering how we all grew up."

"Also," Evan added, "You're tough as shit. We never doubted for a second that you'd be fine."

I snorted a laugh at this and shook my head. Laughing was better than crying at this point.

"One of those had better be for me," I told Jasper, changing the subject away from Dylan. I was staring at the tray of coffees in his hands and he gave me a broad grin.

"Uh, of *course* it is." Balancing the tray on one hand, he grabbed the marker pen from my chart and scribbled something onto the side of one of the cups. "See? Yours."

He proudly handed over the cup, turning it so I could read what he'd written. Where the barista had scribbled "Beck," Jasper had edited it to say "Mrs. Beck - Boss Bitch."

"Cute. You're lucky Beck takes his coffee the same as me." I snickered, taking a long sip of the coffee and groaning. "This is definitely not hospital coffee."

Jasper grinned. "It is when you own the hospital."

I gasped and almost choked on a mouthful of my black coffee. "Holy shit, I'm so sorry. Your dads..."

Jasper's comment about owning the hospital had reminded me that there were a shit load of casualties from Catherine's desperate attempt at a coup. Casualties which left my friends sitting on the board of the world's most powerful company.

What I wouldn't give for a "normal" company structure where crap like blood heirs didn't play a part in who held power.

"No need to be sorry," Evan told me. "The world is better off without those miserable bastards."

Still, now that I looked closer, Jasper held a thin air of sadness about him that suggested he wasn't entirely glad to see his father in the ground.

"Is Eddy okay? They didn't hurt her, did they?" Fear rose back up in me, and my eyes darted to the door as though I expected my sassy girl friend to come waltzing in at any second. If she was okay, that was.

Jasper nodded. "Yeah, we sent Dante a warning, and he got her out just before Graeme's goons showed up. He's keeping her safe until the media circus dies down a bit."

Evan piped up. "Thankfully my sister was away at her fancy mountain yoga retreat when Catherine's hired guns showed up at the dorms."

Thank, fuck.

All of this was a lot to wrap my brain around, so I took another sip of coffee while I processed. "So you guys are Delta now. Like, for real. How does it feel?"

Jasper and Evan exchanged another one of those infuriating looks, but didn't get a chance to answer me when the door burst open and Dylan staggered in with Beck close behind him.

"Hey, you," I greeted him, mustering up a warm smile. It wasn't too hard given how much those few sips of coffee had cheered me up already. Oh, and the fact that they were all alive seemed to help too.

"Riles," he breathed, his voice pained and his face drawn. "I thought..." he trailed off, shaking his head and dropping his gaze to the floor. Straight up, Dylan looked like shit. As far as I could tell, he hadn't slept in days, and his suit was still torn and stained with blood.

"I'm fine," I promised him. "Thanks to someone's sneaky trick with invisible body armor." I shot a look at Beck, who still looked totally unapologetic. "Same goes for you four."

Dylan sucked in a deep breath, his brow furrowing as he looked back up at me. He opened his mouth to speak, but no sound came out. I waved at him to come closer, and his feet practically dragged as he made his way across to me.

"Hey, Dylan," I said, my voice soft and private. "I'm okay. We're all okay."

I reached out and took his hand with mine. In my peripheral, I noticed the other guys quietly leave the room. Even Beck.

When Dylan didn't respond, didn't even look at me but squeezed my fingers tighter, I tugged on his hand.

"Come here," I ordered. "You look like you need a hug as badly as I need to give you one."

He let out a short, bitter laugh but perched on the edge of my bed and wrapped his arms around me. We stayed like that for a little while, until I wrinkled my nose and whispered in his ear. "Now that you know I'm okay, it's probably time to shower. You smell like death."

Dylan started laughing then. A genuine laugh touched with an edge of hysteria and a healthy dose of relief. I laughed with him, until his turned into sobs, and then I just held him. He was Beck's best friend, but he was quickly turning into one of mine too. I knew where he was at. The floodgates had opened, and he just needed to work through it. So I just held onto him and let him cry.

Through the window to my room—the one looking out into the hospital ward—I met Beck's eyes, and he gave me a short nod of approval.

Epilogue

The engine in my brand new Butterfly purred beneath me as I rolled up to the starting line, her nose kissing the chalk mark. I caressed her sleek leather steering wheel before killing the engine and popping my door open to get out.

"Riley Jameson, as I live and breathe. When I got the call to say you were racing tonight, I thought someone was pranking me." Rabbit whooped with excitement, smiling from ear to ear as he held out a palm for me to slap.

I grinned just as wide, unable to hide my excitement. "I wouldn't miss this for the world, Rabbit. You know that. No punk ass bitch is stealing my Widowmaker crown just because I was too busy pushing papers around a desk."

Rabbit hooted a laugh and clapped me on the back before someone shouted his name from across the impromptu gathering of cars. "Gotta go schmooze the fans, girl. Gimme a sec."

He started to leave, and I grabbed his arm. "Wait, where are the other racers?" I arched a brow at the chalked line with only my car—my new Butterfly—sitting on it.

Rabbit grinned broadly. "Only one other racer this time, Riley-girl. Everyone else bailed the fuck out when they heard you were racing." He glanced at his expensive—probably stolen—watch and shrugged. "Dude's got another five minutes to get here, otherwise I'll have to take you on myself. And neither of us wants that." He winked, and I laughed.

"Yeah, because that'd be embarrassing as shit when I leave you for dead," I commented, and he just shrugged with another laugh as he headed over to the guy who'd called out his name.

For a quick moment, I was alone.

All around me, people were chatting, music was playing, engines were revving, and the air smelled of that heady mixture of gasoline, exhaust and beer. It was my happy place.

"What are you thinking about with that silly smile on your face, girl?" Eddy asked, slipping her arm around me in a hug as she arrived.

I hugged her back then did the same to Dante as he reached out to me. "Just excited," I told her honestly. "It's been too long, and this girl needs a proper run." I patted the hood of my shimmering lilac Aston Martin Valkyrie. It was the first real expensive thing I'd bought for myself after inheriting the majority shares in both Militant Delta Finances *and* Huntley Corp.

Turned out that Graeme had left everything he owned to Catherine, and she'd died without a will at all. Typical fucking Catherine, thinking she was invincible.

After Richard abdicated his seat on Delta board, it all passed to me. I was now stupid rich, stupid powerful, and *stupid* overprotected. It'd taken freaking weeks of planning to sneak out for this race without my bodyguards *or* the guys finding out.

"You didn't tell them anything, right?" I blurted out, giving Eddy a nervous look.

She gasped. "Of course not. You know my loyalty lies only with you. It's on them if they got outsmarted into losing you for a night."

Dante snickered a mean laugh, and I whacked him with the back of my hand. "Hey, don't act superior. You're only here because you know you can't stop me."

"No," he replied. "I'm here because I know you're a badass that can handle this course and would never tell you what you can and can't do. Unlike some."

I rolled my eyes at his not so subtle dig at Beck's overprotective nature. The ten months of "peace" since the massacre in Delta's office hadn't really seen Dante and Beck getting along any better, but now that Eddy and Dante lived together things were reaching more of a truce.

"Reckon this guy is going to show?" I asked them both, casting my eyes around the crowd and trying to work out if it was someone I already knew. It'd been a while since I'd raced, though, and new people were constantly popping up.

"He'd be an idiot not to," Dante commented with an odd tone, and I gave him a suspicious look. "I just mean, missing the chance to race against the legendary Butterfly herself? Who knows when you'll next manage to escape your jailers long enough for a race. Right?"

Something about the way he said it felt false, but I was too hyped up for the race to call him on it.

"They're not my jailers," I muttered, unable to resist defending my guys. "We've just had a whole lot of shit going on, you know? Legitimizing Delta's businesses without putting thousands of people out of work hasn't been super easy."

"We know," Eddy said, shooting Dante a warning glare and linking her arm back through mine. "Dante's just got old habits that are dying *hard*. Aren't they, love?"

Dante just rolled his eyes and muttered something we couldn't make out before heading over to talk to Rabbit.

Eddy sighed as she watched him go, but it wasn't a frustrated sigh. It was more of a hopelessly in love sort of sigh, and I smiled. It was nice to see the two of them so loved up with each other. God knew I had my work cut out trying to find girlfriends for Evan, Jasper and Dylan. If for nothing else but to give them something to *do* with their spare time, aside from stalk me.

"Ooooh, shit," Eddy breathed, looking over my shoulder. The sexy, thrumming purr of a sports car engine told me that my competitor had just arrived, so I turned to see who it was.

"Wow," I blurted. "Is that a Koenigsegg CCXR Trevita?"

Eddy snorted. "Like I'd know. But it's gorgeous, whatever it is."

My eyes scanned over the sleek black sports car with fully tinted glass and edgy design, and I let out a little groan. "Oh my god, it is. Eddy, those things cost twice what I paid for Butterfly 2.0. I didn't even know they were *available*."

"Who is it, do you think?" My friend replied, squinting to try and see the driver.

Just then, one of Rabbit's girls strutted out in hot pants and high heels, flipping a flag back and forth between her hands.

"Guess we'll find out at the finish line." I shrugged. "Doesn't matter anyway, he'll be coming in second." I shot Eddy a cocky wink and slid back behind the wheel of my car, clicking on my racing harness—a feature I was all too happy to include in the custom specs, thanks to my recent accidents—and hit the ignition.

I flicked a glance over at my competition, but couldn't make out much more than a silhouette. Not that it mattered. It was probably some rich kid who'd just gained access to a trust fund and went out looking for a thrill ride.

A camera flashed somewhere on the sidelines and lit up his car just enough that I saw his head turn toward me, like he was eyeing me up the same as I was to him.

Good. Because the second the flag fell, he'd only be seeing my tail lights.

The girl in hot pants raised her flag in the air then paused and gave us both a long look to make sure we were paying attention and ready. Just for fun, I revved my engine. The Koenigsegg revved back, and I grinned. Maybe he'd be good enough to make it a fun race.

No time like the present to find out. The flag dropped, and we both shot off across the starting line like bullets from a gun.

It only took a few minutes for me to work out that not only was my competition serious about winning this race, he was also good. Really fucking good.

Excitement ran through me, fueling my every move, every gear shift and every intercept as he tried to pass me on wide patches of road. But shit if he was making me work for my tiny lead.

Either I was rustier than I'd given myself credit for, or this asshole was the best driver I'd faced yet.

Taking another tight corner, he laid on the accelerator harder than I'd ever consider safe or *sane* but it saw him pulling level with me, then inching ahead.

"Oh no," I muttered under my breath as I held tight to the inside lane and pushed my Butterfly harder, faster. "Not today, motherfucker. Not. Fucking. Today."

But no matter how hard I tried, I simply couldn't shake him. He stuck with me, either riding my bumper or edging up beside me the *whole freaking course* until we hit the long straight to the finish line. With barely a few feet separating us, and no corners to slow us down, this would be a clear test of speed.

Heart pumping so hard it hurt, I slammed my foot down on the accelerator the second my wheel was straight. My shiny new baby shot forward like a rocket, but the sleek black Koenigsegg was sticking to us like glue.

Seconds later, we blew past the finish line at way over double the speed limit, and for the first time in my racing career, I didn't know who'd won.

Careful not to harm my car, I reduced my speed calmly, shifting down through her gears and circling back around to where the huge crowd of cheering spectators were gathered with their own cars. One in particular jumped out at me. How could it not? It was bright canary yellow and had a handsome blond playboy perched on the hood with a drink in hand.

"Crap," I groaned, casting my eyes past Jasper for the other three. Yep, sure enough, there was Evan leaning against the door of a cherry red Mercedes with an anonymous girl pasted to his chest. On Jasper's other side, approaching with his hands stuffed into the pockets of a designer hoody, Dylan looked like he always did these days. Angry and secretive. Every time I saw him, a pang of guilt rippled through me. It'd taken him a *really* long time to let go of the crush he'd been holding and now … well shit just wasn't the same with us. Hopefully time could heal things, though. I loved him too much to let his sulking go on much longer.

I pulled my car up in the Winner's Circle, still totally unsure who'd won the race, and hopped out. Eddy had played dress up on my outfit again, and I was feeling pretty badass in my low riding leather pants, flat soled Jimmy Choo boots, and sparkly white tank. The bright red lipstick was just icing on my tough-chick-designer-look, and I knew it made my sly grin all the more obvious as the Koenigsegg rolled up in front of me.

"I fucking *knew* it," I hissed as his door popped open and a familiar face smirked back at me. "Ugh, who else would risk a car like that in a race like this. You shithead!"

"I think I actually beat you," Beck remarked, wrapping his huge hands around my waist and boosting me up against the side of his car.

I groaned, wrapping my legs around his waist. "No way, no one beats the Butterfly."

He chuckled, even as he sealed his lips to mine in a searing kiss. "This time, I think I might have." His lips parted mine, and for a moment, I let him enjoy that brief glimmer of victory before pushing him back a tiny way and peering over his shoulder to Rabbit.

"Who won?" I shouted at the gangster race coordinator.

He grinned back at me, and I knew.

"The queen keeps her crown for another year!" Rabbit announced in a booming voice, making sure *everyone* could hear him. Then sauntered over closer to where Beck held me pinned to the side of his stupidly expensive new sports car. "By a fucking inch, Butterfly. Lucky I had cameras ready, you almost got your ass beat."

He chuckled and left us to it. Or, left me to gloat my victory over Beck while in the background I could hear Jasper yelling some bullshit about Beck getting beaten by his girlfriend.

"I win," I informed Beck with a smug smile, using my thumb to wipe the smear of my red lipstick from his mouth.

He smiled back at me and started dropping light, teasing kisses on my lips. "You can have this one, baby. I win every fucking day when I wake up with you in my arms."

Little baby butterflies erupted inside me, and I ground my hips into him with a groan. "I fucking love you, Sebastian Roman Beckett."

He kissed me again, taking his damn time and blocking out the jeering of our spectators. Fuck them all, we existed in our own damn bubble.

"I love *you*, Butterfly."

And that was the start of our happily ever after...

...or happily for now, at least.

Thank You!

Thank you all so much for embracing Riley, Beck, and the rest of this crazy crew. We've loved every second of writing in this world. It's been one insane race, but we were lucky to have Riles behind the wheel. Girl can drive. If you'd love to see more dark romance from us, flip the page for a sneak peek at our next story, *Princess Ballot*.

XXX, JAYMIN & TATE

SNEAK PEAK: PRINCESS BALLOT
ROYALS OF ARBON ACADEMY

You have been chosen.

Those four words change Violet Spencer's whole life, when against staggering odds, she's selected in the "princess ballot."

Arbon Academy is affectionately known as the school for Royals. Only the rich, powerful, or heir to a throne gain entry ... except for the one scholarship student accepted every five years. It's a worldwide lottery, and one that Violet entered without giving it any serious thought.

But the media got it wrong and Arbon Academy is much more than a simple college for future leaders.

It's a dark world of politics, intrigue, and dangerous guys who will stop at nothing to get their own way. Despite her best efforts at remaining off the radar, Violet finds herself a pawn between two of the most powerful monarchies in the world.

Prince Rafe of the Switzerlands and Prince Alex of the Australasias are bitter enemies both on the soccer field and in the political arena.

Monarchies rule the world now, and every waking breath is a competition for the princes.

Control the ball.

Control the world.

Control Violet.

Whether it's through love or hate, someone will ultimately win.

This is book one in a dark college romance. This is not a RH or traditional love triangle story, but it does include a-hole princes, nasty princesses, and one chick who will take none of their shit, all the while doing her best to make it out alive. HEA guaranteed. Eventually.

CHAPTER ONE

"Violet Rose Spencer."

My head jerked up as my name was called across the speaker on the main floor. The girl next to me snickered, mostly because she was a bitch, but also because it was a well-loved pastime to mock me for my "flowery" name.

My mother had gifted me only one thing, a name from her two favorite flowers, telling the nurse moments before she hemorrhaged and died on the operating table, leaving me an orphan. Apparently, she never mentioned a father, and so far no one had come forward to claim me.

"Violet Rose Spencer, you have five minutes to make your way to the matron."

This time the voice sounded annoyed, but I didn't bother to rush. I wasn't a ward of the state anymore. I'd turned eighteen last week, and they couldn't kick me out. I was only here waiting for my final paperwork—which was probably what this summons was about—before I moved on to college. State college of course, but for the first time I would have control of my life. Freedom to make my own choices, instead of being shuffled around foster and group homes at the whims of people who wanted to play "family" with me.

"Vi!" Meredith yelled, rushing across the room. Meredith Mossman, with her waist-length strawberry-blonde hair, big blue eyes, and curves for days, was the closest thing I had for a friend in this shithole, having been one of the five other girls I shared a room with. "There's someone in the front room waiting for you. A man I've never seen before." Her voice dropped to a whisper. "He's kinda hot in an old dude way."

That gave me a moment's pause, because the paperwork shouldn't require a stranger's input. And a hot stranger at that. Maybe the matron was finally getting some. Might improve the old bitch's temperament.

"Only one way to find out," I said, linking my arm through Meredith's and dragging her along with me. It felt safer not to face them alone.

The matron had an office at the front of the group home. This was where she dished out the good and bad news, disciplined us, and hid away when she was just over kids for the day. And considering Mission State Home was one of the largest in Michigan, housing fifty kids at all times, she was often hiding.

There was a real potential for violence and corruption with this many children under one roof, albeit a large roof, but the matron managed to keep it under control. One thing I could say about this place: I'd never felt unsafe. Unlike many other places I grew up in.

When I knocked, the matron looked up, as did the man who was sitting across from her in the padded chair. The nice chair. If you didn't get to sit in it, you were stuck with the rickety old stool that was propped in the corner.

"Violet, please come in," the matron said as she waved me in. "Miss Mossman, you're dismissed."

Fuck. Looked like my moral support was gone. Meredith gave me a commiserating stare before backing out of the room. The matron got to her feet then, crossing around the desk to close the door. I noticed that she was dressed very nicely, in a tweed skirt suit, the jacket closed over her round figure, the buttons looking like they were working very hard to keep all of her shit contained. Her steel gray hair was slicked back, her lips a garish red, and despite the fact that she still looked every one of her sixty years, she was presenting quite the polished front.

"Violet, please take a seat." She waved magnanimously toward the stool, and I sighed as I pulled it out.

I'd been doing my best to ignore the man sitting there, because men in general made me wary, and strange men were at the absolute bottom of my list of trustworthy species.

Pulling the stool in closer to the desk, I kept a decent distance between the man and me. Despite not staring at him, I still noticed from the corner of my eye how nicely he was dressed. His black fitted suit appeared to be without a single wrinkle or mark. Flawlessly fitting to his broad shoulders.

Additional impressions I got while *not* staring at him was that he was mid-forties, rich, and bored. He just sat there, waiting for the matron to stop fussing, his eyes half-lidded and empty.

"Are you sure I can't get you anything to drink, Mr. Wainwright?" she asked.

He shook his head, letting out an almost inaudible sigh. "No, thank you, Madam Bonnell." He lifted his wrist and a gleaming watch came into sight under the cuff of his suit. "I'm on a tight deadline, as I explained last night when I phoned, and I really do need to be on my way."

He turned to me, and I was finally forced to acknowledge his presence. "Violet Spencer, are you ready to leave?"

He sort of looked about me, like he was searching for something before lifting dark brown eyes back in my direction.

I refused to let my emotions show on my face, working very hard to keep it blank. "Excuse me? Go where?"

At this, the matron cleared her throat. "Apologies, I haven't had a chance to speak with Violet yet, and as such, she has no idea this is happening."

I narrowed my eyes on her. More likely that by the time she got the phone call last night, she was half-way through her Schnapps and Jeopardy, and had forgotten to tell me right until this moment.

I cleared my throat, a weird feeling swirling in my stomach. I had a decent radar for danger, but that wasn't the vibe here. Still, I was nervous to know what this was all about.

Mr. Wainwright shot the matron a disparaging look—a look he did very well—before he reached into his jacket and pulled out a folded piece of paper. He leaned closer and held it out to me.

Warily, I reached out and took the paper, marveling at how thick and heavy it was. I'd never seen paper like it before. My hands shook as I opened it, because for the life of me, I had not a single clue what was happening here.

The writing inside was hand done, in a sweeping, spectacular calligraphy.

Dear Violet Rose Spencer,

We are pleased to inform you that you have been randomly selected from a ballot of over 15 million orphans and foster children for a chance to attend the prestigious Arbon Academy. Our college has a long tradition of producing the finest leaders, professionals, and royalty the world has ever seen.

This is an opportunity of a lifetime. Offered once every five years.

Your tuition, room, food, and essentials are all covered under your scholarship, and you will graduate with the chance to secure a job in whichever field you desire. Our representative will oversee your passport and travel arrangements. We look forward to having you at Arbon academy.

With kindest regards,
Principal Dean Morgan
Advisor to the monarchy.

I read it twice.

"Is this a fucking joke?" I asked the man, my voice wavering as I fought between anger and confusion.

The matron gasped. "Violet. Language!"

Yeah, for sure. Because the previous twelve or so years of chastising me in regards to language hadn't worked, but one more shot was the ticket.

Mr. Wainwright didn't seem to care. "I promise that this is not a joke, Ms. Spencer. Do you remember entering the ballot? It would have been about this time last year."

The matron leaned over her desk. "Yes, you had to go in for blood and a cheek swab, remember? To ensure that you were in good health to be part of it."

The blood part sent the memory hurtling to the forefront of my mind. I hated needles. It was a full blown phobia, so Meredith had held me down—she'd literally sat on me—while they took the blood.

"The princess ballot," I said softly. Mr. Wainwright glared at me then.

"We discourage the use of that name. The fact that some of the previous ballot winners have married into royalty is mere coincidence of circumstances.

We make no promises on your future beyond providing the best education and opportunities."

I snorted. "Okay, sure. Except that *all* of the ballot winners have ended up as royalty in some form, so yeah. Pretty sure calling it the Princess Ballot is appropriate."

He didn't answer, but there was a flicker of something in his dark eyes. That sight bothered me, but I couldn't quite pinpoint why that was. I turned my eyes back to the paper. The *princess ballot* was famous around the world, and not for one second had I ever expected that I would be chosen. Being chosen was like winning the lotto. As the letter said, over fifteen million people, between the ages of fifteen and twenty-two, were entered. Eligible to finish their school or college at the academy.

Arbon academy was the most exclusive, prestigious, and out of reach school in the world. Its location was a closely held secret, somewhere in Europe, and it was the college of choice for royalty and the children of billionaires. How did I know all of this? They had given us a full speech about it when we were eligible to enter.

Fifteen million.

"Ms. Spencer?"

I met the gaze of the man here to change my life.

"How can I trust this is real?" I said softly. "You could be anyone with a piece of paper and expensive suit. I'd prefer not to end up on the black market or in the sex trade."

There was no way I was lucky enough to be chosen for this. It had to be either a joke, a mistake, or something untoward. The matron cleared her throat, her face splotchy and red like I'd just embarrassed her. But the man, again, didn't seem annoyed.

"I have another message for you."

Reaching down, I noticed for the first time that there was a briefcase at his feet. He pulled from it a small device. It was like nothing I'd ever seen before, about the size of a mini-laptop, and when he opened it a familiar face appeared.

Familiar only because I'd seen him on television dozens of times in the past few years.

"Good morning, Violet," the face said, and I jumped because I'd thought it was a video recording, not a video-call.

"K-king Munroe," I stuttered. "Your Majesty."

Holy shit, I was talking to the King of the Americas!

He smiled, probably well used to bumbling morons. "It's a pleasure to make your acquaintance," he said easily. "I wanted to personally congratulate you on this opportunity. It has been twenty years since we've had an American chosen, so this is very exciting for the entire country."

It was real. Holy fucking fuck.

"For your safety, we will not be announcing your name," the leader of the Americas continued, and I paid attention. "But it will be known that an American will be joining the ranks of the upper elite, attending Arbon academy."

"I have no idea what to say," I admitted honestly. "I think I'm still in shock."

I'd probably be in shock for the entire four years of my college degree.

Oh my god! I was going to have the best education in the world, and it was all free. Free food and room and essentials for the next four years. No working five jobs just to get by, while trying to study and better my life.

Tears pricked at my eyes then—I hadn't cried in years, but right now, I allowed myself this moment of weakness. All the while finishing my conversation with the most important man in our country.

When Mr. Wainwright returned the small device to his leather bag, I just sat on my rickety stool like a stunned idiot.

"Do you have any other questions?" he said, and I lifted my gaze to meet his fully, for the first time.

"Just one: when do we leave?"

Also by
JAYMIN EVE

SUPERNATURAL ACADEMY
(URBAN FANTASY/PNR)

Year One

Year Two (2019)

DARK LEGACY
(DARK CONTEMPORARY HIGH SCHOOL ROMANCE)

Broken Wings

Broken Trust

Broken Legacy

SECRET KEEPERS SERIES
(COMPLETE PNR/URBAN FANTASY)

House of Darken

House of Imperial

House of Leights

House of Royale

STORM PRINCESS SAGA
(COMPLETE HIGH FANTASY)

The Princess Must Die

The Princess Must Strike

The Princess Must Reign

CURSE OF THE GODS SERIES
(COMPLETE REVERSE HAREM FANTASY)

Trickery

Persuasion

Seduction

Strength

Neutral (Novella)

Pain

NYC MECCA SERIES
(COMPLETE - UF SERIES)

Queen Heir

Queen Alpha

Queen Fae

Queen Mecca

A WALKER SAGA
(COMPLETE - YA FANTASY)

First World

Spurn

Crais

Regali

Nephilius

Dronish

Earth

SUPERNATURAL PRISON TRILOGY
(UF SERIES)

Dragon Marked

Dragon Mystics

Dragon Mated

Broken Compass

Magical Compass

Louis

HIVE TRILOGY
(COMPLETE UF/PNR SERIES)

Ash

Anarchy

Annihilate

SINCLAIR STORIES
(STANDALONE CONTEMPORARY ROMANCE)

Songbird

Also by
TATE JAMES

THE ROYAL TRIALS

Imposter

Seeker

Heir (2019)

KIT DAVENPORT

The Vixen's Lead

The Dragon's Wing

The Tiger's Ambush

The Viper's Nest

The Crow's Murder

The Alpha's Pack

The Hellhound's Legion (Novella)

Kit Davenport: The Complete Series (Box Set)

HIJINX HAREM

Elements of Mischief

Elements of Ruin

Elements of Desire

THE WILD HUNT MOTORCYCLE CLUB

Dark Glitter

FOXFIRE BURNING

The Nine

DARK LEGACY

Broken Wings

Broken Trust

Broken Legacy

Made in United States
Cleveland, OH
16 September 2025